REDEEMER

SPACE COLONY ONE
BOOK 8

J.J. GREEN

INFINITEBOOK

The world is in such a bad condition that if you don't find what they call a redeemer, every man, woman and child on this planet will be eliminated .

— SUN RA

1

It was time to collect nectar from the Consort of Midnight but Cleve didn't want to go. His mother and father bustled around the cabin, preparing all the equipment they would need: grapples and ropes for climbing the cliff, the soft suits made from flour sacks they would use as protection, bottles to hold the nectar—assuming they were successful, knives to release the precious fluid, drinking water and snacks for the long trek, all the usual paraphernalia. They took the same stuff every year.

This would be his fourth time. He'd begun participating in the ritual when he was ten. On his first trip he'd only been allowed to sit at the bottom of the cliff and watch as the others went up. He'd missed out on the elation of their success, feeling as though he hadn't really taken part. The following year had been better. Then, he'd climbed to the first stage, from where he'd been able to watch as the nectar was harvested. On his third visit, when he was twelve, he'd finally been judged sufficiently mature and experienced to climb all the way to the night-blooming Consort of Midnight. After that, he'd trained often with Dad.

Tonight, he was supposed to be actually gathering nectar. It should have been an honor, an initiation into adulthood. He should have been happy and excited.

He did not want to go.

"Don't just sit there, lazybones," Mom exhorted. "Give me a hand packing these suits."

Cleve got to his feet and trudged to her side. She handed him one of the flour-sack garments and picked up another to fold and stow in a backpack.

"Is there one for me?" Temel asked.

"Of course not," Cleve snapped. "You won't need it."

At ten years old, his younger brother would be keeping vigil at the base of the cliff as he had four years ago.

"But I might still be in danger," Temel said hopefully.

Cleve tutted and shook his head. They were *all* in danger, only his parents didn't want to admit it. He squashed the suit into a ball and shoved it into the base of his backpack.

"Not like that!" his mother protested. She pulled the suit out.

"What does it matter?" Cleve asked, scowling.

"It matters. If you put tension on a seam it might break, and then where would you be? These are only loosely sewn. It isn't possible to sew them tighter. The material is too thick." When Cleve continued to scowl, she rolled her eyes. "If you're going to sulk go back to your corner. I'd rather do it by myself than look at that face any longer."

He strode across the cabin and sat down, his arms folded. That was how he remained until, twenty or so minutes later, everything was ready. His father shouldered his pack and his mother did the same. Temel had a small backpack of his own. Cleve's sat next to the door.

He faced an impossible choice. He could refuse to leave the cabin, abandoning his family to whatever fate might befall them. Or he could go along, risking the nameless fate himself.

"It's time to go," Dad said, opening the door.

Cool night air flooded the cabin, accompanied by a surge in the constant background noise of singing cicadas.

His father glared at him from under lowered brows. "Cleve, are you coming?"

The three figures of his little family were watching him. Mom, her graying hair cropped to ease the summer's heat. Dad, only a little taller than Mom, untidy stubble sprouting on his chin and cheeks. Bright-eyed Temel, puppy fat straining the buttons of his too-small shirt. The three stood in a little group. There were more people in the valley, other families, farmers, store-owners, classmates. But these three were his world.

"All right, I'll come."

He joined them and picked up his backpack, slinging it over his shoulder before stepping out into the darkness.

The Consort of Midnight was half-a-day's trek away, but the journey took longer by night. The trail through the jungle was hard to follow in the dark and they had to keep watch for jaguars. Dad made Cleve and Temel walk in front, where they were less likely to tempt a hungry feline into a risky attack.

When they'd been walking for around an hour and Cleve's mood had evolved from resignation to a rising fear, a hand landed on his shoulder, making him jump.

"Take it easy," said Dad. "I just wanted to say, I'm glad you changed your mind. It wouldn't be the same without you."

His words did little to alleviate Cleve's feelings. His father was still being too casual about the threat. Perhaps it wasn't too late to persuade him to turn back.

"Would it really hurt if we missed it this year?" he asked. "Don't you guys have savings? We could cut down on food and supplies. I could definitely eat less, and so could Temel. Right, Temel?"

"That's not the point," Mom argued. "This isn't only for profit. If we don't collect the nectar it wouldn't only affect us, it would affect everyone who uses the stuff. How would Ma Kristophel make her scented toiletries? And what about Farmer Jake's cordial? Consort of Midnight nectar is the main ingredient. Besides, this is what our family does. It's what we've always done. If we stopped harvesting nectar, who would we be then? What else could we do?"

"I'm sure Ma Kristophel, Farmer Jake, and the rest of the customers could get their nectar somewhere else. Hell, they could climb the cliffs themselves if they want it so badly."

"Don't curse," Dad admonished. "And I don't want to hear any more arguments. We're doing this, and that's final."

"What's that?" asked Temel.

A pale blue light shone through the trees, silhouetting the trunks and gilding the leaves. The light shone upward from the valley so it was clearly not starlight or moonlight. It was also too blue and shimmered in a non-astronomical fashion.

"It's nothing," said Dad.

Cleve knew what it was, though it was the first time he'd seen it. It was the first time this year he'd been outside so late. He'd heard the rumors of the alien encampment glowing blue at night—not brightly, but enough to be noticeable in the darkest hours.

The alien presence was the great unmentionable in valley life. The creatures had arrived months ago, their crescent-shaped ship descending to the valley floor. Hundreds had landed all over the globe, it was said. Since then, they'd slowly constructed domes over each ship.

No one had done anything about it as far as he knew. News of what went on in the rest of the world was hard to come by. There was an hour-long radio broadcast every evening, but Mom and Dad had forbidden him from listening to it lately. He guessed it was because they didn't want him to worry, yet not knowing what was going on was more worrying.

It was probable that people had tried to make contact with the aliens or even attack them, and they'd failed. Now all that could be done was to tolerate their presence and hope they didn't mean any harm. He hoped so too. There was plenty of land for them to settle if that was all they wanted. He had a horrible feeling it was not, and that it wasn't safe to roam in the area of their dome.

He walked on, first in line on the trail, Temel behind him, then Mom, then, last of all, Dad.

Why did they have to harvest the Consort of Midnight nectar?!

Why couldn't they leave it one more year?

Why did they have to hike through uninhabited areas in the early hours of the morning when no one else was about?

"Here we are," said Mom, relief in her tone.

So she was scared too. She just didn't want to admit it.

They'd arrived at the cliff base. Cleve had been so preoccupied he'd almost walked past it.

A rough, rocky surface rose above their heads, the top obscured by shadows and vegetation. In amongst the jagged, irregular shapes of plants was a soft luminescence. The Consort of Midnight was blooming, right on time. The trumpet-shaped flowers of the rare species would be heavy with nectar. The air seemed to carry their delicate scent, even here, far below.

"I can see it!" Temel exclaimed.

"You can see *them*," Dad corrected. "They're right across the cliff, see?" He pointed, moving his finger from left to right. Speaking to Mom, he continued, "It's going to be a bumper harvest. We can live all year on it. I hope we brought enough bottles."

"I packed some expandable ones," she replied.

"Good thinking." Dad rubbed his hands together gleefully. "We have a long night ahead of us. Let's get started."

Cleve glanced at the blue, spectral light in the distance and then at his little brother. "Maybe... Maybe I should stay down here with Temel, as it's his first time."

"He'll be fine," said Dad. "Won't you, son?"

"Sure, Dad. You go up, Cleve. I bet you'll harvest more than Mom or Dad."

"Not likely," said Mom. "It takes time and practice to get it right, but if you do, Cleve, I'll give you a small bonus to share with your brother. How does that sound?"

"Cool," Temel breathed.

Dad was already swinging the grapple. Foliage crowded the trail, and the sharp metal hooks bashed through the leaves. "Stand back," he warned, before slinging the grapple up the cliff face.

Dad had been harvesting Consort of Midnight nectar all his life. He knew this area like the back of his hand—as he often mentioned. But the surroundings changed every year. The cliff crumbled a little. New plants grew and old ones died. Yet Dad's throws remained true. The grapple caught on the gnarled trunk of a small tree. He tugged on the rope. When it didn't fall down he jumped onto it, dangling by his hands and wrapping his legs around it. The rope bore his full weight.

"Cleve," he said, "this one's yours. Mom and I will go farther down. Temel, you come with us."

"But, Dad..." Cleve demurred.

His father ignored him.

As his family walked away down the trail, he threw his backpack to the ground, tore the fastening open, and pulled out his suit. He swore as he put it on, using all the words he'd learned but could never say in front of his parents. It didn't make him feel any better.

When he was suited up, the flour-sack material hanging loose on his body, he pulled the hood over his head and face. This was the only part of his kit his parents had purchased. The hoods were expensive. A transparent shield covered his face and a thick, closely woven cloth covered him to his shoulders. He slipped thick gloves onto his hands. Then, his heart heavy with foreboding, he lifted his backpack onto his shoulders again and began to climb. Hand over hand, rope gripped between his thighs and feet, up he went.

Harvesting nectar from Consort of Midnight blooms was easy. It was the fact that the plant only grew on vertical surfaces and at least fifteen meters above the ground that made it hard.

That, and the bees.

Bees loved the nectar as much as humans did, if not more. They built their hives close to the source and fiercely defended it.

The first bee smashed into Cleve's visor, almost causing him to lose his hold on the rope. He was still many meters from the Consort of Midnight plants but they knew his intention. Another bee arrived and landed right in front of his nose, crawling curiously across his vision. Cleve switched his attention to the rope. He didn't dare look down but, judging from the distance to the nearest flowers, he was high up. A fall from this height could kill him.

The sounds of his mother and father climbing and talking drifted over.

"You doing all right, Cleve?" Mom called.

"Uh huh. Where's Temel?" Bees buzzed all around him. They pushed their stingers toward his face and gathered thickly on his gloves and suit.

"He's right underneath me. Don't worry about him. You got your first nectar yet?"

"Not yet. Nearly there."

He wished he could see her. It would be more reassuring than hearing her. He couldn't see anything except the bees and the cliff face, faintly lit by the luminescent blooms and the distant glow of the aliens' dome.

He reached his first flower. The trumpet poked out, long and slender. Holding tightly with both hands, he kicked the cliff. Loose, sandy soil tumbled down. He pushed his foot into the hole and rested a large portion of his weight on it. Now came the really tricky part. He eased one shoulder out from the strap of his backpack, and swung the bag around to his front.

The bees were going crazy. He could barely see what he was doing.

More by touch than sight, he took a bottle out and unscrewed the lid. After stowing the lid in a pouch on the side of the bag, he felt for his knife. He took great care to avoid the blade as he pulled it out. A cut or tear in his suit would allow the bees in and he would be lucky if he only suffered a few stings. Some nectar collectors had been stung to death.

He placed the neck of the bottle below the base of the bloom and pierced the petals with the tip of the knife.

Nectar gushed out.

Dad had been right that this would be the best night to gather the nectar. A lifetime's experience had told him down to the space of a few hours when was the perfect time to do it.

"I got some!" Cleve yelled. "Mom! Dad! I got some nectar."

The bottle was full and still the nectar poured out. Cleve hastily replaced the lid, put the bottle in his bag and retrieved another. He managed to fill it a quarter full before the nectar slowed to a dribble.

Bees swarmed over his hands, the bottle, and the flower, drinking the dregs with their long tongues.

"Mom!" Cleve called. "I got my first nectar!"

No answer came.

Somewhat annoyed, he called again, "Mom! Dad!"

The forest was silent.

"Mom?" His voice was quieter this time. Were his parents joking around? Maybe they were teasing him about his earlier worries.

"Mom, if you're there, please answer."

Nothing.

"Dad?"

Cleve fastened the lid on the quarter-full bottle and put it in his bag along with the knife. "Temel?"

Above, the vegetation rustled.

He froze.

Something was there. A creature. It couldn't be a jaguar. They didn't climb this high. Was it a monkey?

The thing was climbing down toward him. It moved awkwardly, as if unused to the environment.

Cleve tore his pack off his back and flung it at the creature. Without waiting to see the result, he launched himself from the cliff and slid down the rope so fast it grew hot under his hands.

Landing with a thump on the trail, he flew down it in the direction his parents and brother had taken.

"Temel! Temel, where are you?"

"Here," a small voice squeaked. "I'm here, Cleve."

He tried to follow the sound but only met solid cliff face beyond the cloaking foliage. "Keep talking. I can't find you." His eyes wide, he looked over his shoulder.

A dark shape moved closer, scraping along the track. It was large and its outlines weird. It looked like nothing he'd ever seen.

"I'm here, Cleve," Temel called.

How would he ever save his brother from the animal? Maybe he shouldn't lead it to him but away from him. Had the creature killed Mom and Dad? Was it—

A hand clasped his ankle and he nearly jumped out of his skin.

"Come inside," said Temel. "We can hide."

He had found an opening in the cliff. Cleve ducked down and slipped through the gap. He barely fit. Temel crouched at the end. Cleve squashed up close to his brother.

The meager light went out. The thing had found them and was

covering the entrance. But it was too large. It would never be able to get in.

Cleve held his brother tightly.

Temel whispered, "If we wait long enough it'll give up and go away, won't it?"

"Yeah, for sure," Cleve replied quietly, forcing confidence into his voice. "We just have to wait."

But what had happened to Mom and Dad?

2

It was like old times. Cherry studied Aubriot's crouching, shadowed form as he hid behind a tree trunk, peeking out, keeping watch on the Scythians. The aliens had plagued humanity since the early days of the Concordian colonization, and she and Aubriot had spent years of their lives fighting them. Only this time the Scythians had actually landed, and the planet she and her former lover were defending was not Concordia but Earth, the cradle of human civilization.

In all the years she'd known Aubriot he hadn't changed and would never change, while she'd aged and begun to grow stiff. She shifted position in the ferny undergrowth to ease her aching joints, causing the fronds to rustle.

"Shhh!" Aubriot hissed.

"They're a hundred meters away," she retorted in a harsh whisper.

"Doesn't matter. They might still hear us. We don't know what they're capable of."

She silently grumbled, though he'd made a fair point. In the past, Concordians had gone to huge lengths to hide themselves from the hostile aliens, assuming they used sight to search. But the mechanical Scythian spiders had hunted the colonists through their scent and nearly succeeded in wiping them out.

She pushed down a leaf and peered over it. The structure the aliens were building seemed nearly finished. Construction had continued day and night since they'd arrived eighteen days ago. First, trundling robots had laid down a low wall surrounding the ship, squirting a pale, faintly lustrous liquid that hardened on contact with the air. Later, machines with articulated limbs placed blocks on the base, each layer tapering slightly inward. The result was a dome roughly a hundred and fifty meters in diameter. Aubriot called it an igloo. The top was out of sight but the construction noises continued. They had to be closing the top of the dome by now.

She reached out to grab Aubriot's sleeve and tugged it. When he looked over his shoulder she jerked her thumb toward the trail. He shook his head.

Why he wanted to stay, she didn't know. There wasn't anything more to see.

Moving as quietly as she could, she rose to her feet and walked, stooping, into the forest.

Back at the Earthers' settlement, the low houses and narrow streets were mostly quiet. Nearly all the local inhabitants had moved out as soon as they could after the Scythian ship appeared. Earthers didn't have the technology let alone firepower to defend their territory from a space-faring species, and they weren't stupid enough to try. They'd fled, getting as far from the threatening presence as they could.

Yet, according to the grapevine, Scythian ships were landing all over the planet. What would the Earthers do when there was nowhere left to hide?

Cherry went immediately to Wilder's hut. In answer to her knock, she heard a faint *Door!* through the wood. A moment later, a flustered-looking Wilder pulled the door open.

"I'm never going to get used to this ignorant tech," she complained.

"You'd better. We might not have the luxury of responsive devices ever again."

Wilder grimaced. "Don't remind me. What's happening at the construction site?"

Cherry followed her into the hut. "Nothing new. I think they're nearly finished."

"Want some tea?"

"Sure." The Earthers' drink was nothing like what Concordians called tea, but it was light and refreshing. "Where did you get it?"

"I found a house someone left in too much of a hurry. They hadn't packed up any of their food as far as I could tell. We can eat for days on what's in the cupboards." She handed over a mug of steaming liquid. "I just made this. I'll make myself another one."

"Should we stick around that long?" asked Cherry. "There doesn't seem to be a lot of point. Maybe we should take our lead from the Earthers and find somewhere to hide out. The Scythians must have a plan for what to do after they've finished building their dome. I'm guessing it involves destruction and slaughter."

Wilder lowered herself onto the sofa with resignation. "At the very least we should get Miki and Nina away from here. We have to look after them now Kes is gone. What does Aubriot say?"

Before answering, Cherry rested her elbows on the windowsill and gazed out into the deserted street. It was only wide enough for one of the Earth vehicles. The basic automobiles had to be manually driven. There was no planetwide net for them to connect to—nothing to navigate by or prevent collisions. It was a wonder the Earthers managed to use them at all.

Earth also lacked good infrastructures to support food supplies, medical treatment, education, and other essentials. It wasn't that the planet didn't have these things, but provision was patchy and uneven and depended entirely on conditions in the local area.

History lessons aboard the *Nova Fortuna* had told of the decline of technological development on Earth due to the rise of the Natural Movement, nevertheless it felt odd to return to humanity's birthplace and find it more backward than its colony.

"You know him," Cherry replied. "He's all for attacking the Scythians as soon as possible, before they get a foothold. He would do it alone, only even *he* understands it would be suicide."

"Before they get a foothold? They already have one. And what would we attack them with? Our bare hands? Firing on them from the *Sirocco* is out of the question. That ship's our only way home."

"You don't need to convince me how stupid it would be. We do need to get away from this place. I don't think watching the Scythians is going to tell us anything. Maybe we'll leave in the morning. I would have liked to figure some things out but I've given up."

"Like what?"

"Like why there are no doors in that dome, for one thing. It was the same with the Scythian city in Suddene. No doors. Only soft, squishy material you could push through. There doesn't seem to be any of that stuff in the construction material they're using here."

"Maybe it's permeable to gases. The Scythians can't breathe Earth's atmosphere."

"Okay, but how are they planning on getting in and out? Unless they don't intend to ever leave their domes they need exits. That wall looks solid."

"Just because it looks solid, doesn't mean it is," Wilder countered. "There might be seams that are invisible to human eyes."

"Yeah, you're probably right."

A figure appeared at the end of the street. Cherry opened the door and beckoned.

A moment later Aubriot stepped through the entrance. "You disappeared in a hurry."

"I didn't have a reason to wait around. We weren't seeing anything new."

"How would you know if they did anything new if you weren't there to see it?"

"So did you notice something different?"

"That's not the point."

"Ugh, get yourself something to eat. Wilder's found a new store."

Wilder pointed toward the kitchen. "It's all in there."

Aubriot strode past them, glowering.

"One thing's for sure," Cherry went on, "if the Scythians wanted us dead we would already be checked out. There's no stopping their spiders. Once they get a whiff of a scent they follow it, slicing through everything in their paths until they..." She swallowed, recalling seeing

Garwin hacked to pieces and the loss of her own left arm. "If the Scythians wanted to eradicate all humanity they would have started by now. They have something else in mind."

"You haven't figured it out?" asked Aubriot, emerging from the kitchen with a sausage of cured meat. He took a bite and leaned a shoulder on the wall before somehow managing to chew and yet maintain his usual supercilious expression.

Cherry glared at him, refusing to take the bait. They'd been romantic partners, of a sort, for so many years. Of all the Concordians she'd been one of the few to give this man of Earth the time of day. She'd allowed him into her heart, prickly and arrogant though he was, and in return he'd betrayed her. It was a betrayal he'd never apologized for, never even appeared to see a need to apologize for, and she'd long ago moved past the point at which she could ever forgive him.

Yet circumstances forced her to be around him. Despite all his many, many faults, Aubriot was their best military tactician. If she and the people she loved were going to survive, she had to tolerate his presence.

Wilder gave in. "Are you going to enlighten us?"

Aubriot smirked. "Don't you remember the Scythians' demands you refused, Cherry? Before they launched the biocide?"

"Oh, shit." She moved from the window and slumped into a chair, putting her head in her hands.

"What?" Wilder asked. "What were the demands?"

It had been the worst time of Cherry's life. After the Scythians had returned to Concordia and annihilated Oceanside, they'd made a proposal. The Leader at the time, Meredith, had wanted to accept but Cherry had overruled her, firing off a refusal. Her decision had resulted in countless deaths, including most of the peaceful Fila. The aliens' biocide had just about destroyed life on Concordia, and all because she hadn't wanted to give in to the Scythians' demands.

Aubriot poked her shoulder. "What's your answer going to be this time?"

"To what question?" Wilder insisted.

Cherry replied woodenly, "They want to live here. They want to colonize Earth, with human beings as their slaves."

"And they can do it," said Aubriot. "On this piss-poor planet, with its Iron Age tech and Neanderthal natives, it'll be easy. It's over. Earth's screwed."

3

The head of the Global Advancement Association was a stooped old man. To Cherry's eyes Dakarai Buka looked even older than Ethan had been when he died. Perhaps late eighties or early nineties. A strong puff of wind could blow him over. That explained why he hadn't been present when the Earthers had returned Kes. He was too frail to be riding horses, flying around in helis, or waiting out on the prairie to meet strange humans who had arrived from another world.

Naturally, he spoke no English. He relied on the Earther translator, Itai, to communicate with the Concordians, as they did with him. Itai sat next to the old man, leaning close as he listened to the quiet words. He was as silver-haired as the old man but perhaps thirty years younger, ruddy cheeks above his clipped gray beard giving the impression of vigorous middle age.

When Buka stopped speaking Itai gave a nod and turned to the room. "The GAA has received a report that the Scythians may have begun their attack. Two people have gone missing in the vicinity of one of the domes. A mother and father. Their sons managed to evade capture by hiding in a hole too small for the creature to enter."

Vessey asked, "When did this happen?"

"Two days ago."

"Why have we only just been informed?" The *Sirocco's* captain looked nervous. She'd been all for abandoning the Earthers and returning to Concordia the minute the Scythians had appeared. It had only been strong dissent from Aubriot that had dissuaded her.

"The region is remote. We only received news of the incident ourselves a few hours ago."

"What else do you know?" asked Aubriot. "When did the attack take place? What do the Scythians look like?"

The head of the GAA laid a bony hand, freckled with sunspots, on Itai's arm. The translator leaned toward him again.

"Mr Buka would like to know why you're asking about the appearance of the Scythians. We thought you were familiar with these aliens."

"We've never—" Aubriot began.

But Vessey talked over him. "No Scythian has ever landed on Concordia as far as we're aware. Their assaults on our planet have taken place from orbit or via automated devices."

The old man smiled wryly and he spoke again.

Itai translated, "So Earth is honored by this special privilege."

"They've landed because Earth is weak," Aubriot said loudly. "It doesn't have the tech to fight back. But it's more than that. When the Scythians discovered humans were living on Concordia they tried to wipe us out. You see, our planet used to be theirs a long time ago, before they ruined it and made it uninhabitable to their form of life. Finding another intelligent civilization living there upset them. Only they couldn't kill us all easily, so they changed their minds and decided they would re-colonize, with us as their personal servants. We turned down their kind offer, and they tried to sterilize the planet instead. You're lucky they didn't do that here. Concordia had a much smaller population and better transportation. We survived the biocide attack with mass vaccination. You'll never manage the same thing on Earth. If the Scythians launch their biocide, it'll destroy you and all life. They don't seem to want to do that—yet. They've switched to the colonization plan again. They must have abducted those people in order to study them. They'll need to know all about our anatomy if they want to control us."

By the time he reached the end of his short speech, a leaden silence had fallen in the room. No one seemed able to speak. Cherry cast her gaze around the small space. The GAA had taken over a subterranean building that had to be centuries old. The concrete walls were stained and worn shiny by the passage of bodies. What had the place been in its previous life? Offices? A prison? Aubriot had said the region it was in had once been very cold, which explained why construction had been underground. The Earthers had figured out how to repair the ancient geothermal energy mechanism to supply power.

Buka spoke.

Itai said, "We would like to know how the Concordians plan on helping us defend ourselves against this invasion."

Vessey spread her hands wide. "You must understand, there's very little we can do. As I've explained before, it was fortunate that the Scythians didn't attack our ship when they arrived. They seem to have recognized the weapon we carry, which is the same type used to defeat them in the past. If we fire on their ships we will inflict significant damage. That is what currently holds them back. Yet if we do attack, they will surely destroy us in the end. We're at stalemate for now. How long the situation will last, I cannot tell. My personal belief is that the Scythians have more ships on the way and they're only waiting for them to arrive before removing the *Sirocco* from the equation."

"So you're going to leave?" Itai demanded.

Though Buka hadn't spoken, his frown indicated his translator had expressed his sentiment accurately.

"Nothing's been decided yet."

"You're going to abandon Earth, your home planet?"

Vessey looked uncomfortable. "The expedition to colonize deep space set out from here centuries ago. Concordians have no memories of Earth. They view Concordia as their home planet. And we have plenty of problems of our own. The *Sirocco* was heavily delayed on her journey. Our planet desperately needs the material we gathered if our people are to survive."

"So now you've got what you need you will leave us to our fate? Your own kindred?"

"If we could help, we would, but I'm not sure..."

All through this exchange, Aubriot's jaw muscle had been twitching, to Cherry's amusement. He *hated* not being in charge.

Should the *Sirocco* have departed at the first sight of the aliens? Probably. It would have been the sensible thing to do, given all the points Vessey made. But the captain wasn't expressing the majority opinion of the ship's personnel. She didn't dare give the order to leave when so many Concordians were against it. Most of them wanted to help Earth. That was the reason Vessey had stuck around. She didn't have the authority or strength of will to enforce an unpopular decision. Aubriot might have managed it without significant repercussions, but not her.

What was his take on the situation? He'd seemed all for fighting the Scythians at first, in his typical antagonistic manner. But recently he'd appeared to begin to change his mind. Though combative, he was also pragmatic. Whatever stance he took in the end it would come down to one thing: would it suit him personally?

Buka said via Itai, "Where do we go from here? Must we plead or beg you to stay and help? You have so much to offer—technology, skills, and knowledge that has been lost to us. Will you really deny us your aid? Surely there must be something you can do."

"We will continue to monitor the situation," Vessey said tightly. "The news about the abduction was useful. Please keep us informed about any further details that arrive and anything else you find out about the Scyth—."

Aubriot interrupted, "You didn't answer my questions earlier. Do you have a description of the aliens? When did the attack take place?"

"It took place at night," Itai replied. "The boys who escaped could only say the creature was large, about two and a half meters tall and wide."

"Two and a half meters *wide*?" Cherry echoed.

"That's what the children said."

She couldn't imagine what the Scythians looked like. The only large aliens she'd met had been at the Galactic Assembly. But that had been half a lifetime ago, and the Assembly was half a galaxy away. It would have been nice to have their allies around, if not to offer military backup then at least to give advice. Humanity was on its own, however. The distress signal the *Sirocco* had sent out when the jump drive failed had gone unanswered.

Buka made several more attempts to get Vessey to commit her ship's resources to Earth's defense, but the captain remained firm on wanting to wait and assess further developments. The meeting broke up without any decisions having been made. The old man rose unsteadily to his feet and Itai helped him from the room.

Vessey sunk her head into her hands.

Aubriot said, "You're gonna have to piss or get off the pot."

She shot him an angry look. "Thanks for your support just now."

"What did you want me to say? You know you don't have the backing of the crew."

"Well if you or anyone else has any suggestions about helping the Earthers I'm all ears."

"Cherry and I are still investigating the Scythians. Until we know their weaknesses it's hard to develop a plan to defeat them."

"I seriously doubt that's even possible."

"If we can't defeat them on Earth," Cherry interposed, "how will we defeat them on Concordia? Sooner or later they'll go back to see if anyone's still alive, and then they'll finish the job they started."

"That's a good point," said Aubriot. "We could learn valuable lessons here."

Vessey lifted her gaze to the ceiling. "The kind of lessons that involve a lot of bloodshed, no doubt."

"Hopefully more of the Scythians' than ours."

"If they even have blood," Cherry added.

Vessey rose to her feet. "I'm going back to the ship, providing she still exists. Keep me updated about anything you find out."

"Before you go," said Cherry, "Wilder had an idea she wanted me to run past you. She said she wants to go with Niall to find the source of the signal we detected near the seed bank."

"Why does she want to do that?"

Cherry shrugged. "It might be significant."

"I don't see how. The Earthers themselves didn't know about it. It must be something left over from before the collapse of civilization, like the seed store."

"Let her do it," said Aubriot. "It isn't like she'll be any use if it comes to a fight."

Cherry spluttered, "Wilder helped develop and maintain the armaments on Concordia!"

"Yeah, but there aren't any armaments here."

"Tell her from me," said Vessey, "that anything she can do that might contribute to Earth's independence is welcome, but she cannot use the shuttle and only she and Niall are to go. Our resources are already stretched to their limit." She left the room.

"That went about as well as I expected," said Aubriot.

"Which part?" Cherry asked.

"All of it."

"I guess we couldn't expect anything better. I'm going to find Wilder and tell her what Vessey said."

She stood up to leave, but Aubriot grabbed her hand. Stiffening, she halted and carefully pulled it from his grip.

He rolled his eyes. "After you've talked to Wilder, have you got anything else you have to do?"

"Why?" she asked warily.

"I was wondering if you wanted to hang out."

"Are you kidding?"

"Don't look at me like that. It's a reasonable question."

"It would have been a reasonable question twenty years ago, before we knew each other properly. Before you..." She swallowed. After all this time, the memory still hurt.

"Christ, you know how to hold a grudge, don't you? That should be water under the bridge by now. Can't you let bygones be bygones?"

In answer, Cherry stalked from the room.

"You fucked Kes, didn't you?!" Aubriot's angry response rang out. "I know you did. You act like you're so superior, but you're no better than me."

4

"**W**hat *is* this place?" Niall asked.

Wilder replied, "You mean, what did it used to be?"

The field of broken concrete spread out for hundreds of meters. Twisted shards, uplifted by tree roots, protruded from the ground, and thorny weeds covered the gray surface in dense patches, but it was clear the site had once been large and significant. A network of buildings had once occupied a part of it, though now the walls only stood at waist height.

"Your guess is as good as mine," she went on. "It must be from Aubriot's time."

Niall shook his head. "It's hard to believe he's that old."

"He hasn't *lived* all those years. He spent the journey on the *Nova Fortuna* in cryosleep, then when we went to the Galactic Assembly time dilation hit us, and then—"

"Oh yeah, I was forgetting you went on that trip too. So you're how much older than me?" He was trying to keep his expression deadpan but a cheeky smile leaked through nonetheless.

"Do you mean chronologically or emotionally and intellectually?"

Laughter burst from Niall. "Come here, old lady." He pulled her into his arms. "You're older and better than me in every way and I don't mind admitting it."

"Huh, took you long enough."

They kissed until the roar of an approaching engine broke through their pleasant distraction. The *Sirocco's* shuttle was a bright spot of light in the blue sky.

Wilder and Niall backed off a little more. The shuttle settled on a relatively empty spot, the engine cut out, and the noise died. A moment later the hatch opened and Zapata beckoned them, calling out, "Don't hang around on the concrete. It isn't made to absorb heat."

They ran over the hot surface and climbed up to the open hatch.

"Thanks for helping us out," Wilder panted.

"No problem," the pilot replied. "But you understand I can't wait around for you, right? It'll be a while before Vessey notices the shuttle's missing but if she does I'll be in a world of shit."

"Sure, we get it. We've packed enough supplies to last us a few days."

"You think it's going to take you that long?"

Niall replied, "We don't have any idea what we might find. We might be finished in a day or a week, or we might need even more time."

"Well, comm me when you need picking up and I'll get there as soon as I can, the captain's diversions permitting."

"Thanks," said Wilder. "We appreciate it."

"I don't know what Vessey was thinking," said Zapata, returning to the pilot's cabin. "How are you supposed to go so far north on a planet with virtually no long-distance transportation?"

"We approached the GAA for one of their helis but they said they couldn't help us." Wilder settled into a seat and fastened the belt. "They said they're in too much demand. They're booked up months ahead."

Zapata halted at the cabin entrance. "Figures. It's really something to see how low Earth has sunk since our ancestors left it, right? This place used to be an airport, with hundreds of airplanes flying in and out every day."

"What's an airplane?" Niall asked.

"Like a heli but with wings and wheels."

"Huh?"

Zapata waved a hand dismissively. "Never mind. I'll explain another time."

It had been months since Wilder had been to the island where the ancient seed vault was located, yet nothing seemed to have changed. Zapata landed at the coast as he had when she'd been one of the party to search for the seed store. Kes had been in the team too. An ache expanded in her chest. It was still hard to believe he was gone. As she walked with Niall away from the landing site and into the forest, the noise of the shuttle's takeoff behind them, she recalled the older man's silver-streaked red hair and kind, cheerful expression.

He'd been a good man. He'd been there for her at her lowest moments, the parent or older brother she'd never had, and she struggled to accept she would never see him again.

"Are you okay?" Niall asked, watching her.

She heaved a sigh. "Let's find this signal beacon."

She took out the locator from her pack. The signal originated in a spot beyond the seed vault, on the other side of a low mountain. Trees grew thickly up the slope and all around. With no tracks on the uninhabited island, they were in for a tough trek.

"It's that way," she said, pointing directly at the mountain. "Do you want to go up and over or take the long way and go around?"

Niall squinted up at the peak. "I'm not sure that up and over isn't the longest route." He peered at the screen. "Do you think the signal might be coming from the far side of the seed vault? Maybe we could go inside the mountain. That would certainly be easier than trying to force our way through the forest."

"I didn't think of that." Wilder studied the map more closely. "I suppose it's possible. When I came here before we didn't go right into the depths of the vault. We found the seeds we needed and left. I don't know how big it is. It might take up the whole mountain." She lifted her gaze to the slope. "That would make it huge."

"On the other hand, why would the people who built the vault have set up a signal beacon so far from the entrance? It doesn't make a lot of sense."

"Nothing about the signal makes any sense. That's what makes it so intriguing."

"I hope," said Niall, "after we go to all the trouble of investigating it, it's worth the effort."

"You're getting ahead of yourself. I'm just hoping we find whatever's making it."

"We won't find anything if we don't get moving. What do you think? Up and over, around, or through?"

Recalling the skeletons of desperate people she'd seen in the vault, Wilder didn't relish the idea of re-entering it. "Let's try going around the mountain. It'll be chilly on higher ground and harder to find somewhere flat to camp."

"You don't want to go into the vault?"

"I will, but as a last resort. It isn't nice in there."

"I'll take your word for it."

They lifted their packs onto their backs and set off, pushing through dense scrub. Niall went first, using his heavier bulk to forge a path. Brambles snagged at their clothes and low branches made them stoop. Wilder didn't remember it being this hard. She guessed the original party must have been lucky, stumbling across the remains of the original track leading to the vault entrance.

They toiled on for an hour before Niall halted and said, "Do you know where we are?"

The higher ground was out of sight. Vegetation crowded so closely that visibility was limited to three or four meters. Wilder was scratched, sore, and tired.

She replied, "I thought you did. You're the leader here."

"You're the one who's been here before."

"Not to this part. We went directly to the vault."

"Well, my question stands. Where the hell are we?"

Wilder surveyed the surroundings. "This isn't going to work. We need someone who's used to wandering around in wild places. We've barely stepped out of a lab all our lives."

"Shall we go back?"

"I don't think we have a choice."

An upside to their mistake was that their return passage was easy to find, marked by the crushed ground cover and disturbed and broken foliage. Another upside was that they arrived at their starting point in half the time of their outward journey. Soon, they were looking up at the mountain again from the original spot.

Niall said, "Unless you fancy doing the same again, only climbing, it looks like we have to enter the vault."

"Enter the vault? You make it sound like a sim." In truth, the prospect did hold fantastical potentialities. "Just so you know, there are human remains in there. It isn't the nicest place to be."

"The dead can't hurt us. Let's do it. Do you remember the way?"

Wilder led him in the direction she roughly remembered. When they passed the piece of metal grid suspended high on a tree branch, remnant of the ancient walkway, she knew she was on the right track. Within another few minutes, the broken double doors gaped open before them, revealing darkness.

The sun was grazing the forest canopy.

She asked, "Do you want to make camp here and go inside tomorrow? It'll be night soon."

"All the more reason to go in now. We can bed down in there if we get too tired to go on."

"Yeah, but..." She couldn't think of a rational objection. "Okay."

She retrieved her headlamp and put it on.

Niall did the same. "You go first this time."

"Thanks." She ventured into the dark.

The seed vault was just as cold and lonely as it had been last time. Scattered remains of torn seed packets and the boxes that had contained them littered the floor. Animal and human scavengers had taken the seeds themselves. The Concordian team had been scavengers too, of a kind, though they needed the seeds for planting, not eating. The packets they'd found were now safely aboard the *Sirocco*, only awaiting the journey to a new planet to fulfill their biological destiny.

As Wilder pushed deeper into the mountain, memories of her

earlier visit flooded back. She recalled the passageway where they'd found the skeletons and wordlessly guided Niall away from it. The vault was vast. She realized the first time she'd visited her party had been extremely lucky to stumble across the cache of seeds they'd discovered. Everywhere else seemed ransacked.

After an hour or longer of wandering, they seemed to have finally reached the limit of the vault. At the end of a passageway a smooth wall confronted them and a set of stairs led straight down. It seemed obvious to descend. If there was a way through to the signal site it was here, though for some unknown reason her guts tightened at the notion. Perhaps it was only that they'd walked in the dark for so long and so deep in the mountain under tens of thousands of tonnes of rock. She stepped down the stairs and Niall followed unquestioningly. He didn't know this area was new territory to her.

The metal stairs resounded with their footsteps, perhaps the first human footfalls that had hit them in centuries.

"Are you sure this is safe?" Niall asked.

"Absolutely not. Hold onto the handrail in case the treads collapse."

The concrete shaft was square and the stairs ran around the edges. The light from their headlamps didn't penetrate the central well.

"This is odd," Niall commented.

"I know. Where are the storage rooms? Where are the seeds? What was the point of this part of the vault? Why would the builders make it hard for people to reach whatever's down there?"

They continued to walk down the stairs. The place had the feeling of something secret, an area deliberately hidden. Perhaps the seeds stored at the bottom were precious. Or were they dangerous?

The beam from Wilder's headlamp hit a concrete floor.

They'd reached the end of the stairs. Stepping from the final tread brought them to a plain, square landing with a single, unadorned metal door, tightly shut.

"*Shit*," Niall breathed. White bones draped in dusty rags gleamed in the rays from his lamp. "These are the remains you told me about?"

"These are *different* ones. Yuck." Wilder tried the door but it resisted her.

"He or she must have been trying to get in."

"So it seems. We don't have a way in either. This is a dead end. We should go back."

"Don't give up so easily." Niall stepped to the door and also tried the handle.

Unsurprisingly, the door didn't open.

"What's this?" Wilder asked. As she'd moved out of his way, her headlamp had lit up a section of wall containing a series of numbers. Some numbers were set in grids, others were in rows. Beneath them all a series of bumps protruded from the surface.

"A puzzle!" Niall exclaimed. "They're all puzzles." He pushed one of the buttons. "It's mechanical. I bet if we put in the correct answers the door opens."

"Cool." Wilder assessed the first puzzle. She forgot about the skeleton in the corner and all her feelings of fear and foreboding dropped away.

Niall leaned his head close to hers as he also took in the details of the problem.

3 2 1 0

1 9 2 0

0 8 1 ?

7 5 2 4

Wilder got it first. "The space is a missing number, and it's two. Add together the first two digits then multiply by two. The answer's six." Without waiting for Niall's agreement she pressed the relevant key.

The next puzzle consisted of two rows of numbers.

? 7 2 7 3 7

? 7 5 7 6 7

Niall said, "Seventeen, twenty-seven, thirty-seven... It's one and four." He pressed the keys.

Wilder was already working on the third problem.

So they continued all the way down.

"These are too easy," Wilder complained.

"I don't know how that dead person couldn't figure them out," Niall agreed.

They reached the bumps.

"Were these for blind people?" Wilder speculated, running her fingertips over them. Next to the rows of bumps was a single, plain button. "How can we show our answer? We can only either press the button or not press it."

While they'd been working no sound had come from the door so she'd assumed it hadn't opened. She tried the handle again in case she was wrong. The door remained locked.

Niall had closed his eyes and was touching the buttons. "Can't feel anything unusual."

"Let me try."

The bumps were shaped as an irregular pyramid. One bump sat at the top and another sat beneath it. Below those were two bumps in a row. Three bumps were in the third row, then five, then eight, then...

"Ugh," she said, annoyed at herself for taking so long to understand. "It's the Fibonacci sequence."

"Of course. How many are in the last row?"

"Thirteen."

Niall pressed the plain key twenty-one times.

With a click, the door unlocked.

5

T he Scythian were increasing their abductions. All over the globe, people were disappearing. The attacks always took place at night and targeted individuals out alone or in small groups, usually in remote, rural places.

Since the aliens' brief visit to the planet two years ago, the majority of Earthers had moved their activities underground wherever possible. The situation was similar to how it had been on Concordia: with little to no defensive capability, the best strategy was to hide. Yet a subterranean lifestyle was impossible for many. Topography, lack of digging and construction equipment or the necessary skills prevented it. Other communities had underestimated the threat, and though the vanishing of their members had raised their awareness, their efforts were last-minute. Plenty of Earthers remained vulnerable to the attacks.

When yet another report of an abduction had arrived from the GAA Aubriot's response had been *Two can play at that game*. The idea was for the Concordians to grab a Scythian of their own. It would send the message that Earth wasn't going to roll over and accept defeat without a fight. It would also give the Earthers vital information about exactly what they were up against.

As well as Cherry and Aubriot, the team of Concordians

preparing for the mission in a wood half a klick from a Scythian dome consisted of Maddox, Dragan, Maura, and Acton.

Cherry watched Maddox turning the pulse rifle over in her hands doubtfully. Even after all these years, she found it hard to look at the woman without the image of her sitting astride Aubriot, both stark naked, popping into her mind. Maddox had never spoken to her about the incident. She hadn't apologized, but nor had she tried to rub it in Cherry's face, though the sly smile she'd given at the time was also something Cherry had never been able to erase from her memory.

Maddox looked up, and her gaze drifted to the space where Cherry's left arm should have been. "Are you sure you're coming too?"

"Why wouldn't I?" she retorted hotly.

"Cherry's one of our best fighters," said Aubriot. "She was at the Battle of Sidhe, defending it against the Scythian spiders. Of course she's coming."

Like Maddox, none of the other team members had received extensive military training. Maura and Acton were fellow scientists, and Dragan was an engineer. Cherry had tried to dissuade him from volunteering. As one of the people to design and build the *Sirocco*, she'd felt his skills were too valuable to put at risk. But he'd insisted and, after registering the desperation in his eyes, she'd relented.

She guessed he wanted to atone for what he'd done. Or rather, what he'd nearly done. As one of the Final Day Five—the apocalypse cult that had formed during their long space voyage—he'd come close to killing Wilder. At the last minute he'd come to his senses, protecting her from his deluded associates. She'd forgiven him and they were friends again, but maybe playing an active role in Earth's defense was his way of forgiving himself.

Aubriot said, "We have time for some training before we set off. Maddox and Dragan, come with me. Maura and Acton, you're with Cherry."

Cherry took her pair to the edge of the woods and proceeded to deliver a severely truncated version of basic training she and Aubriot had developed years ago on Concordia. At the time, she had never imagined she would be repeating herself on Earth.

They had three hours before they set off. The plan was to reach the Scythian dome at midday. They hoped the night-time abductions indicated the aliens were nocturnal. If they couldn't grab one, at least they should be able to get a good look at the creatures and the interior of a dome. It was clear the purpose of the structures was to provide the aliens with a breathable atmosphere, but other than that no one knew what went on inside them.

Was it crazy to launch an attack in broad daylight? Perhaps. It went against the grain. Dangerous activities were usually safer done in darkness. But the Scythians had developed interstellar space travel. The idea that they wouldn't have systems to detect movements around their domes day and night wasn't feasible.

Cherry spent most of the available time in target practice and familiarizing her pair with their armored EVA suits. There had not been much time to develop and manufacture the suits during the rush to leave Concordia, so the *Sirocco* only carried a handful, but they would be essential for the attack.

Too soon, the preparation time was up.

Aubriot approached through the trees, asking, "You guys ready?"

"As we'll ever be," Maura replied.

"Cool. Let's get to the heli."

The Earthers' heli would drop them close to a dome. There seemed little danger of the Scythians firing upon it on its approach. The aliens had ignored the air vessels when they passed over and their structures didn't appear to contain ground to air armaments. What would happen when the Concordians attempted to break into one was another matter.

The pilot only nodded as they boarded. The language barrier remained a problem. Itai, the Earthers' translator, had said he was teaching others the Concordians' ancient version of English but it would take time until they were proficient. For now, everyone was confined to hand gestures and facial expressions to communicate. Cherry hoped the pilot truly understood that if the mission was successful and the Concordians emerged with a Scythian, he might have to risk fire to land and collect them.

As was the case with all the Scythian domes, this one sat on open land, far from areas of human habitation. The ivory dome was a blister on the green landscape, strangely incongruous and out of place. For the first time, Cherry saw the upper surface, which was smooth and complete.

How did the aliens leave it? They had to have a way. No one was in any doubt they were responsible for the disappearances.

"You sure that stuff's gonna work?" Acton asked Aubriot nervously.

He shrugged and lifted the package on his lap. "I've been told it's an effective explosive. Whether it'll punch a hole in the side of the dome, who knows?"

The Earther pilot said something and then the heli plummeted from the sky, eliciting gasps from the passengers.

"Visors down," Cherry ordered. "This is it."

As soon as the landing skids touched the ground they piled out. The pilot had set them down roughly fifty meters from the dome, as instructed. Aubriot raced toward the dome, carrying the explosive. The heli whined as the pilot took off to retreat to a safe distance. Cherry tightly gripped the trigger that would set off the detonator.

The others seemed frozen. Had they forgotten the plan already?

"Get down!" she urged.

Snapped from their trance, the four Concordians squatted and turned their backs to the dome.

Cherry scanned the structure. The smooth surface remained whole.

She comm'd Aubriot. "Not seeing any response so far. You're good to go."

He'd reached the dome.

Still, the aliens didn't respond.

Aubriot slapped the package against the wall so hard Cherry winced. Intellectually, she knew the explosive wouldn't go off without the trigger but that didn't stop her from *feeling* it would.

Then he was on his way back. "Blow it."

"Not yet. It isn't safe. You'll get hit by the shockwave."

"Do it. We don't know how long we have."

She set her jaw, refusing to answer. Damn the man and his stupid heroics.

"Cherry! Bloody well do as you're told."

He'd almost reached her.

"Shut up and get down." She swiveled, crouched, and pressed the button.

At the same time as she heard the *Boom!* a force knocked her on her face. The sharp-edged trigger box was underneath her belly. She scrambled onto her knees and tossed it to one side before turning around for a look at the dome.

A dark, jagged-edged hole gaped in the wall. A dusty haze filled the air and shards of white material were spread far and wide.

They'd done it.

"My suit's leaking," said Acton. "I think a piece of the dome hit me."

"You know what to do," Cherry replied as she leapt to her feet.

Acton would run back to the cover of the forest and wait to be picked up.

One man down already, she sped with the others toward the hole. Nothing was visible within it. The Scythians didn't appear to light their dwellings. So they were definitely nocturnal?

Something appeared at the hole. At first, Cherry couldn't make it out. Its form was so odd, so unlike anything she'd ever seen, she couldn't take it in. Its skin was bronze and papery and stretched tightly over a skeletal frame. Two large, white eyes, bisected by a vertical black line, stared out.

A pulse round flashed. Aubriot had fired.

But the creature was gone.

A beat later, Aubriot was at the hole. He halted, waiting for the others to catch up. In another second Cherry was at his side. Together, rifles lifted, they peered in.

The interior was pitch black. It seemed to absorb the sunlight, reflecting nothing. Cherry switched her visor to night vision. Now, she could see a little, but it was only another wall a couple of meters in from the outer one. It appeared to ring the dome, as if it was an inner layer of protection.

"It's full of CO2," Aubriot remarked.

She hadn't noticed, but her visor reading agreed. The gas was pouring from the breach.

"Dragan's with me," said Aubriot. "We'll go to the right. Cherry, you go left with Maddox and Maura."

"No, Maddox is with you."

"Not since you lost Acton."

There was no time for arguing. She roughly gestured for the woman to follow her and stepped into the dome. Taking point, she walked into the dark passageway. No aliens were in sight but she couldn't see far due to the curvature of the dome.

"Did anyone get a good look at that thing?" Maura asked.

"Not me," replied Maddox. "I only saw—"

"Stay focused," Cherry snapped. "If anything moves, shoot it, remember? And if it's near enough and hurt enough, try to grab it."

"Yeah, we remember," Maddox replied sarcastically.

The levels of atmospheric carbon dioxide increased as they walked farther from the breach. Everything else stayed the same. The white outer walls were a rich, light-absorbing black on the inside, mirrored by the interior wall, which extended overhead, running parallel as it curved beyond view.

One minute. That was the agreed time they would spend trying to capture an alien. Even so short a time was highly risky considering the hole they'd blown was their only exit.

Forty-five seconds had passed. How far had they come? Perhaps only thirty meters. They'd been walking slowly.

"See anything?" Aubriot comm'd.

"Not a thing. You?"

"Zilch."

"Get ready to leave in ten seconds."

"I might just—"

"No. That's not what we agreed."

"But we might not get—"

A shriek, quickly cut off, broke through his words.

"What was that?" Aubriot asked.

"I thought it was from your end."

"Maddox!" Maura yelled. "Where's Maddox gone?"

Cherry swung around. Maura was alone. The passageway was empty.

"She was right behind me," Maura sobbed, "and then she wasn't."

"Maddox has gone missing?" asked Aubriot.

Cherry ignored him.

It didn't seem possible that an alien could have snuck up behind them silently, snatched Maddox. and retreated out of sight without Maura noticing. She would have turned immediately she heard the other woman cry out. The Scythian would have to be lightning fast to do it.

"We're on our way," said Aubriot. "Get out of there before they take someone else."

So quick to abandon your girlfriend?

Cherry pushed the spiteful thought aside.

How had the Scythians taken Maddox?

The answer niggled at the edges of her mind. It was something to do with the Scythian city on Concordia.

She had it.

"Maura, go back. When you meet Aubriot, tell him... Never mind. Just go back. Now."

There was no time to check the other woman had followed her order. Cherry punched the interior wall. As she'd predicted, her fist sank in, followed by her arm up to her elbow. She leaned her shoulder against it and pressed with her right knee. Slowly but surely her body sank into the spongy substance. Then she was through it.

Maddox was vigorously struggling with one of the bronze-skinned creatures. It held her around the waist with its... Whatever they were, they were not arms. And it didn't have hands but long claws. The thing bent over her and tugged at her suit. The claws were incredibly sharp. They scythed through the armor and the suit split like overripe fruit. Cherry's mind flew to the Scythian spiders and Garwin's horrific death. Maddox's struggles became more frantic. Without oxygen, in a couple of minutes she would be dead.

The creature didn't seem to have noticed Cherry. It was too preoccupied with killing Maddox.

Where was its head, its brain? Near the eyes, presumably.

Cherry took aim. She was in grave danger of hitting Maddox too, but if she delayed the woman was dead anyhow the second those claws reached flesh.

She fired.

The Scythian fell, but it didn't die. It writhed on the floor like a mad thing, bucking, jerking, whirling.

Maddox took a step past it and its claws raked the leg of her suit. She screamed as blood ran from the gashes, but she didn't stop until she reached Cherry's side.

"Where did you come from?" she asked. "How do we get out of here?"

She must have been snatched so quickly she hadn't noticed being pulled through the wall.

"This way," Cherry replied.

The Scythian seemed to be weakening. Its movements had slowed to twitches but it edged closer. Cherry shoved Maddox into the wall face first and pushed with all her might. The sponge absorbed her until she was gone.

Cherry faced the alien for a good look at it.

She finally understood about the Scythian city on Concordia.

The creature was dying. Its eyes slowly opened and closed.

She fired off another shot.

It was still.

As she emerged on the other side of the wall, she found herself suddenly grabbed. Aubriot lifted her onto his shoulder and began to pound down the passageway.

"Put me down!" she shouted. "Put me down! Stars, I can run, you moron."

Maddox must have gone ahead. Cherry's night vision picked up the residual heat of splashes of her blood on the floor.

They were outside, and still Aubriot didn't set her on her feet. She was forced to let him carry her all the way back to the waiting heli. He threw her into a seat and then climbed aboard. Instantly, the heli lifted into the air. Cherry was thrown to the side as it banked.

They were all here. Acton sat at the back of the craft, Dragan beside him. Maura and Maddox sat in front of them. Maddox's visor was up and her face deathly pale as blood ran from her wounds. Aubriot was beside Cherry, staring out the window. They hadn't managed to capture an alien but they'd made it into and out of one of their domes and—

"Shit," Aubriot said, "would you look at that!"

Before even following the direction of his gaze, she knew what must be happening. Her close look at a Scythian had revealed a key fact. It explained the weird configuration of their ancient city, all walls and no doors.

A circular opening at the top of the dome had appeared, and the aliens were emerging from it. Tinted transparent spheres over their heads and tanks on their backs—no doubt supplying the CO_2 they breathed—they beat thin-skinned wings against the air and flew.

6

The purpose of the puzzles at the door remained unclear to Wilder as she walked with Niall down the tunnel beyond it. It was clear the puzzles were part of an intricate mechanical lock but why they'd been placed there was a mystery.

"I still can't believe that person at the entrance couldn't figure them out," she commented.

"You aren't *still* thinking about that?"

"I can't figure it out. It's bugging me."

"Really? I couldn't tell. You've only been talking about nothing else for the last five minutes. How about thinking about something different? Like where this tunnel is taking us."

She poked her elbow into his side. "One problem at a time. I'll work on the door lock, you concentrate on the cryptic destination."

"Seriously," said Niall, suddenly grave, "we could be walking into danger. That was probably the reason for the puzzles you're obsessing about. They must have been designed to keep people out. They were a safety measure."

"Then they weren't a very good one. We made it through without too much difficulty."

"That skeleton didn't."

"No. But why?"

"Because he or she couldn't figure them out. That's obvious."

Wilder chewed her lip. "Do you think there was something wrong with them? Like they had low cognitive function?"

"What's the point of speculating?" Niall added, after a pause. "Not everyone would be able to solve those puzzles so easily. And if you didn't know the Fibonacci sequence, it might be hard to figure out at first."

"Yeah, but that person *died* trying to figure it out. They took however long they had left and still didn't understand it."

"They might not have had very long left. Hey, look!"

Wilder swept her headlamp in the direction Niall's was pointing. The monotonous concrete of the dusty tunnel was broken by a door.

"And this one doesn't have anything to solve to open it," Niall added. He grasped the doorknob and turned it.

"You shouldn't just open a door like that," Wilder chided. "Wasn't it you who was saying we could be walking into danger?"

The interior reminded her of a starship cabin. A single bunk stood against the wall, the bedclothes neatly made. There was a desk and chair and a small cupboard, presumably for personal items and clothes. Above the cupboard was an empty shelf. Despite its tidiness, the room had an abandoned, forgotten air.

"Well," said Niall, "at least we have somewhere comfortable to sleep tonight."

Wilder gave a shiver. "I think I'd rather sleep on the floor in a sleeping bag." She crossed the room to the bed and touched the covers. The fibers parted under her fingertips. Experimentally, she pushed both hands down on the mattress. It sank beneath her hands and she found herself pressing against the bed frame. "This place is incredibly old."

"Is that so surprising? I thought the seed vault was built in the days before the appearance of the Natural Movement."

"It was, but something gave me the impression this area is newer, an add-on, you know? At a later date."

"Maybe you're wrong."

"Maybe." Wilder bent down to open the cupboard door, but it was jammed shut with rust. "I bet there's nothing inside it anyway." She stood up. "This was someone's room once but apart from the bedding there's no sign of their things. The shelf and desk are empty. There are no pictures on the walls. Whoever lived here packed up their stuff and left."

"Let's carry on looking around," Niall said. "If the rest of it is as neglected as this room there hasn't been anyone here for a long time, so it's completely safe."

As they walked down the corridor they encountered similar rooms, all containing single bunks and minimal furniture, all in a state of extreme age. Unlike the seed vault, the place was so far underground no rodents or bugs had colonized it. It was lifeless. Wilder began to long for the surface.

"How big do you think this is?" she asked.

"We've walked a long way. Farther than the diameter of the mountain at its base, I would say. We're now under the surface on the other side, which means it's impossible to guess how big this place is. It could extend the width of the island."

"Have we passed the signal beacon yet?"

"I don't know. I lost the signal not long after we entered the vault."

A pair of doors appeared in their way. Accordion-style, they encompassed the entire width of the tunnel. A small rectangular window glinted in the light from Wilder's headlamp as the beam hit it.

"Interesting," she murmured, stepping closer. She peered through the window but saw nothing but empty space in the rays from her lamp. "That's a big room. Way bigger than anything we've come across so far."

"Let me look," said Niall.

Wilder moved away from the window and inspected the doors. A simple handle was set into one of them halfway up. She grasped it and tugged. With a metallic screech, the doors parted, folding up as they opened.

She sensed, rather than saw, a vast space. The light from her lamp faded into darkness, and the air felt different. While the tunnel had felt close and stuffy, here currents wafted against her skin. She called out, "Hello?"

Her voice echoed back three or four times.

"Shhh!" Niall hissed.

"Why? A few minutes ago you said this place is completely safe."

"There's no point in taking unnecessary risks."

"I just wanted to confirm my suspicion, and I was right. This room is huge. It must reach as high as the surface. I wonder if it's a natural cavern." She set off to explore.

"Slow down," Niall urged. "You have no idea what's ahead. Oh."

"Oh, what?"

"The signal. It's reappeared. I can see it now."

"Then let's find it! Lead the way."

Holding his interface in two hands, Niall swiveled to get his bearings. "This way." He moved off, checking the screen and the ground in front of him alternately.

Wilder followed, glancing from side to side, but she saw only concreted ground.

Niall proceeded on a diagonal from the double doors, crossing the wide area in silence.

After a couple of minutes, Wilder asked, "Are we close yet?"

"Nearly. Uhhh..." He veered to the left.

"Wait, there's something ahead of you." Her light had reflected from glass and she'd caught a glimpse of their two figures, shadowy under the bright spots of their headlamps.

It was another set of double doors. Two large windows were set into them.

"Look!" Wilder exclaimed. "It's a control booth."

The walls of the room through the doors were covered with equipment. Screens, dials, gauges, buttons, and sliders on panels festooned it. Ropes of wires ran between them, bound with tape.

Wilder's heart raced. "What's it for? And what's it doing down here?" She felt as though they'd stumbled across something significant, though she had no idea what it could be. "Can we get inside?"

Niall's hands were already on the handles. He pushed cautiously but they didn't budge. "No, it's locked."

"Maybe there's another set of puzzles." But the walls to each side of the doors were blank.

"They must have locked them for a reason," said Niall. "The equipment must be dangerous."

"Not after all this time." She tried the handles, but she didn't pull. She pushed, and the doors opened.

Light filled the room and a holo flashed to life in the center. Wilder gave a little jump and grabbed the edge of the door.

The translucent holo was of a man wearing old, patched clothes, little more than rags. He was speaking but not in English.

After a few moments, Niall asked, "Can you understand anything he's saying?"

"Not a word."

One thing was clear, however. The man was not giving a friendly greeting to the visitors from the future. His eyes were narrow and spittle flew from his mouth as he spoke.

He was angry.

7

***

Cherry cradled the man's head. Blood from the wound on his chest welled up with each breath he took. As he exhaled, it coated his lips and face in a fine spray. So much blood. She could feel it, wet and warm on her thighs where he lay on her lap.

He was saying something, murmuring words she couldn't catch. She leaned down, bending her body over his, turning her head so her ear was closer to his mouth. She could hear him now, but she couldn't understand him. Of course. He was an Earther, speaking their language. Of course she couldn't understand.

He was speaking his last words, probably giving her messages to pass on, messages of love, perhaps apologies, who knew? Who knew what he was saying? None of them could understand and no one would know what he said with his last breaths.

She nodded anyway.

He was too out of it, too far gone to remember that she was from another planet light years distant, that she spoke another language and the history of her people was very different from his. She gave another nod. "I understand. I'll tell them."

Relief lit his fading eyes. Then they lost focus and his body relaxed.

Cherry held onto the slumped form. She was back on Suddene inside Chimera, the chamber built to house Concordia's fifth armaments silo. She was holding Isobel, Kes's wife. Inside the dark tent the iron smell of blood had been strong. Little Nina had been quiet and still as her mother died.

"Cherry."

What would she tell Kes? How would she explain that Isobel was gone?

"Cherry, he's had it. It's over."

How would she tell Kes?

"Give him to me."

As Aubriot tugged the body from her grasp, she looked up, confused. What was he doing here in the tent?

But she wasn't in the tent. Trees surrounded them and she was sitting within ferny undergrowth.

"Are you all right?" Aubriot had laid the pilot's body out.

She blinked. "Yeah, I'm fine."

"You don't look fine. You're covered in blood, for one thing. Not a lot we can do about it now. Come on, we need to get moving." He reached down as if to lift her to her feet.

"I told you I'm okay," she snapped, standing up. "And, while I remember, you didn't need to carry me out of the dome. I'm not a kid you can haul around."

"Pardon me for wanting to save your life. Don't worry, the next time you're in trouble I won't make the same mistake. We'd better get moving."

"*I* wouldn't mind a little support," said Maddox.

The rest of them were there too: Acton, Dragan, and Maura. How had she not seen them?

Maddox did look as though she would need help with walking. The gouges the Scythian had inflicted on her leg looked painful, though she wasn't bleeding heavily. Yet Cherry hadn't failed to notice a coquettish tone in her remark. She scowled. Wouldn't the woman ever give it a rest?

"We should head west to get back to base," said Acton.

"I agree," Aubriot said, swiveling as he looked at the sky. "Sun's over there," he went on, pointing, "and it's the afternoon, so we go that way." He held out a hand to Maddox, who limped over to him. "If we can manage without any rests, we should make it back before sunset."

He set off, an arm around Maddox. The others followed in a line. Cherry took a final look at the pilot and the crashed heli before joining the end of the line.

TWENTY OR THIRTY Scythians had erupted from the dome. Cherry would never forget the sight of the creatures bursting out in such numbers, climbing aloft on the power of their wide wings. Once, on Concordia, she had disturbed nocturnal flying animals sleeping in a cave in the mountains, and their reaction had been the same—a flurry of urgent movement, a frantic explosion of life as they escaped into the air.

Only the Scythians had not been surprised or scared, they'd been out to get revenge for their murdered comrade. At least, that was how it seemed as they flew after the heli. Or perhaps they didn't care about the Scythian she'd killed. Perhaps they were only angry about the hole in their precious dome, still leaking CO_2.

The Earther pilot had wrenched his vessel's engine up to maximum output and angled the nose-tip down to maximize acceleration. Her passengers hung forward in their harnesses.

Aubriot opened a window and the wind howled in.

"What are you doing?" Cherry yelled.

"What do you think?" He shifted in his seat and leaned out of the window, pulse rifle under his arm.

"Stars, don't hit the rotors!"

But he had the right idea. She did the same. Luckily, from her position she could shoot with her right arm. Aubriot was forced to shoot left-handed.

The Scythians swarmed after them in a bunch, making an easy target. She got off two rounds. One hit a Scythian's wing. Through the tint of the creature's visor she seemed to glimpse its mouth opening but any sound it made was blocked off. It separated from the rest, its flight erratic. It began to whirl and tumble over and over, losing altitude. What happened to it next Cherry didn't see. She'd hit another Scythian in its midriff. The creature clasped at the wound, no doubt in agony. But the movement caused it to drop down from the bunch. Appearing to realize it was falling, it beat its wings to regain height, but the pain from the wound was too great and it stopped flying again, reaching for it.

A window shattered. There was a zing accompanied by a metallic ping.

"What the hell's happening?" Maddox shouted.

Aubriot replied, "They're firing back."

At first, Cherry didn't understand. She hadn't seen any flashes of pulse fire, yet it was undeniable that the Scythians were attacking the heli. But how? They weren't holding anything in the claws on their wings. They couldn't or they wouldn't be able to fly.

Another zing.

The round must have passed close by her head but there was no ping. Where had it gone? After glancing around the craft's interior to check no one was hurt, she returned her attention to the Scythians and fired again. They'd spread out now, probably to be harder to hit.

She saw their weapons. Within each pair of prehensile feet was a metal object somewhat like a pulse rifle only smaller. All pointed at the heli.

Aubriot hit an alien, the pulse round exploding against its scrawny neck. The wings folded and it plummeted from the sky, the wind turning it lazily as it fell.

The heli was maintaining distance from the pursuers. If anything it was pulling away, but not fast enough. All the Scythians had to do was hit the engine or a rotor and it would crash. Cherry looked down. They'd reached the forest. Would crashing into trees be safer or more dangerous than crashing on open land?

She fired again, letting loose a stream of rounds, but aiming backward was hard and both she and her targets were moving. She couldn't hit a thing.

The heli swerved. Her stomach lurched as it sank. They were losing speed.

Had the heli taken a hit?

She faced forward. The pilot was hunching over his controls and blood oozed from a wound on his back.

It was only then she noticed the hole in his seat back. The zing she'd heard earlier had been a round hitting it. The projectile had passed through it and into the pilot. He'd been hit and hadn't said a thing.

Aubriot reached forward and grabbed the man's shoulder. He moved. He was conscious, but barely. He pushed himself upright and gripped his controls again. The heli swooped upward, throwing everyone back. But its flight was erratic. The pilot couldn't maintain control. They began to fall again.

Acton blurted, "We're gonna crash!"

What followed was hard to recall exactly. Cherry remembered the jerking of the heli as the pilot, seeming to lapse in and out of consciousness, grabbed and let go of the controls. Aubriot unfastened his harness and reached over the seat, trying to get to the controls himself. Cherry yelled at him, telling him to sit down and fasten his harness.

The forest canopy loomed upward and swung from side to side, matching the motion of the aircraft. A peek over her shoulder revealed the Scythians hovering, beating their wings impossibly fast as they watched, their bronze forms bizarrely out of place in the deepening blue sky.

The scene seemed to freeze in silence.

Then the forest rushed toward her, the crash of breaking branches and battering of foliage burst in her ears... Everything cut out.

When she woke up she was hanging upside down and her head felt thick with blood. She groped for her harness catch and released it, the understanding of what would happen dawning too late. She hit the ceiling of the heli and crumpled, groaning in pain.

Others were moving around her, dragging themselves free.

Where was Aubriot?

What had happened to the Earther pilot?

The heli was a bashed-in mess. The rotor blades had torn free, and the cabin was bent and deformed. She sat marveling at it. How had she managed to extract herself from that disaster?

"Hey," said a voice close to her ear. "You okay?"

"Nothing broken, I don't think," she replied to Aubriot.

"Can you help me with the pilot?"

"WE SHOULD HURRY UP," said Maura. "Maddox, can you go any faster? Maybe we can carry you."

"I'm doing the best I can," she snapped.

"I know what you're thinking," said Aubriot, "but the Scythians won't come after us in here."

"He's right," said Dragan. "There's no way they can maneuver through the trees. Not with those massive wings. And they can't shoot at us if they're walking."

"But they could fire on us while they're flying."

"Canopy's too dense," Dragan replied shortly.

Cherry walked on in silence. They had learned a lot. They now knew the Scythians were primarily fliers, not walkers. They also knew their weapons fired projectiles, not pulse rounds. And that their domes were vulnerable to regular explosives. They had other vulnerabilities. Sunlight was too bright for their eyes. Their visors had been tinted. And they couldn't breathe Earth's atmosphere.

The knowledge had come at the cost of the Earther pilot's life but it was invaluable. Surely there was a way to defeat these creatures. If the Earthers mounted a sustained attack, perhaps they could drive them off the globe.

Her shoulders slumped as she recalled a vital piece of information. How could she have forgotten? Aubriot had talked about it at the meeting with Buka, the head of the GAA, but he hadn't followed his train of thought to the natural conclusion.

The Scythians had a deadly weapon in their arsenal: the biocide.

Even if they could be persuaded to give up on their plan of colonizing Earth with humans as their slaves, they would never leave peacefully. They would do the same as they had done on Concordia. They would release their deadliest weapon and render the planet all but uninhabitable.

Everything that had been learned about them didn't matter. It didn't matter what the Earthers or Concordians did. The situation was hopeless.

8

As Wilder watched the man's holo talk and wondered what to do next, a second voice spoke from the darkness behind her.

"Whoa!" She started and swung around. Her headlamp caught a man's face in its beams.

"He's armed!" Niall blurted and clutched her arm, attempting to drag her away. His light had flashed against the muzzle of the rifle slung over the man's shoulder.

Wilder resisted. "He isn't aiming at us. I think it's safe."

The man had continued to talk, and he raised a hand as if in an attempt to reassure them. But, like the holo, his words were unintelligible.

Niall leaned closer to her. "This one's real, right?"

"I think so, but I'm sure as hell not going to touch him to make sure."

"Where did he come from? Did he follow us in here?"

"He must have, but..." An odd feeling was nagging at her, something that intellectually she knew couldn't be right no matter what her gut was telling her. "Let's go in the room. I want to get a proper look at him."

As she'd hoped, when they went into the room where the holo

was playing, the stranger did the same. He seemed to be appraising them as much as they were appraising him.

He was tall, taller than most Earthers she'd seen, and he wore unusual clothes. A neatly fitting pin-striped suit clothed him from his neck to his knees, and he didn't wear pants but closely wrapped strips of cloth around his calves. His boots were black and looked new except for the fact they were coated in thick dust. His hair was the oddest part of his appearance. It was long but it had been gathered into a bun on the top of his head. For an Earther he was impressively clean shaven.

But was he an Earther? Could Wilder's feeling be correct, and, if so, how? How could it be possible?

He seemed to conclude his assessment. He lifted a hand and gestured toward the interface Niall was carrying.

"Does he want me to give it to him?" Niall asked.

"Try it and see what he does."

The stranger took the interface, said something Wilder assumed meant 'thanks', and took it to a console, where he sat down.

Wilder joined him and peered over his shoulder. The man didn't object. He placed the interface on a smooth black pad and then touched another with his fingertips.

"What's he doing?" Niall asked.

"How would I know?"

The man inclined his head and was still. Was he concentrating? It was hard to tell. His eyes remained open though unfocused.

"Niall, look at his chest. Is he even—"

Light burst from the chamber they'd just left, paling the room's light into insignificance.

"Look at that place!" Niall exclaimed, returning to the open door.

It was even larger than Wilder had guessed. The ceiling hung thirty meters above them and the space was about a hundred and fifty meters long and wide. A seam circled the entire floor about seven meters from the wall and the two sections were made from different materials. The outer was ordinary tile while the inner was metallic. Long tubular lights were suspended from the ceiling.

"He must have done that," said Niall. "He turned on the lights."

"Look, he's shut off the holo too. I didn't notice at first."

"I wonder if he owns this whole setup. Maybe he was broadcasting the signal so someone would come and rescue him."

"He doesn't look in need of rescuing." The more she'd seen of the man and his behavior, the greater her conviction that her feelings were correct had grown. "This is going to sound crazy, but I think I know him."

"That does sound crazy. You can't possibly know him. He's an Earther, and this is the first time we've been here. Unless you think you saw him somewhere else?"

"I did see him somewhere else. Somewhere not on Earth and a long time ago. I remember him from when I was a little girl."

"That's insane. Are you feeling okay?"

"I'm fine and I know I'm right."

"I suppose it's possible he had a doppelganger, or maybe you're mis-remembering."

There was no point in trying to convince Niall. Besides, she was sure the man would prove she was correct soon.

He straightened up, turned, and smiled. "Hello. I'm pleased to make your acquaintance. Could you please tell me your names?"

Staring, Niall made eye contact with Wilder and then returned his gaze to the man. "H-How come you're speaking English? Did you find out where we're from when you checked our interface?"

"He learned it," Wilder explained. "He learned it just now. That's right, isn't it?" she asked the man. Except he was not a man.

"That is correct. I have analyzed the data on your device. I may pronounce some of your words incorrectly at first. I would appreciate it if you would inform me of the correct pronunciation."

"Happy to," Wilder replied. She introduced herself and Niall. "Do you mind if I try to guess your name?"

"If that's your wish, I will comply."

"Huh?" said Niall. He touched her shoulder. "What are you doing? We're going to be here a long time if you try to do that."

"I don't think so." She frowned. The name she'd been trying to remember had been on the tip of her tongue but had slipped away. Concentrating, she searched her memory again. She'd been young

when she'd learned it, and she'd been on the periphery of everything
that had gone on.

She had it. "Are you called Strongquist?"

He smiled. "You have met my counterpart. Many things are
becoming clear to me. You must be from the colony the other
Strongquist set out to help."

Niall breathed, "What the hell?"

"We named the planet Concordia," she said.

"So the mission succeeded. That is gratifying to know."

"It did succeed, only... A lot's happened since then."

"I would be interested to hear about it. Your interface only
contains recent information."

"I can tell you everything. I was there from the start."

"You were? I don't understand. Even if you were one of the scientists suspended in cryosleep, you should have died of old age many
years ago. Unless perhaps you were only recently revived?"

"That's another long story."

"I would also like to know why you have returned to Earth."

"I get it," Niall announced. "He's a Guardian."

"Finally," Wilder replied sarcastically.

"Hey, I never saw one." He stepped closer to the android, who
regarded him with a questioning look. "So he looks like one of the
androids who arrived on the *Mistral*?"

"As far as I can remember he's the original Strongquist's twin. It
must have been easier to reuse his design."

"Actually," the android demurred, "the second Strongquist is a
copy of me. Not that it really matters. Is he among your party?"

"He died," replied Wilder. "I'm sorry. They all died defending the
colony."

"I see. So they fulfilled their intended function. Steen would have
been pleased."

"Steen?"

"One of the Makers. The holo that was activated when you
entered this room was a recording Steen made before the team shut
everything down and left."

"He didn't seem too happy in it," Niall remarked.

"He grew very bitter toward the end of the project," Strongquist replied. "He would rail about the sacrifice he'd made for people he had no connection to and would never meet. I think in the beginning his focus was on the scientific challenge of the project. It was only as it drew near completion he saw beyond it to the dull, unsatisfying, and dangerous years that remained ahead. He also saw more clearly what he'd given up—the chance of escaping Earth. His message is full of anger and does not contain useful content. It is probably not beneficial to watch it, though I am able to translate it if you wish."

Niall had wandered to the doorway and was leaning out, resting one hand on the frame. He whistled. "They built a starship in here?"

"That is correct. It was a truly magnificent feat, considering the state of Earth at the time. The materials and parts had to be sourced from all over the globe or manufactured here in unfavorable conditions. And it all had to be completed in secrecy. The Natural Movement as an entity had disintegrated during the collapse of civilization, but the general anti-scientific sentiment continued. Plus, anyone with a supply of food or still-functioning items of equipment was a target. That is why the scientists came to Svalbard, where they would be safe from marauders and scavengers."

Wilder asked, "Do you know what happened to them after they launched the *Mistral*?"

"My knowledge of the past stops at the moment I shut down. There may be other messages or evidence that answers your question. As it is extremely unlikely the team was able to enter cryosuspension the logical conclusion would be they all died many years ago."

Niall turned his attention away from the chamber and back to the android. "Why did they create the signal beacon?"

"I was not aware of it until your arrival triggered my reactivation. I perceive it now but don't know its purpose. When I was ordered to shut myself down all I knew was that my assistance might be required again. I didn't personally anticipate ever meeting anyone from your planet, but the team might have hoped a delegation might arrive on Earth one day. Or perhaps they simply hoped their work would not be forgotten."

Wilder mentally added, *Not forgotten by people who understood.*

The android's story made sense of the puzzles at the entrance. Only someone with an understanding of arithmetic and a basic interest in mathematics would be able to open the door. To anyone else the site would remain an enigma. The person who died must have hoped it contained food stores and had starved to death trying to get in.

9

Cherry stuffed the remainder of her belongings into a bag. She hadn't brought much down from the *Sirocco*, and in her brief time on Earth she'd only acquired a few additional items. Everything fitted into a couple of bags. She took a last look at the small room she'd occupied for the last weeks, and then walked to the door.

Itai was standing on the other side of it.

They each took a moment to get over their surprise, and then the Earther looked her up and down, taking in the bag hanging from her shoulder and the other she'd put on the floor in order to open the door.

"So it's true," he said.

"I'm sorry, but I'm in a hurry." She picked up the second bag and tried to move around him, but Itai stepped sideways to block her exit.

"You're really leaving? All of you?"

"Nothing's been decided yet. But we are returning to the ship for now."

"How long will you be gone?"

"I don't know. We have things we need to discuss."

"You could do that here, with us. Buka is open to more discussion."

"I'm sure he is. Look, would you move out of my way? The shuttle is scheduled to depart in fifteen minutes."

Itai rested a hand on the door frame. "They'll wait for you. You're too important to leave behind."

Cherry sighed. Even two-handed she was no match for a fully grown man, and the last thing she wanted was a fight. She felt guilty enough as it was. This might be the last time she spoke to an Earther, and she didn't want to depart the planet on bad terms.

"Can't we talk about this?" Itai asked. "There's still a lot to talk about."

"Maybe there is, but we have things to talk about too. So if you wouldn't mind...?"

"Please, hear me out."

She put down her bag again. "You have one minute."

"You say 'you' have things to talk about too as if you're different from us, but we're both human. Concordians are the same as us. If you leave you'll be abandoning your own kind. How will you be able to live with yourselves knowing you refused to help your cousins when they were in need?"

"We have helped you. We risked our lives breaking into a Scythian dome. We drew them out into the open in broad daylight. Now you know what they look like and what they can do, you're in a better position to fight them. We've done a lot already. You seem to be forgetting we could have left at the first sight of them."

"I know, and we do appreciate the fact that you stayed. Only..."

He was out of arguments yet he still didn't want to let her go.

She said gently, "We understand what you're up against. Believe me, we really do. But we have others to think about. Our people are waiting for us. They desperately need the seeding material. If we don't return soon we could be too late." The last point was speculation though she wasn't about to admit it. The *Sirocco* had been absent from Concordia for so long, no one knew what they might find upon their return. The colony might not have survived or the Scythians might have dealt a second dose of biocide, rendering the planet entirely sterile.

Lifting her bag from the floor, she pushed past Itai. He didn't resist. As she reached the end of the passageway, Buka hobbled into view, leaning heavily on a walking stick.

He raised a hand and said something she didn't understand. She hurried away. Word had gotten out that the Concordians were leaving. She didn't want to wait around for more Earthers to accost her. Things could turn nasty.

When she made it to the shuttle she was the last to board.

As Zapata flew them up to the *Sirocco* the mood in the passenger cabin was somber. Everyone seemed to be wrestling with their feelings. Cherry's were mixed too. Since her realization that, regardless of the aid the Earthers received their future was doomed, she'd battled with her conscience over the best course of action. Kes would have probably wanted to stay if he'd been alive. Aubriot had the same attachment to the planet of his birth. For her, Concordia was her home and her first allegiance, yet she also felt a duty to the Earthers.

She wished Ethan were here. Not only would he have known in his heart the right thing to do, he would have confidently and decisively led the Concordians to do it.

Aubriot slid into the next seat. "I bet you're glad you got your way."

"What?" She squeezed herself up against the window. Aubriot was not particularly bulky but he was strong and, for the first time since she'd known him, his presence felt physically threatening.

"Don't play innocent. You got what you wanted all along."

"You mean leaving Earth? Nothing's been decided yet."

"And yet here we are *leaving Earth*. Seems to me the decision's been taken. Only no one's told the Earthers. Vessey's recalled us all to the ship so no one gets lynched when she gives Buka the bad news."

Lynched. He'd used that word before. It was something to do with hanging.

"If you really think the Earthers will kill us if we don't help them maybe it's better that we leave, and soon. We've already done a lot for them and they aren't the least bit grateful. They seem to expect us to sacrifice everything we have and even our lives to protect them, as if we don't have our own planet to protect."

"So that's what you've been telling everyone. It's no wonder the mood changed." He was clenching and unclenching his fists as they lay on his knees.

"You really think I orchestrated this whole thing?" It was true that, following the mission to break into the dome, she'd expressed her worries to other Concordians. She'd explained her realization that Earth was in an impossible bind, faced with the choice between enslavement and destruction. The people she'd talked to might have discussed her thoughts with others, but none of it had been deliberate. If other Concordians had come to the same conclusion as her and related their change of heart to Vessey it wasn't her fault.

When Aubriot didn't answer, she went on, "You said it yourself—Earth's screwed. It doesn't take a genius to figure it out. Anyone who lived through the biocide would come to the same conclusion eventually, so save your blame for the ones who are actually responsible for this situation—the Scythians."

Aubriot still didn't answer. He only stared at the back of the seat in front of him, continuing to clench his fists. He seemed to be undergoing some kind of mental crisis.

"What I don't get is," she said, "you *know* Earth can't be saved. You saw it first, right? That day we got back from spying on the Scythians building their dome. You saw it then. You said as much. Why can't you accept it's over for the Earthers and it's time for us to move on?"

He jerked his head around to face her, his features rigid. "Because I can't," he spat. "Cherry, you never saw Earth in its heyday. There were billions of people. The night sky lit up with the lighting from vast cities. Roads and railways traveling thousands of miles. Planes and shuttles filling the skies. Container ships sailing across the oceans, transporting food and products between continents. Art, music, books, vids, sims, dancing, circuses, restaurants, sports, clubs, societies..." He caught his breath before continuing, his tone softened, "Medicine, manufacturing, construction, technology, research, finances, law courts..." He paused again. "Then the Natural Movement shit on everything and now it's gone." He added quietly, "It's like a bloody country town in the arse end of nowhere. Everything's gone. *Everything.*"

She hadn't realized his return to a changed Earth had affected him so badly, but it was hard to be sympathetic toward someone who never sympathized with anyone except himself. "What did you expect? The Guardians told us things had gone downhill after the *Nova Fortuna* left. I don't know what you thought you would find."

"*Something*," he muttered. "A sign of what went before. There were paintings, Cherry. Already hundreds of years old in my lifetime, worth millions, billions, even. Beautiful works of art. Where are they now? If they still survive they'll be rotting in a basement somewhere with no one to appreciate them. There were buildings, ancient monuments, surviving from great civilizations. You could go and see them, walk around them and imagine the famous people who lived and died in them. Where are they now? Who remembers those people?"

"Just you, I guess."

Was he finally grieving Kes, his remaining link to his past? Aubriot hadn't shown any emotion regarding his fellow Earther's death. It was hard to imagine Aubriot feeling anything for anyone, but it was possible. More likely, he was missing the one person who remembered how important he'd been in Earth's former incarnation.

Aubriot nodded, saying, as if to himself, "Just me."

10

Vessey looked better than she had in a while. The rumor was she hadn't touched a drop of alcohol since the *Sirocco* entered Earth orbit. Her skin was clearer, the bags under her eyes less heavy, and her demeanor was more assured. More key to her improvement than going teetotal, Cherry guessed, was the fact that the captain felt the ship's personnel was finally behind her.

She greeted the shuttle passengers brightly as they disembarked and chatted to a few who were her personal friends. Perhaps spurred by the responses they gave, she announced an immediate meeting.

It was a little too soon. It would have been better to give people time to settle in and get used to being aboard the ship again. But, with some grumbling, the Concordians left to put their luggage in their cabins before going to the meeting room.

In particular, it would have been a good idea to give Aubriot time and space to accept they'd done all they could for their Earther cousins, and that now they were going to put their own needs first. Cherry watched as he stomped off angrily. She contemplated saying something to Vessey but the damage was done. Canceling the meeting the minute she called it would make her look indecisive and weak. They still had a journey of several weeks ahead, assuming the jump drive worked.

Cherry decided to go straight to the meeting. The cabin she now shared with Miki and Nina after taking on the girls as—she felt—an inadequate adoptive parent, was on the other side of the ship, and her minimal luggage wouldn't get in the way. Several others had the same idea and when she arrived the room already had some occupants. Vessey arrived and nodded at her. She walked to the front of the room to wait, clutching the back of a seat nervously.

When everyone had arrived, she gave a cough to quieten the murmuring. "Thank you for coming at such short notice. I think we all know why we're here. The situation on Earth has become untenable. The Scythians have constructed domes all over the planet and hundreds of Earthers have gone missing. It's clear that the aliens have embarked on a program of subjugation of the human population and colonization of the planet."

She gave a voice command and the lighting dimmed. "Also, I would like you to look at this."

A holo lit up the room. It was a spacescape, showing Earth with its thin layer of blue, luminous atmosphere.

Vessey said, "Display Scythian vessels."

Brilliant spots appeared, high above the atmosphere but clearly also in orbit. Cherry counted five.

"There are more," Vessey said. "What you can see is only what the computer can display on the holo. Scythian vessels surround the planet."

"How many?" someone asked.

"Twenty."

There was a whistle and several gasps.

"We've known the number for a while, but now I can tell you the scan data indicates that many are transports. They brought the smaller colonization vessels after discovering Earth was undefended a couple of years ago. The *Sirocco* must have come as quite the surprise upon their return."

"And her gun," came a comment from the audience.

"Exactly," said Vessey. "We've been lucky. If the Scythians had attacked us with the same ships they used to attack Concordia, we couldn't have defeated them in the end. The *Parvus*'s weapon has bought us time, but it's my belief that time will shortly run out. The aliens must have called for military backup. We need to leave, and soon, if we're to make it back to Concordia."

A hand rose. It was Maura's. "But the Parvus's weapon deterred the Scythians before. Why wouldn't it work now?"

Cherry replied, "The Scythians had already released their biocide when the Parvus started attacking them. They had no reason to stick around and risk their ships. They thought the biocide would kill us anyway. If they really want Earth, the Parvus's weapon won't be a deterrent, especially not in this part of the galaxy where there are no Assembly members to come to our aid."

"But the Scythians must know where we're from," Maura argued. "What's to stop them going to our planet and attacking us again?"

"Nothing at all," said Vessey, "but Concordia is easier to defend. We've done it before and we can do it again. Maybe we can convince the Scythians to leave us alone, especially if they already have Earth as their prize."

Maura asked, "Give up our origin planet in return for being allowed to live on theirs?"

"The Scythians might accept the tit for tat. It's impossible to know, but, regardless, we can't protect Earth with our one ship, and Earth's population is too large and spread out and their infrastructure is too weak for it to protect itself." Vessey took a breath. "It's a lost cause. It's time we accepted that and moved on. We've gathered everything we need to re-seed Concordia so there's no reason for us to wait any longer. We're going home. We'll make the first jump in forty-eight hours."

"When are you going to tell Buka?" asked Aubriot. "He's gonna kick off."

"Naturally, I expect Mr Buka will be extremely disappointed. I hope he can understand and accept my decision with grace. Regardless, we leave in forty-eight hours."

"What about Niall and Wilder?" Zapata asked.

Vessey replied, "What about them?" Before the pilot could answer, she quickly scanned the room and added, "Shit. I'd forgotten about their plan to investigate the signal. Does anyone know how far they got?"

"They, er..." said Zapata. He squared his shoulders. "I flew them to the island."

"You what?! I gave you express orders not to—"

"I'm sorry, but I thought it was less dangerous than letting them attempt to reach it on an Earther ship."

"Ugh. You're probably right. But this direct contravention of my order will not be forgotten. As you flew them there you can damned well fly back and pick them up. Comm them to let them know you're coming so they're ready to leave as soon as you arrive."

The meeting broke up. As the attendees left, Cherry realized she couldn't see Miki or Nina. Maybe they'd missed the notification. The girls had been shadows of their former, cheerful selves ever since their father's death, and their mood hadn't been lightened by the fact that they hadn't been allowed to return to the surface since his funeral.

How would they feel about returning to Concordia? They would be leaving Kes's grave behind and would never be able to visit it. And when they arrived home, what would they find? Did the house they'd shared with their father even exist anymore?

Similar prospects applied to everyone on the ship. Many had left loved ones behind who must have died and no one knew the truth about the current state of their planet, but the girls were young and they'd loved Kes so much, they could be even more traumatized.

Cherry steeled herself as she walked to their cabin, preparing to break the bad news.

The atmosphere on the ship had changed. Enthusiastic chatter floated along the passageways as the Concordians discussed Vessey's decision. In the long years of the journey the mood had not been so upbeat. It was understandable. Though they would be flying to an unknown fate they would also be flying from known danger and a hopeless cause.

Now the decision had been made, and the right decision, guilt began to eat at Cherry. It felt bad to abandon their cousins in their hour of need. She was glad she wasn't the one who had to break it to Buka.

When she arrived at the cabin, it was empty.

She comm'd Miki, guessing they were probably working in the Ark. Its re-conversion to a storage facility wasn't quite complete and the girls had been helping out as a welcome distraction.

Miki didn't answer the comm, so she tried Nina.

The result was the same.

It was odd. Wherever they were on the ship they should be reachable, and as their bunks were empty they obviously weren't asleep.

Why weren't they answering?

Then she saw the small devices on their bedside tables.

What the hell?

She strode to Miki's table and picked up the ear comm. Why in all the galaxy had she taken it out?

She scanned the cabin. The light on her interface was flashing. A message was waiting.

Cherry, please don't be mad, but we decided we want to live on Earth. Nina overheard the captain talking about the plan to go back to Concordia really soon. We don't want to leave with you guys. We know it's dangerous but we want to be on Earth, near Dad. We don't want to leave him all alone down there. So we're going to stow away on the shuttle. Don't try to find us. We hope you have a safe journey home. Thanks for everything you've done. You were like another Mom. We love you. Have a good life.

Love, Miki and Nina.

11

It was surreal to sit with a Guardian and tell it all that had happened on Concordia since the arrival of the *Nova Fortuna*. Wilder had never imagined she would meet another one so long after all the others had been destroyed. She'd certainly never imagined she would meet one on Earth. It was a lot to take in.

She told Strongquist about the First Night Attack, when saboteurs had turned off the electric fencing and sluglimpets had invaded the camp, killing colonists horribly by dissolving their flesh. And she told him how Ethan and Cariad had saved many lives with their calmness and quick-thinking.

"That was the night the *Mistral* arrived," she said. "It was a lucky coincidence. If it hadn't been for the Guardians many more people would have died, possibly everyone. The sluglimpets were relentless in those days. We found out later that the Fila had eradicated their food source in that area, so they were starving."

"The Fila?" Strongquist asked.

"Sorry, I'm getting ahead of myself. I'll explain about them in a minute."

"Before you go on, I heard Niall, refer to me as a Guardian earlier, and you used the same word again just now. This was the name the colonists gave us?"

"The other Strongquist explained... Can I call you Strongquist II? It's confusing."

"Call me whatever you like. I can be known by another name if it helps."

"Strongquist II is fine, I think. Though..." She vaguely recalled Cherry had an antipathy toward the Guardians and had probably disliked the original Strongquist. But changing his name wouldn't make anything better. The resemblance to the first Strongquist was an unmistakable reminder. "Never mind. We can call you Strongquist II. Where was I? Oh, yes. Strongquist explained they were there to protect the colony from the descendants of the Natural Movement members who had infiltrated the project. That was how they got the name Guardians." She paused. "You have to understand, I was young when all this happened. I wasn't there for the First Night Attack, thank the stars. I didn't go to the surface until later. What I'm telling you is secondhand."

"I only need to know the gist."

"Well, there were lots of problems in the beginning, and not only due to the saboteurs. The scientists—they called them the Woken—and the generational colonists, the Gens, both thought they should be in control of the colonization attempt. There was a *lot* of anger, a lot of fighting. Between the Natural Movement saboteurs, sluglimpet attacks, and the vying for control, it was a miracle the colony succeeded. To be honest, the presence of the Guardians made things worse in some ways. They were armed, you see, and the Woken turned them into a militia to subdue the Gens. You can imagine how well that went down."

Strongquist II nodded. "An unfortunate and unforeseen consequence. The Makers did not anticipate that result. They thought they were helping the colony and that without their intervention it was doomed."

Niall commented, "Their intentions were good. And this..." he gestured at the vast chamber outside the office "...this monumental effort shows the lengths they went to in order to safeguard the survival of human civilization. And it worked, right? I have a question,

Wilder. When was it the colonists realized the Guardians were androids?"

"That was after the cave settlement was sabotaged, I think."

Strongquist II asked, "So they managed to maintain the subterfuge for some time?"

"Oh, months, if not a year."

"The Makers were conflicted about whether to divulge our true nature to the colonists. Some felt it would cause distrust if it was known we were not human."

"It did, as I remember. Most Gens hated the Guardians." Wilder thought of Cherry again. "Though, to be fair, that was mostly the Woken's fault. Who likes the person aiming a gun at them? Uhh, where was I?"

"The sabotage of the cave settlement," said Niall.

"Right. You know, it's funny but the revelation about the Guardians seemed to bring everyone together."

"A common enemy," said Strongquist II.

"Perhaps. Anyway, it was around that time we discovered the Fila. They're an intelligent alien species who had colonized Concordia decades before the *Nova Fortuna* arrived. But we didn't know about them because they're aquatic. They were living in the seas, oceans, rivers, and lakes, and we didn't even know they existed. They also didn't know about us at first, not until we started living and working near water."

"So humanity has made first contact with an extra-terrestrial species? How interesting. Do the two sets of colonists coexist peacefully?"

"The Fila have left Concordia," Wilder said sadly, thinking of Quinn, who she would probably never see again. "The ones who survived the biocide, that is."

As Strongquist II opened his mouth, clearly about to ask for further explanation, she held up her hands. "This is going to take all day. I have an idea. How about you return with us to the *Sirocco*? Concordia's history is bound to be somewhere in her data banks. You can learn all about it there. And I'm sure everyone will be fascinated to meet you."

"I'd be delighted to accept your invitation. Shall we leave now? How did you come to Svalbard?"

"What?!" Niall exclaimed. "No way. We can't leave without having a look around. Right, Wilder?"

"I guess so." She frowned. "Yeah, of course." This might be the only chance she had to see the place where the famous *Mistral* and Guardians had been built. She asked Strongquist II, "What's left to see? What's the power source for the lighting, for instance?"

"A fusion reactor."

"Holy shit," breathed Wilder. "You have a freaking fusion reactor on site?"

"Only a small one. I recall the team planned to shut it down. It must have re-started as you entered the outer door. It's pleasing that it still works after all this time."

"Show us," said Niall. "I want to see everything."

The site put anything Wilder had ever seen on Concordia to shame. It extended far deeper into the mountain and the surrounding land than she'd thought. Many workrooms contained equipment she didn't recognize, but that was clearly highly sophisticated. Strongquist II explained these were the areas where the Makers had constructed the androids. In other places she knew the purpose of the machinery was to create the many parts that made up a starship, including the a-grav. It was astounding to think that humans had invented the precious drive centuries ago, only for the knowledge to be nearly lost.

It *was* lost here on Earth.

"I'm blown away," Niall remarked as they left yet another work site. "Just when I think I've got my head around the scope of all the scientists and engineers did I see something else that's amazing. It was hard enough building a starship on Concordia, where we had the entire colony behind us and priority for all its resources. How the hell did the people here manage to do everything they did, in secret, and scrounging materials or making things from scratch?"

Strongquist replied, "You're forgetting they had a much larger population to draw upon. As I understand it, the scientists had developed an underground network in response to the rise of the Natural Movement."

"They were *driven* underground from the sound of it," said Wilder.

"That may be a more accurate description. They had the advantage of technical knowledge and skills to maintain effective channels of communication. While the world was falling apart around them, they used their intelligence and training to survive, building communities of like-minded people. The resources of earlier generations remained available to those who understood how to use them. There were abandoned space programs and myriad other scientific endeavors all over the globe."

"That makes sense," said Niall. "Earth's population must have still been in the billions then. What I don't get is, why didn't the scientists and engineers use their advantages to try to re-establish an advanced civilization? I mean, I appreciate that they built the *Mistral* and you androids. If they hadn't I might not be here. But wouldn't it have been easier for them to put their skills to use on Earth, trying to rebuild civilization where they could also be more certain of the outcome, rather than trying to save a colony light years across the galaxy?"

"Do you think they didn't?" Strongquist II asked. "If you search the archives you will find many instances of attempts to do exactly that. All failed, often with much loss of life and permanent injury, not to mention the destruction of irreplaceable equipment. Eventually, the consensus was that once civilization passes a certain point in a downward trajectory, recovery is impossible, in the short term at least. Therefore the scientists faced the choice of saving a space colony they knew was well-planned and heavily resourced or making their own colonization attempt on another planet. In truth, despite Steen's ravings, the latter option was not viable. The team managed to build the *Mistral*, but a ship the size of the *Nova Fortuna* was beyond its capabilities. Moreover, there were far more people wanting to leave the planet than the two thousand the original colony ship carried. Who would have chosen who was to go or stay, and based on what criteria?"

Wilder gazed around the workroom, with its dusty benches and tall stools, its dry sinks and rusted faucets, its silent machines and dark corners filled with useless items left behind. Her mind conjured shadows of the men and women who had worked here, laboring for a purpose from which they would personally derive no benefit, striving for a cause to benefit humanity, not themselves.

She imagined the camaraderie of the united endeavor, the thrill of the intense work and the anxiety that something might go wrong, that they might not achieve their goal, or the willfully ignorant majority of humankind might discover the site and attack. And they did it all knowing they would never find out if they achieved their goal, whether all their effort would be worth it.

Perhaps it didn't really matter to them. Perhaps it was enough to simply try.

"You've seen the main work areas," said Strongquist II. "Would you like to see the residential accommodation?"

"I think we passed through a section on our way in," Niall replied. "I'm not interested. Are you, Wilder?"

She shook her head. The rooms where people relaxed and slept were predictably similar across the ages, but that wasn't what put her off. She felt a strong connection to the people who had lived and worked at the site. Now they were gone, lost in time.

"I'm glad we came here," she said. "Especially glad we met you, Strongquist II, but I think we should report in and tell our captain what we've found. It feels important though I'm not sure how just yet."

"Let's go up to the surface and comm Vessey," said Niall.

The android said, "I will show you the way."

12

The stairs wound around and around. Every five meters or so motion-activated lights would blink on above, revealing another section with no apparent exit. At the same time, lights below would turn off, plunging the lower levels into darkness.

"How much farther is the exit?" Niall asked.

"Only ninety-eight meters," replied Strongquist II.

"Ninety-eight meters? I thought you said this was the quickest way back."

"It is, by five point zero five meters."

Niall grumbled something Wilder didn't catch, but she could guess at his complaint. His thighs and calves had to be aching as much as hers. The android might have chosen the shortest route but it was also the most strenuous. Naturally, as a machine it hadn't factored physical exertion into its choice of exit.

She was puzzled. The stairs they'd descended at the far end of the seed vault hadn't been anywhere near so tall. The corridors had sloped downward, accounting for some of the additional height they were now scaling, but it couldn't be all of it. "Where exactly are you taking us? You know we have to go back to the airstrip, right?"

"There's a gully running across the lower slope of the mountain.

That's the quickest way to the place where your shuttle landed, if I understood your description correctly."

"Why didn't the Makers enter via the seed vault? Why did they create this entrance?"

"In the early years the vault was the only entrance. This was constructed in later years, for safety. People would turn up at the vault from time to time, following a rumor of a massive storehouse from the old days, stuffed to the rafters with grain and dried and preserved food supplies. Often, they were starving when they arrived. Hunger made them desperate and violent, and chance encounters with the scientists resulted in some deaths. So this shaft was sunk at the far end of the gully. Only those who knew the way were able to find it. If, by chance, a stranger who had heard about the project arrived, they could still enter via the vault entrance by solving a few puzzles. It was a basic safeguard and yet surprisingly effective."

Another set of lights flicked on. Still, no door appeared.

"There is a third exit from the site," said Strongquist II, "a much larger one, for equipment and materials. A dirt road ran from it to a hidden harbor on the far side of the island. The forest must have overgrown the road by now."

The last comment had sounded wistful. Wilder glanced at the android over her shoulder. Its head was down, its expression hidden. She hadn't had much to do with the machines in the early years of the founding of Concordia. Mostly all she knew about them was from Cherry, who had described them as creepy. This one didn't seem creepy. In fact, if she hadn't known what it was, she would have been surprised to discover it wasn't human. Was the emotion in its face and voice programmed in order to fool the colonists or did it really feel it?

Just when she felt she would need to take a rest before climbing farther, and perhaps abandon her backpack, the next set of lights revealed a metal door set into the rough-hewn wall.

"At last," said Niall.

He was the first to reach it. He turned the knob but it didn't move. "It's rusted." He tried again to no effect. "Don't tell me we have to go all the way back down."

"Allow me," said Strongquist II as it reached the landing. "It's a simple mechanism." It gave the knob several blows with its fist. Flakes of rust fell from the door and frame. Gently, Strongquist II grasped and turned the knob. A loud creak resounded and the door opened. Sunlight burst from the gap, drowning out the meager interior lights.

"We've been in here all night," said Wilder. "I can't believe it."

"I can." Niall stepped through the opening and raised a hand to shield his eyes. "Come and take a look at this."

They were high up on a rocky crag protruding from the mountainside. A forested vista spread out before them and beyond it lay the ocean, the beams of the rising sun gilding the waves.

"It's so beautiful," Wilder said. "It could be Concordia."

Strongquist II joined them. "Your planet must be very Earth-like. I heard it was supposed to be. That's why it was chosen."

It was odd to hear it describe her home planet as Earth-like when to her it was the other way around.

"How long will it take us to reach the airstrip?" Niall asked.

"Approximately two and a half hours," replied Strongquist II, "depending on how fast you walk."

"Then we should comm Zapata to pick us up."

"I'll do it," said Wilder. "Boy, do we have a surprise for everyone."

But before she could comm the pilot, his agitated voice sounded in her ear. "Wilder, Niall, can you hear me? Please respond."

"We're here," she said. "What's up?"

"Thank the stars. I've been trying to contact you for hours. Vessey's hopping mad."

"She found out you brought us here? Shit." Wilder pulled a face at Niall. "Sorry about that. We'll tell her we insisted or something."

"That isn't the problem. We're leaving for Concordia soon. She wants everyone aboard pronto."

"We're leaving? But what about the Earthers? What happened to the plan to help them fight off the Scythians?"

"The plan's changed. Are you at the pick-up site?"

"Not yet. We should be there in under three hours. And we have another passenger for you."

"No, absolutely not. We're not taking any Earthers with us. Vessey's strict orders."

"Um..." Wilder looked at Strongquist II, who had been listening to her end of the conversation. "I think she might change her mind about this one."

"I doubt it, but I guess that's on you. I'm gonna be making at least one more trip to the surface so I can take him or her back down when Vessey says no."

"It isn't a him or a her, technically," Wilder replied.

"Huh?"

"Never mind. See you in a few hours." She cut the comm.

"We didn't discuss my accompanying you to Concordia," Strongquist II said mildly.

"Ugh, you're right. I just assumed you would. It seemed logical. You're a Guardian, and I associate them with my home planet."

"Do you want to stay here on Earth?" Niall asked. "What would you do?"

"I would like to apprise myself of all facts pertaining to the current state of affairs before making my decision, in particular regarding these Scythians you mention."

"Makes absolute sense," said Niall. "Let's go. I don't want to keep Vessey waiting. She's already pissed off."

Strongquist II walked to the side of the crag where it met the mountain slope and stepped down. Niall followed him, and Wilder was about to do the same when something in the distance caught her attention. Two large birds had flown into view. The pair circled and she watched, fascinated. Before coming to Earth she'd only ever seen birds in educational vids at school. Roughly guessing their position, which was in the area of the pickup point, she concluded they had to be very large indeed. The birds disappeared behind the mountain.

"Wilder," Niall called, "what are you doing?"

"I'm on my way."

She climbed down from the crag.

～

STRONGQUIST II LED them on a tough march through the forest. As Wilder watched the android effortlessly navigating the dried stream bed, often stopping to allow them to catch up, she wondered why the Makers had left it behind. It had said that the Strongquist sent to Concordia was its copy. Did that mean Strongquist II was a prototype? Could it be defective and that was why they hadn't sent it? And if it was defective, did it know?

Or was there another reason for the android's presence at the abandoned site? The Makers had activated the signal before they left, so they clearly expected or hoped that one day someone would detect it and come looking. As they entered the site Strongquist II was triggered to turn on, yet it didn't know why. Or did it know and it just wasn't telling them? Could the androids lie? She couldn't remember, but Cherry might. She'd been involved with them from the start. Making a mental note to ask her friend when she got back to the ship, Wilder hurried on, scrambling through the undergrowth.

By the time they neared the rendezvous point, she was hot and sweaty despite the cool temperature. She was also panting and tired as well as sore from thorns that had caught in her skin. The Makers were either hardier than her or they rarely left their site.

Strongquist II was waiting for her and Niall at the head of the track. Beyond him lay the wind-churned ocean.

"I thought we'd never make it," said Wilder. "I can't wait to get aboard the shuttle and relax."

"Yeah," Niall replied, "I'll happily take an angry Captain Vessey over another trek through the wilderness."

As they neared the android, however, it held up a hand, warning them to stay back.

"What's wrong?" Wilder asked.

"An aircraft is at the site. I don't recognize the design."

"Oh, that's just Zapata and the shuttle. He must have arrived early and he's waiting for us."

She walked around Strongquist and out into the open. The vegetation petered out as it neared the shoreline, where slabs of rock stepped down to the sea. The remains of the airstrip stood on higher ground. Wilder turned, expecting to see the familiar lines of the shuttle and perhaps the friendly pilot standing next to her, getting some fresh air before the return journey.

Zapata was not there and neither was the shuttle.

Two slim points faced her, joined by a silver crescent covered in intricate yet chaotic swirls.

A Scythian ship!

With a sharp intake of breath, she turned to run back to the forest.

At the same time, a shadow descended over her and there was a burst of downward, fetid air. Something fastened tightly around her waist and lifted her from her feet. Suddenly, she was meters from the ground, looking down at the upturned face of Strongquist, who quickly disappeared into the trees.

Her immediate impulse was to tear at the feet that gripped her around her middle. They were covered in knobbly skin and were oddly prehensile. She fought her instinct. She was already so high that falling would kill her. All she could hope for was the bird would set her down somewhere and not try to kill her in flight.

It had to be one of the two birds she'd seen before. She'd never heard that some Earth birds attacked humans. Why hadn't anyone warned them?

She craned around to get a look at the creature. Close up, she wasn't even sure it was a bird. It didn't have feathers but pale brown skin, stretched out over a skeletal frame to form its wings. She looked up for a view of its head...

She screamed.

The thing wore a transparent helmet and it was looking at her. Round white eyes, each with a central, vertical black line stared into her face. A lipless mouth opened. Wilder caught a glimpse of layered jagged scales, and then it spoke. It was talking. There seemed no other word for it, though she couldn't hear anything it said. Even if sound had permeated its helmet, the wind at this height was too noisy to hear anything else.

Understanding hit her like a bolt of lightning.

She looked at the ship below, now little more than a silver crescent on a distant shore. She looked at the creature again.

It was a Scythian.

The Scythians could fly.

And it would kill her. There was no doubt about it. They hated humans for taking over their origin planet. No one they'd kidnapped had ever been seen again.

All strength left her. With shaking fingers, she plucked feebly at the feet around her waist. Better to drop to a quick death in the ocean below than face whatever fate awaited her inside a Scythian dome.

She hoped Niall was safe, hiding among the trees. She'd seen two of the creatures. Where was the other one? The skies around were empty. The island was far below now. The alien ship was a sliver of bright metal on a thread of rocky shore. They were higher than the mountain peak. She struggled to breathe.

Why was the alien flying so high? What was it planning to do with her?

The great wings beat hard and the Scythian banked to the left, sending her legs trailing.

Let me go! Let me go, you disgusting creature.

Even at this height and in the freezing gale she could smell it. A rank odor emanated from its feet and the skin she was pressed against.

What was it doing here? The island was uninhabited. There were no humans to capture or kill. Had the Scythians detected the signal too? Had they come here to investigate?

It was descending. Its banking had turned into a spiraling glide downward. Slowly, the ocean drew nearer. Cringing, she looked up into its face again. It continued to talk but it was no longer looking at her. Its focus was on the shore or perhaps its aircraft.

She followed its gaze.

There was the other one. The massive wings were unmistakable. But it wasn't flying. The wings were only partially outspread as it crouched on the rocks. What was it doing?

A terrifying image of the other Scythian feasting on Niall flashed into her head, gnawing at him with the gray, scale-like teeth.

But that couldn't be right. The aliens would suffocate if they took off their helmets.

There was Strongquist II!

The android stood at the alien's head, one hand on its long neck, the other arm holding the muzzle of the pulse rifle against its helmet.

That was why the creature that had captured her was descending. Strongquist II was threatening to kill its partner if it didn't bring her back. Naturally, no words had been exchanged. None were needed.

She could breathe easily again and the roaring of the wind had lessened. They were about three hundred meters high now and dropping lower every second. The white tips of the waves were clear, the hull pattern of the alien vessel defined.

What would her captor do? Would it put her down gently on the rocks? Did it understand she would be hurt if it dropped her more than a few meters?

She couldn't see Niall, which was a good thing. Strongquist II must have told him to hide in the forest. The android really was a Guardian. It was protecting them.

A hundred meters.

Fifty meters.

Strongquist II watched carefully. She made eye contact and gave a small wave to show she was okay.

Below, the water surged.

The Scythian had to fly closer to the shore if it was to set her down safely.

Another gliding circle, and they were thirty meters up.

Closer to the shore. You have to fly…

The feet opened.

She shrieked.

Perversely, she reached for the open, taloned 'fingers', clutching at them. But the alien was already swooping out of reach.

The ocean rushed up at her impossibly fast. She plunged into icy water. Just before it closed over her head she managed to take a breath. Then she was in the frigid ocean. Bubbles resounded in her ears. Water pressure crushed her eardrums and lungs. Her eyes opened on darkness. How deep had she gone? Which way was up?

She kicked and pushed down with her arms. Was she going in the right direction? It was cold, so cold and the current pushed and pulled at her. Where was the sunlight? It should be above but she couldn't see a thing.

She needed to breathe. The coldness made her want to gasp. Her chest worked as she fought the desperation for air. Was she swimming correctly or was she only thrashing around in the water?

Quinn, where are you when I need you?

The Fila had tried to teach her to swim on one of the rare occasions she'd taken a break from her work, but she hadn't been very good at it. Her arms and legs refused to coordinate.

Quinn, I need you. Where in the wide galaxy are you, my old, dear friend?

Her thoughts were turning fuzzy. The darkness seemed to grow. It closed in.

I have to breathe.

Sorry, Quinn.

Sorry, Niall.

I must breathe.

Something touched her head. Snapped back to alertness, she swept it away. What was it? Was it one of those predatory fish she'd heard about? The thing touched her arm, but before she could hit it, a clasp fastened around her biceps. She tried to prise it off with her free hand, only to realize it wasn't a clasp but another hand. Someone had grabbed her. She was being saved!

Relaxing her body, she allowed herself to be towed. Moments later, her head broke the surface and she inhaled air in a great whoop.

Strongquist II bobbed next to her. "Are you hurt?"

"No, I don't think so," she panted. "Thank you! Thank you for saving me."

A wave lifted them closer to shore. Along with it came the body of the Scythian that had captured her. The massive wings were spread out but the rest of its body and its head hung out of sight.

On land, the other alien lay on a slab of rock, dead.

13

As they journeyed back to the *Sirocco* Niall was quiet and pensive. He stared out of the shuttle window, brooding. When Wilder reached to take his hand he didn't resist but his grip was limp and apathetic. Bewildered by his attitude, she didn't know what to say. He seemed angry but she didn't know why.

Zapata had arrived while Strongquist II had been helping her from the water, and there hadn't been time to talk about what had happened. The pilot had insisted they left as soon as possible, reasonably speculating there might be more hostiles in the area or on their way. As everyone had been getting ready to leave, she'd changed from her wet clothes into one of his spare flight suits. The garment swamped her but at least she was dry and warm.

She didn't know exactly what had gone on between the time the Scythian had snatched her and the moment she'd seen Strongquist threatening to kill the other one. Perhaps it was something that had happened that had upset Niall.

Or was he annoyed because she'd stepped out into the open, ignoring the android's warning about the strange ship? How could she have known it was a Scythian craft and not the *Sirocco*'s shuttle? It was an easy mistake to make. He might have done the same too.

"Is something wrong?" she asked.

"No, why?"

"Uhh, no reason."

I nearly died. Don't you care?

She released his hand. He didn't react.

She turned away from him. Two could play the ignoring game. "Strongquist, what happened while I was up in the air? How did you manage to catch the other Scythian?"

"It was not difficult. The alien landed just beyond the trees. It clearly suspected there was more than one human in the vicinity. I asked Niall to show himself—we were both hiding by then—in order to entice it under the canopy. It took the bait, and I pounced on it from behind. The hard part was dragging it out onto the rocks. I am stronger than humans but my strength has its limits. And, of course, I had to prevent it from flying off. So I shot at its wings, disabling it. The creature became more passive after that."

"I bet it did."

"I had several concerns. The alien who had captured you might not have cared about the threat to its partner's life. Or they may have been unable to communicate. Or my one might not have told yours that it was in danger. Any number of things might not have gone according to plan. As it was, the event that surprised me was your captor dropping you into the ocean. That decision was its undoing, for it allowed me a clear shot at it without any danger of hitting you. The obvious next step was to dispatch the alien in my control."

"Why do you think my one dropped me instead of handing me over?"

"I cannot answer with any certainty. I am only familiar with human psychology. If I were to speculate, I would say it may have never intended to participate in an exchange and was only stalling until it felt it was sufficiently close to attack me. Perhaps, according to their culture, the one I injured had lost honor and its life was forfeit, so its partner did not care if I killed it. Who knows? It's impossible to say."

"I hope we never find out," Wilder mused, shivering, though she was no longer cold. She didn't want any more close encounters with Scythians. Her first sight of them had been a shock. After the attacks in Concordia's early years, living under the threat of their return most of her life, and the later decimation of the colony, she'd given a lot of thought to what they were like, yet she'd never imagined anything so horrible as the creature that had carried her high into the air. Why had it done *that*? Strongquist was right. It was impossible to say.

DISEMBARKING at the *Sirocco* took longer than usual. Before taking them to the bay, Zapata had to deliver their cargo to the hold, which turned out to be a tricky process. If it hadn't been so precious, Wilder suspected he might have been tempted to abandon it. But after half an hour or so of maneuvering he managed it and they could finally fly around to the bay.

It seemed like the entire ship's personnel had turned up to greet them. The news of their adventure must have spread. Wilder was first to exit the hatch.

Cherry stepped forward from the group to give her a hug. "Thank the stars you're okay. I was worried about you." Stepping back, she added, "Why the heck are you wearing *that*? Thinking of training to be a pilot?"

Before Wilder could answer, however, Cherry turned white and her mouth fell open. Her gaze was fixed on something over Wilder's shoulder.

Niall and Strongquist had exited the shuttle.

"Bloody hell!"

The exclamation had come from Aubriot, who stood with the others who had waited to see the new arrivals.

"It can't be," Cherry breathed.

Aubriot stepped forward. "*This* is the Earther?" he asked Vessey.

"Who else could it be?" the captain snapped. "I assume you're already familiar with Niall and Wilder."

Zapata emerged from the shuttle. "Got everything into the hold, Captain. I didn't think I'd manage it but I did in the end."

"Thank you. I'll take a look at it all right away. Would you mind taking our guest to the mission room and making him comfortable,

Cherry? Dragan, could you come with me? And I'll need a couple of biologists."

Niall said, "I'd like to take a look too, if you don't mind."

"I thought you might want to recuperate after your ordeal, but the more the merrier."

"I'm fine. It was Wilder who got put through the mill."

They left and the group began to break up. Today's show was over. Cherry hadn't moved a muscle.

Strongquist's features were impassive as he watched Aubriot walk up. His gaze followed Aubriot while he inspected him from the toes of his boots to the top of his head.

"Fuck me," Aubriot said, turning to Cherry. "It's really him."

"It isn't a he," she replied icily, "it's an *it*."

Wilder mentally checked herself. Cherry was right. Strongquist wasn't a person. It was a thing. Yet her attitude toward the android had changed since it had saved her life. She'd begun to see it as a person. It was hard not to. Even if it hadn't been her savior, it looked like a person, sounded like a person and even mostly behaved like one.

"And it isn't the Strongquist we knew," Cherry continued. "I saw him cut to pieces with my own eyes."

"*Pftt*," said Aubriot. "You know what I mean. It's his twin or whatever."

"I don't know what Vessey's told you," Wilder said, "but this Strongquist saved me from the Scythians."

"Yeahhh," Cherry drawled, her expression not changing, "they have a habit of doing that."

Aubriot took a step back as something seemed to occur to him. "You found him at the seed vault?" he asked Wilder. "I thought we searched that place pretty thoroughly."

"We didn't see half of it. We left after we found what we were looking for, remember? But he wasn't in the vault. Didn't Vessey explain? The signal was coming from the place the Makers built the *Mistral* and the Guardians."

"She didn't explain shit." Aubriot tutted and shook his head. "The woman's not fit to lead. So you found the construction site? What was there? I mean in terms of equipment. Did you have a look around?"

While Wilder listed what she could recall from Strongquist's tour, Cherry continued to stare at the android. He appeared unperturbed by her scrutiny. Eventually, Wilder became uncomfortable on his behalf. "Someone should take Strongquist to the mission room. I can do it."

"I am happy to answer any questions," the android said. "It appears my arrival has caused some agitation."

"Oh, I've got plenty of questions for you," said Aubriot, "and I want to hear more about the place the *Mistral* was built."

"Why are you so interested?" Cherry asked suspiciously. "What difference does it make? Don't tell me you're still thinking about protecting Earth."

"It's a whole new discovery. Throws a new light on things."

"It doesn't throw a light on anything. One android and some starship-building equipment isn't going to save the Earthers from the Scythians."

"Why the pessimism? Oh, that's right. You don't give a shit about Earth."

"Why should I care about *your* home planet? You'd happily sacrifice everyone on this ship for a war we can't win."

Wilder interjected, "I thought Vessey had decided we're leaving?"

But neither of them heard her. They continued to bicker.

They hadn't gotten along since breaking up years ago, but lately their animosity seemed to have intensified. It didn't help that, as two of the most experienced and competent people on the ship, they often had to work together.

"Come with me," Wilder told Strongquist.

"Wait," said Cherry, noticing they were leaving. "You haven't heard the news. Miki and Nina have gone down to the surface. No one knows where they are."

14

Wrinkling her nose, Cherry squatted down and grasped the edge of the Scythian's wing. When she lifted it a noxious smell escaped and she wrinkled her nose more. "Gross!"

"They aren't the most pleasant life form I've encountered," Maura commented.

"That's putting it mildly," said Acton. "I've seen quite a few odd species since arriving on Earth but nothing compares. These creatures are abominable."

Cherry straightened up. "What can you say about them?"

"Apart from the obvious," Maura replied, "that they're aerial, CO_2-breathing, and predatory, it's hard to say anything just yet. We're taking samples to analyze in the lab, and then someone will perform a full autopsy. Probably Dr Clarkson."

"Did you say predatory? Do you think they're here to prey on humans?"

"I haven't seen anything to indicate it. The one that snatched Wilder didn't try to take a bite out of her as far as I'm aware. What I meant is their forward-facing eyes, sharp teeth, and grasping and slashing appendages tell us they evolved to catch and eat prey, that's all. Humans have some aspects of predator anatomy too but Concordians are vegetarian."

"Yeah," said Acton, "let's not jump to that particular nightmare scenario just yet, if you don't mind."

The dead Scythians only took up a small portion of the hold. Most of the rest of it was occupied by the Scythian vessel Zapata had towed back. Though it followed their ships' usual design, it was the smallest Cherry had ever seen. Niall and Dragan were attempting to open a humped section at the widest part of the crescent. It was easy to guess why: it had to be where the aliens sat while flying it. The hump probably contained the control center, though what the engineers would be able to discern from inspecting it was uncertain. So far, they hadn't even gained access to the strangely marked vessel.

Vessey stood to one side, watching.

Cherry approached the captain. "Aubriot and I are ready to go planetside as soon as Zapata's rested."

"I'm not sure what you mean."

"What?" she spluttered. "You know exactly what I mean. We have to find Miki and Nina and bring them back."

"I told you the matter is still under consideration. I've been consulting with Buka about exactly how to handle it. Luckily, I haven't given him formal notice of our plans to leave, so there's still room for negotiations."

"*Negotiations!* These are two teenage girls we're talking about. Kes's daughters. What's there to negotiate? We have to get them back. We've delayed long enough waiting to pick up Wilder and Niall."

"What you're forgetting is that Wilder and Niall are essential crew. Miki and Nina went to the surface of their own free—"

"They're kids! They don't have any idea what they're doing or the danger they're in."

Her tone stubborn, Vessey continued, "They have as much information at their disposal as everyone else aboard this ship, and though they might not be quite adults yet, they are intelligent and capable individuals. If they don't want to leave their father's grave site, that's up to them. I have a responsibility to *all* the *Sirocco*'s personnel, not just those two. If it were only a matter of picking them up it would be different. But I can't risk more of my people searching an entire planet to find them, delaying our departure for who knows how long." As she'd spoken, the captain's voice had grown louder and more strident. By the time she finished she had the attention of everyone in the hold.

"Are you talking about Miki and Nina?" Niall asked.

Cherry replied quickly, depriving Vessey of the chance to spin the facts to fit her agenda, "They got it into their heads they need to stay on Earth and not return to Concordia. They don't want to leave Kes." She choked up. *She* didn't want to leave Kes either. But he was dead. He had no knowledge of and didn't care who might visit his remains.

"You have to understand," said Vessey, "Buka suspects we plan to leave. Miki and Nina's actions have given him bargaining power and he's using it. Whereas before we could come and go as we pleased, now he's saying we need to request permission to land, that the 'increased use of air space' must be managed for safety. It's complete nonsense, of course. All they have is a few helis. We'd be in more danger of colliding with a flock of birds than hitting one of their aircraft."

She swallowed before continuing, "Painful as it would be to leave the girls behind, the simplest solution would be to do just that, which, after all, is exactly what they want."

"You don't know that," Cherry protested. "They could have changed their minds already and be looking for a way to come back. We don't know where they are or who they're with. They could be wandering around the countryside trying to find where their father is buried. Or Buka could be holding them against their will, refusing to allow them to comm us. We don't know anything, and the only way to find out the truth is to go down there and find them, speak to them face to face, and hopefully persuade them to come back to the ship."

"What about these?" Maura touched a dead Scythian with the toe of her boot. "The latest development changes things, doesn't it? The aliens have been snatching humans, presumably to study them, but now we have two specimens of our own to study, plus one of their ships."

"So?" Vessey asked.

"So we can offer the Earthers information about the enemy in exchange for returning Miki and Nina."

"You clearly don't know the first thing about diplomacy. As soon as Buka knows we're prepared to offer something valuable for the girls he will up the stakes, demanding more and more concessions and delaying the process in order to squeeze as much out of us as he can, while also getting us to stick around as long as possible. I'm not prepared to accept further delay. We need to leave soon, before it's too late."

Cherry had a horrible feeling it was already far too late, that there was no hope of saving her planet. She was also not persuaded by Vessey's reasoning, though she had to concede that diplomacy was not a personal strength. Maybe the captain was right. "Do you mean we should pretend Miki and Nina aren't that important to us?"

The captain replied resignedly, "*If* there is a way to get them back quickly and simply I'm happy to hear about it. But what Maura is suggesting would take weeks, firstly to gather data and then to bargain with Buka."

The discussion had captured Dragan's attention too. "What if we offer to give them the bodies and the ship in return for Miki and Nina? Straight exchange. If Buka doesn't know where they are, that would light a fire under him to find them. The whole thing could be over in a day or so."

Vessey shook her head emphatically. "*We* need these bodies and the ship. We can use the information we glean from them to protect Concordia when the Scythians inevitably return."

Cherry had another reservation. If Miki and Nina had to be dragged, screaming, back to the *Sirocco* they might never get over it. It could damage them forever. They stood a better chance of staying alive, but at what cost? She had learned the hard way, while caring for Wilder when she was a teenager, that forcing them to do what *you* thought was best rarely brought good results.

There had to be a better way. She just didn't know what.

"I have an idea," Niall announced. He walked to the alien nearest the ship and grabbed its wing tip.

"An idea about what?" Cherry asked.

"Uhh, sorry. I meant about opening the ship. Could someone give me a hand?"

Niall and Dragan dragged the corpse to the small vessel and up onto it. The helmeted head flopped and bounced, the lax features sagging. Niall pressed the tip of a claw against the hull.

"I get it," said Dragan. "There's no patterning on that spot. Maybe it's a sensor."

"That was my guess," Niall agreed, "but it didn't work."

"We could try another claw or another part of its body."

"Try its foot," Cherry offered.

"A foot?" asked Dragan.

"They hold stuff with their lower limbs and use their wing claws for cutting and slicing. You're forgetting they fly. They would fly onto the ship and open it, not climb onto it like a human."

"Makes sense," said Niall. "The one that snatched Wilder held her with its feet."

"Whatever you say." Dragan hauled the creature around until its feet were nearest the bare patch on the hull. It didn't seem to take much effort, though the Scythian had to be three times his mass.

Niall tried each toe of one foot in turn. At the third try, the humped section split from the rest of the ship. "We're in!"

15

It was hard for Wilder to pay attention as Aubriot questioned Strongquist II. The news about Miki and Nina was extremely worrying. The girls were smart and resourceful but they'd spent most of their lives on a starship. They would have struggled to survive by themselves on Concordia, let alone on a planet with a poor infrastructure and where the inhabitants had gone into hiding.

She itched to ask Aubriot what was being done to find the missing children and if there had been any news of them. Had her and Niall's trip delayed the search? She would feel terrible if it had.

But Aubriot was busy drilling the android for information.

"Did these Makers, as you call them, give any indication of where they were going when they left?"

"As I've already told you," Strongquist II replied patiently, "all I know is that after the *Mistral's* departure they planned to abandon the site. There was no reason for them to stay, and they feared the launch of the starship would attract unwelcome attention. Though few of Earth's inhabitants possessed significant military capability then, the number of intruders had increased and there was a realistic threat of a sustained attack. Furthermore, the Makers had no reason to stay once their work was done."

"All right," Aubriot replied tetchily. "Where do you *think* they might have gone? Where would it have been logical for them to go?"

Wilder asked, "Why do you want to know? What difference does it make? The *Mistral* left Earth centuries ago. The Makers are all dead and it's a different place now."

He turned to face her sharply. "Because those people were the last of the peak of scientific and engineering achievement in human civilization. They weren't the country bumpkins messing around with ancient artifacts they don't understand living down there today. You think you're smart, right?"

"Well..."

"You are. You're a freaking genius. Niall and Dragan aren't far behind you. Imagine a hundred of you. A thousand. The cream of human intelligence. Do you think people like that would fade away, living out their lives tilling the soil and brewing their own beer? If you lived on Earth now, if you'd grown up there, is that what *you* would do? Would you be satisfied with that kind of life?"

Wilder recalled the long years on the *Sirocco*, with little more to do than keep the ship running and maintain the growing systems. "I would be bored out of my head."

"I know you would. So would the Makers. Wherever they went, whatever they did, there's a chance they left stuff behind that we can still use."

"That we can take back to Concordia? The Ark's already full and the Scythian ship takes up most of the hold. We don't have space to stow anything big."

"Use to defend Earth!" Aubriot spat, glaring.

If a man could be said to be beautiful he was it, but when he got angry he turned ugly fast.

Wilder leaned slightly away from him. "But I thought we were leaving—as soon as we get Miki and Nina back."

"That might be what Vessey thinks, but that woman doesn't have her head screwed on straight. If we give up on Earth, what's the point? We might as well throw in the towel." He continued more softly and as if partly speaking to himself, "The kids aren't so important. We have bigger issues at stake. Much bigger." Narrowing his eyes, he returned his attention to Strongquist II. "Do you have a list of all the equipment at the construction site?"

"Not an exhaustive one, I'm afraid, only a general understanding. And as I was showing Wilder and Niall around I noticed some things were missing."

Aubriot swiveled aggressively toward Wilder again. "You toured the site? Why didn't you tell me?"

"You didn't ask. What did you think I would do? Just leave?"

"I want to know what you remember. Everything. Write it down and send it to me." He swiveled back to Strongquist II. "One more thing. What's in your programming about the Concordia colony?"

"Nothing at all. I was not constructed for the same purpose as my counterparts."

"You don't have any protocols to follow about assessing personality types and their fitness to lead?"

What a strange question. Why was he asking that? She vaguely recalled a run-in between Aubriot and the Guardians.

"I do not."

Aubriot regarded the android suspiciously, as if he suspected him of lying.

She asked, "Do you know what purpose you were constructed for?"

"I believe I am a prototype. Perhaps the first successful model. The history of my manufacture was never explained to me."

"But you are programmed to protect humans," she said. It seemed obvious from the android's behavior when the Scythian snatched her.

"That function overrides all others, including self-preservation."

Aubriot rose to his feet and slapped Strongquist II on his back. "Useful bloke to have around. Just remember, you don't need to interfere in the ship's politics. Got it?"

"I don't anticipate doing anything in that regard."

She watched Aubriot leave. As was his habit, he hadn't said he would see her later or anything like that, and it wasn't only because he didn't do platitudes. He knew she disliked him and that was unlikely to change. There was no point in social niceties between them.

She had a bad feeling about his mention of 'ship's politics'? He clearly disagreed with Vessey's decision to return to Concordia. What exactly did he have in mind?

Strongquist II was watching her expectantly. She didn't know what to do with him. Apart from Aubriot, everyone else seemed to have forgotten about the android's existence in all the excitement over the Scythian bodies and their ship.

"Um, you should wait here until Captain Vessey decides what to do with you."

"As you wish." Strongquist II rested his hands on his knees.

Wilder walked to the door. She desperately wanted to shower and change into her own, clean, clothes, but something occurred to her. "If you were charged with choosing between defending Earth and returning to Concordia, what would you choose?"

"I am reluctant to give a reply. I don't believe I have sufficient knowledge of the situation on the respective planets to make an informed decision."

"Fair point. What if you had access to all the available information? Would you tell us then?"

"I will give my opinion, for what it may be worth."

"I'll ask Vessey to give you access to the ship's database. You can find every—"

"What?!" Cherry had arrived. "What did you just say?"

"I was telling Strongquist I'll get him access to the *Sirocco*'s data."

"Are you out of your mind? Have you gone crazy? Why the hell would you think it's a good idea to allow that thing access to our data?"

"He has a high level of computing power."

"*It*, not he."

"Okay, *it*. It's difficult to not think of it as a man."

"Try harder. Have you forgotten all about Faina?"

Wilder put a hand over her mouth. "*Shit*."

She hadn't exactly forgotten. She'd been present when the Guardian had appeared on Concordia decades after it was supposed to have destroyed itself smashing the *Mistral* into a Scythian ship. Hell, she'd gone with Kes to the site where the escape capsule had crashed. After that, she hadn't had much to do with Faina because she'd gone to live with Quinn on the *Opportunity*. It had been Cherry who had followed the android into the ancient Scythian city.

Faina's programming had been compromised by the aliens. They'd sent her to the planet to re-activate the defense systems that would destroy approaching starships. The android had been turned against them, her functions subverted.

"What do you know about that thing?" Cherry demanded. "You don't have a clue about it, do you? All you know is that it was at the *Mistral*'s construction site. That's it."

Wilder stared at her.

"And now it's here, with us, on the only ship with the only people who stand the tiniest chance of putting up a fight against the Scythians. You think that's a coincidence?"

Strongquist II hadn't moved while they talked. He sat still with his hands on his knees, facing the bulkhead. Cherry strode up to the android and peered behind his ear.

"May I ask what you're looking for?" he remarked mildly.

She peered behind his other ear and then inspected his neck, pulling at his collar to look down it. "Where is it?"

"Where is what?"

"You know what I mean. Where's your off switch?"

"My... *off switch*? I'm not mechanical per se. I have an inbuilt power pack and—"

"How can we turn you off?" Cherry demanded. "All the Guardians had a mole or a freckle somewhere on their neck that could be pressed to turn them off. Where's yours?"

"I understand what you mean. That was a feature of the later model. I can only be deactivated and activated remotely. I have no external controls."

"Figures. How do we deactivate you remotely?"

"The computer on Svalbard can emit the signal."

"Double figures. Stars, you're a liability."

"I had anticipated being an asset."

Cherry turned to Wilder. "I'm going to tell Vessey we need to return it to the surface, fast. It's too much of a security risk. We can look for Miki and Nina at the same time. Are you up for that?"

"Absolutely. I just need to get changed."

"Be quick. I'll stay here with it to make sure it doesn't do anything shady. If Vessey won't let us take it back to the surface I'll try to persuade her to destroy it. Actually, maybe it would be better to destroy it right now."

Strongquist II's eyebrows rose.

16

D akarai Buka stared mournfully out from the interface. He seemed to have aged in the brief interval since Cherry had seen him. Captain Vessey stood to one side of the screen, her arms folded tightly over her chest. She looked furious, perhaps understandably. As she'd explained after summoning all the ship's personnel to the bridge, Buka had told her he had important news to convey but he would only give it with all the Concordians present.

"It's as if he doesn't trust me to relay news from Earth to you truthfully," she'd concluded.

Maybe the suspicion of the GAA's leader was correct. The captain's eagerness to leave Earth and all her problems far behind was no secret. Cherry suspected that if Miki and Nina hadn't pulled their stunt Vessey might not have agreed to his demand.

The old man's eyes drooped and his lips sagged as he spoke. From off screen came Itai's translation. "I received a report half an hour ago from a distant province in South America. You may remember the incident where Scythians snatched a mother and father while they were out in the jungle with their two sons? Thankfully, the children were unharmed, though their parents have never been found. This report comes from the same area."

Buka took a deep breath before continuing, via translation, "Last night, the aliens emerged from their dome, flew to the nearest village, and murdered every man, woman, and child. Only one young woman managed to escape. She walked through the night and the morning to reach the nearest habitation and tell others of the massacre. I say she managed to escape, but it would be more accurate to say the Scythians let her go, for she...she..." he wiped his eyes and breathed in deeply again "...she has what I believe to be a message carved into the skin of her back. I won't show you it. It is too distressing. But after a doctor cleaned up the wound I had a copy drawn."

He held up a sheet of paper. "Can any of you tell me what this might mean?"

The paper was covered with short, vertical lines. Cherry winced, imagined the many cuts they represented. At the top of the paper—presumably in the area of the woman's neck—were two lines standing alone. Below them were eight rows of eight lines.

"Sixty-six," said Vessey. "Sixty-six in total."

"Yes, we can count too," Buka snapped.

Wilder asked, "Is that how many people were killed?"

"Sixty-nine people died, seventy if you include an unborn child, so the numbers only roughly correspond."

Niall said, "The Scythians have four toes on each foot. It would make sense they use base-eight for their number system."

"What's base-eight?" Itai asked, not waiting for Buka's response.

"It's just a different way of counting, from zero to seven instead of—"

Wilder gasped and clapped her hand over her mouth. Tears started into her eyes.

"What's wrong?" Cherry asked. "Have you figured out what it means?"

"It's not complicated," she replied in a strangled tone. "It's a simple representation. Two equals sixty-four."

"Two what?"

"Mr Buka," Vessey said, "we'll discuss this matter and get back to you." She cut the comm. "Wilder, explain."

"It's easy," Niall said heavily. "Two Scythians equals sixty-four humans, give or take."

"I see," Vessey said. "The two Scythians you killed. The massacre was retaliation for their deaths."

"Well, technically it was Strongquist who killed them, but..."

The aliens had implemented a brutal deterrent against further attacks.

A pall settled over the bridge.

Aubriot asked, "Does Buka know about the Scythians Strongquist killed?"

Vessey replied, "Not unless someone has gone behind my back to tell him. He doesn't know anything about the trip to investigate the signal and neither do any other Earthers."

"So he doesn't know we have one of their ships either. We need to keep it that way."

"That was my plan, for now."

The screen flashed. Buka was hailing the ship.

"He didn't wait long," someone muttered.

"You'd better answer," said Wilder.

"I'd better?" retorted Vessey. "Why?"

"We need to maintain a dialogue. Miki and Nina are down there!"

"Yes," said Cherry. "We have to get them back."

Vessey bit her lip and studied the assembled Concordians from under hooded eyes, as if trying to get the measure of their feelings about the missing girls.

Cherry repeated forcefully, "We have to get them back. They're just kids, and they're the children of a highly valued and respected member of this team. I can't believe you're contemplating leaving them behind, not after everything Kes did. If it weren't for him we would have starved to death. The least we can do to honor his memory is to not abandon his children."

"She's right," Aubriot said. "Can't ditch the nippers."

Cherry rolled her eyes. He didn't care about Miki and Nina. He was only jumping on the opportunity to keep the *Sirocco* in orbit, hoping there might be a way to protect his beloved Earth.

"They are half-Earthers..." someone mumbled.

Cherry stared at the crowd but couldn't figure out who had spoken. It might have been Marcus, blinded by Wilder when he attacked her. The man seemed to seethe with silent hatred for everyone and everything. Judging from other expressions, the sentiment of the Concordians was mixed. No one else spoke, probably not wanting to commit themselves.

Vessey said, "Every day, the possibility of Scythian military backup arriving grows greater. The longer we delay our departure the more likely it is we'll *never* depart. Is that what we want?"

Silently, the interface blinked.

"Aren't our hands tied anyway?" Maura asked. "Any attack on the Scythians will be avenged on the local population thirty-two fold. Many Earthers are in hiding but some have nowhere safe to go. We have to consider them."

"We do," Vessey agreed, "but let's not get our priorities mixed up. Are we for the Earthers or our own kind? Do we try to save someone else's planet or our own?"

"Now, hold on," Aubriot said. "Don't turn this into them and us. We're all human beings. And you're lining up the situation here with some airy fairy notion of what might happen somewhere else. For all we know Concordia could be dead. Like it or not, Earth might be our only chance for survival. Seems to me that after all this time, that's the real situation."

"I wish Kes were here," Wilder murmured. "He would know what to do."

"If Kes was here," Cherry said, "we would already be planetside searching for the girls."

"All right," Aubriot announced, slapping his knees before standing up. "Vessey, you're not a bad person, but you're no leader. There. I said what's been obvious to anyone with eyes to see right from the start. All through this mission you've been shilly-shallying, dithering, going backward and forward, and it's getting us nowhere. It's clear what's needed here is a firm hand."

A voice called out, "And we can guess who you mean."

Aubriot shrugged. "There's no point denying it. I *do* think I could do a better job. But don't forget, I could have gone around—"

"Sit down!" Vessey blurted, turning pale.

"I could have gone around behind the captain's back rallying support," Aubriot repeated, speaking over her, "but I haven't. At heart, I believe in democracy."

Cherry snorted.

"I said, sit down!" Vessey's gaze roamed the room but no one was looking at her. All attention was on Aubriot. She slumped into a seat.

"I propose a vote of no confidence in our captain. If the majority thinks she's competent to lead, fair enough. I'll shut up and let her get on with it. If she loses the vote, we'll elect a new captain. Someone who'll make a decisive plan about what we do next. Maybe that'll be me, maybe it won't. What do you say?"

Chaos erupted as everyone started shouting at once.

"Who are you to tell us what to do, you freak?" someone yelled above the rest. "What's wrong with you?"

"Yeah," a second voice added, "how come you never seem to get any older? Everyone's aged on this trip except you. What's that about?"

Aubriot looked taken aback. His gaze flicked to Cherry, the only person who knew his secret. She stared back at him blankly.

Before the thread could be followed, however, someone else exclaimed, "You can't have a vote of confidence about the captain of a ship! That's mutiny."

"But he's right," came the reply. "We need someone to make a concrete decision, someone who can think of the best way out of this mess."

"I say we vote!"

"No, he's only doing this because he knows Vessey wants to leave, and she's right. Concordians for Concordia. What did the Earthers ever do for us? They killed Kes with their nasty disease."

Cherry tried to figure out who had spoken. It had sounded like Maura but she wasn't sure. It wasn't possible to tell in the sea of flushed, angry, and agitated, faces. The volume of voices rose.

Aubriot was looking at her, a peculiarly intense expression on his face. As soon as he caught her gaze he nodded toward the corner of the room. She followed his direction. Zapata stood there, leaning his back against the bulkhead, arms folded over his chest, head down, like he was fed up with all the arguing. She felt the same.

Still, what was Aubriot trying to signal?

She looked back at him. He nodded in the direction of the pilot again, more emphatically. Then he said to the crowd, "I'm just stating my opinion. Everyone's entitled to their opinion." He made a subtle gesture, flicking his fingers at her.

He wanted her to leave? With Zapata?

He wanted her to leave with Zapata.

She grabbed Wilder's arm. "Let's go."

"Where?"

She stood on her tiptoes to whisper, "To get the girls."

Understanding dawned in the younger woman's eyes. They quickly eased through the mob of over-excited Concordians.

"Zapata," said Cherry. "Can I speak to you outside?"

"Sure, anything to get out of here."

It was quieter in the passageway. When she explained her proposal to the pilot, he hesitated but only for a few seconds. "Vessey's gonna want to kill me, but what the hell. This mission's turned into a free for all, and I hate the thought of those girls down there by themselves."

Cherry was partly elated, partly furious. She finally had a chance to find Miki and Nina and bring them back. On the other hand, she was playing right into Aubriot's schemes. He didn't really care about the girls. He was only using them to undermine Vessey's authority and force her to keep the ship in orbit around Earth a while longer.

Everything was about him and what he wanted, as usual.

17

A s Wilder stepped down from the shuttle, she surveyed the surroundings. It was here that Miki and Nina would have snuck away from the vessel, probably the instant Zapata had left it. By the time the Concordians had boarded, the girls would have been long gone.

Where?

It was a bleak place. The site the Global Advancement Association had picked for their headquarters was in the north of a large continent, not as northerly as the seed vault, but sufficiently high latitude to give a distinct chill to the air. Unlike the island of the seed vault, the area wasn't forested. A small settlement stood a kilometer or so away, and a few low buildings huddled beyond the landing pads. Flat plains stretched out in all directions to the featureless horizon.

No, it wasn't featureless.

Wilder squinted and shielded her eyes with her hand. To the east a small bump broke the monotonous view. Light from the low sun glinted on the structure.

"Is that what I think it is?" she asked. Cherry and Zapata were chatting as they exited the shuttle.

Cherry checked and replied heavily, "Yeah. It's one of their domes."

"So close to the GAA?"

"They're all over the place."

"But why didn't the group move after the aliens arrived?"

"There can't be many underground complexes on Earth. The association probably didn't have a lot of choice except to stay here."

"It's this way," Cherry said, heading for the buildings.

They didn't get far before several figures emerged from a door.

The shuttle's arrival had been noticed.

Cherry said, "Now we find out how serious Buka was about asking permission to land." She halted. "I don't think it's a good idea to leave our only method of getting back to the *Sirocco* unattended."

"You think they'll try to steal the shuttle?" asked Zapata. "They'd have a hard time piloting that thing."

"That wouldn't stop them from taking it." She glanced at the vessel and then the small delegation approaching. "Are there weapons aboard?"

"Always."

"Then I suggest you go back and lock yourself in."

"What about you guys?"

The danger of what they were doing was beginning to dawn on Wilder too. She'd been focused on finding Miki and Nina, who were like sisters to her. But now that Dakarai Buka suspected the Concordians were about to abandon Earth, who knew what he might do in order to encourage them to stay? And here they were, walking right into his hands. "Maybe we should get a couple of those rifles."

"I thought about it," Cherry replied, "but no. If we act too aggressively it's only going to inflame the situation. Let's tread carefully for now."

"I'll be waiting for your comm," said Zapata. "Good luck."

While the pilot retreated, Wilder said, "Tread softly? That doesn't sound like you."

"I guess I'm getting old."

One of the men arriving to greet them was Itai, the translator. "We're delighted you decided to pay us a visit, though it's somewhat unexpected."

Cherry replied, "I apologize on behalf of our captain for not seeking permission to land. We're here on an urgent matter that couldn't wait for formalities."

"I see. I'm sure Mr Buka will be eager to hear about it and do all he can to help. Please come with me. Your, er..." he glanced at the shuttle "...pilot won't be joining us?"

"He's busy running flight checks. We don't expect to be here long."

It was Wilder's first time at the GAA headquarters. From the bare, utilitarian style of the place it seemed to be a former military bunker or some other governmental building. Naturally, everything above ground was long gone, though the concrete rooms and passageways remained. Someone had mentioned that the GAA had resurrected the ancient geothermal energy system powering it.

They descended with Itai to the lower level, and he took them immediately to a small room. The leader of the GAA was waiting.

The old man didn't get to his feet. He gestured for them to sit down, murmuring something Itai didn't bother to translate, probably a greeting. He continued, "We appreciate your quick response to this terrible tragedy, and we understand why you didn't follow protocol and request permission before landing."

Terrible tragedy?

For a heartbeat, horror seized Wilder as she inferred he was talking about Miki and Nina, and that something awful had happened to them. Then she realized he meant the massacre at the Earther village. Vessey had cut the comm after he delivered the news. He hadn't heard from the ship since.

"We, uhh..." Cherry stumbled over her words as she also took a second to catch his meaning. "We were so sorry to hear about it. I don't think you've met my colleague. This is Wilder, one of our engineers."

The old man nodded at her then returned his expectant gaze to Cherry.

Wilder said, "We were all devastated to hear what happened. Is there any more news?"

"The location of the attack is very remote and the government has few resources. We haven't received any updates yet but I expect more information will reach us in the coming days. I'm eager to hear about your plans to help us now the Scythians have taken this next, horrific step. Did any of you make sense of the markings on the girl's back?"

"We're still working on it," Cherry said. "We're actually here for another reason. We want to collect the two girls who arrived when the shuttle came to collect us the other day."

"Two girls?"

"They were supposed to stay on the ship but they stowed away and snuck out while no one was watching. We're here to take them back."

"Their names are Miki and Nina," Wilder added. "They're teenagers." Buka and Itai seemed genuinely puzzled, though she was wary of trusting her impression. She wasn't good at reading people.

The two Earthers spoke for a while. Itai left the room. Buka, Cherry, and Wilder sat in awkward silence, the language barrier a gulf between them, until he returned a few minutes later.

"There are no girls from your ship here," he announced.

"But they have to be," said Cherry. "Where else could they go?"

"I can assure you, no Concordians are present in this base."

"They must be hiding. They're intelligent, and one of them is strong-headed. They must have found somewhere—"

"It isn't possible. We've recently taken in about fifty refugees and we're packed to the rafters. There's only one way in and out of this place. They couldn't have got in without someone noticing."

"Could someone be helping them?"

"Why would anyone do that? We're living on rations. Why would anyone give up their food to a pair of strangers?"

Wilder said to Cherry, "They must have gone to that settlement out on the plain."

"It's deserted," Itai responded quickly.

"That doesn't mean they aren't there," Wilder retorted.

Cherry said, "I'm still not convinced they aren't here, somewhere."

Buka spoke. He seemed agitated.

Itai listened and appeared to weigh his words before translating, "We're naturally concerned for the welfare of the adolescents, but we have weightier matters at hand than two runaways. Mr Buka would like to know the options you may have discussed for the defense of Earth."

"As I said—" Cherry's words were cut off as Buka spoke again. She waited.

"We believe your ship to be armed," Itai said. "Otherwise the Scythians would have attacked it. You could destroy the Scythian settlements, or fire upon their ships. The aliens should receive a clear message that their invasion will not be tolerated."

Cherry snapped, "If it was as easy as that don't you think we would have already done it?"

"I don't know," Itai translated. "Would you? Wouldn't it be easier to avoid any risk to yourselves and leave us to our fate?"

"Avoid any risk to ourselves?!" She rose to her feet. "You realize you're talking to one of the people who broke into a Scythian dome? Someone on our team nearly died."

Buka also stood up, leaning on his cane. Spittle flew from his mouth as he spoke.

Itai said woodenly, "Our pilot on that mission *did* die, one of the very few we have. Hundreds more of us have been snatched. An entire village was annihilated. And you expect sympathy because a few of you put yourselves in danger?"

Wilder touched Cherry's arm. "We aren't getting anywhere. We should go take a look at that settlement."

"I apologize for Mr Buka's anger," Itai said. "He is under a lot of pressure. The GAA is one of few organizations with the reach to mount a response to the invasion, but even we lack equipment and skills to act effectively."

"Look," Cherry said, "what you don't understand is..." She hesitated.

Wilder squeezed her arm, fearful she was about to spill the beans about the Earthers' hopeless predicament and the *Sirocco*'s imminent departure. "Sit down."

As Cherry took her advice, Itai said, "What don't we understand?"

Wilder replied, "The situation is complex. It's going to take us a while to figure out a strategy for helping you. We need time to work on it." She felt like shit for lying to them. Despite Aubriot's challenge to Vessey's leadership, it seemed a foregone conclusion that the Earthers were on their own. Realistically, there wasn't anything the Concordians could do. Everyone would realize that eventually, even Aubriot.

"And in the meantime," Itai said, "you want us to find these girls?"

"That's right," Cherry replied.

"I will speak with Mr Buka and we'll see what we can do."

The men talked. Buka appeared to calm down. He glanced at Cherry and Wilder. After a little more discussion, he nodded.

"Phew," Wilder murmured. "I think he's agreed to help us."

Cherry was watching the men suspiciously. "I'm not so sure."

Buka addressed them as if he was taking his leave, and then hobbled toward the door.

Itai said, "We will arrange a team to search the base top to bottom."

"I thought you said it wasn't possible they're here," Cherry said.

"I, er, may have been wrong. Please wait. If we find them I'll let you know immediately."

Buka had left. Itai stepped toward the door.

Cherry got up and followed him. "Can we search too?"

"I'm afraid not."

He shut the door.

Cherry turned to face Wilder. "I don't trust—"

A noise had interrupted her.

It was the sound of a lock snicking shut.

18

Cherry closed the comm to Zapata.

"Did he say where he's gone?" Wilder asked.

"Not exactly. He's found somewhere in the middle of nowhere with no visible habitations. He'll wait there."

"For how long?"

"As long as it takes for us to get out of this mess."

"You're sure he won't just go back to the ship?"

Cherry shrugged. "What can I do? It's up to him what he does." She had abandoned her chair and was sitting on the floor, leaning on the wall. She rested the back of her head against it. "I've known Zapata a long time. He's usually pretty reliable. Did you know he flew me to Suddene once, in the middle of a storm?"

"I didn't. When was that?"

"During the Biocide Attack. I had to get there to..." She sighed. "Never mind. It was when Isobel died." She closed her eyes and rubbed them.

"Are you okay?"

When she opened her eyes she found Wilder watching her with concern.

"I'm just pissed at myself," she explained. "Coming down here was dumb. How could we have been so stupid? Now Buka has four bargaining chips—us and the girls. We've played right into his hands. Vessey's going to be furious." She slapped her forehead. "And I went and told him you're an engineer. He knows how valuable you are. He knows our captain won't want to leave without you."

"We didn't get a chance to think this through."

"It was Aubriot's fault, pushing me to go right there and then, to sneak out while Vessey was distracted. If it hadn't been for him we wouldn't be here. Damn that man. I hate him."

"What *is* it with Aubriot?" Wilder asked. "Someone at the meeting said about him not getting any older. I've noticed it too. It's weird."

"Everyone must have noticed by now. He won't get away with it much longer."

"Get away with what?"

"I suppose it won't hurt to tell you. It'll come out in the end, one way or another. You know Earthers used to genetically engineer their embryos?"

"I'd read about it, yeah. They used to remove abnormalities and congenital diseases, then progressed to enhancing intelligence, physical attributes, etcetera."

"Well, you can imagine the level of engineering Aubriot's parents could afford. They used an experimental treatment on him, designed to eradicate aging."

"*Eradicate* aging?! I mean, I can understand they could maybe delay it. You're telling me he's immortal?"

Cherry gave another shrug. "Even he doesn't know how long he'll live, but, for now, the treatment's working. As far as I can tell, he hasn't aged a day since he was revived on the *Nova Fortuna*."

Wilder whistled.

"If only being immortal compensated for being an asshole," Cherry continued. "I honestly don't know what I ever saw in him."

"Apart from his perfect body and devastating good looks."

Cherry gave a sly smile. "There is that. But even they don't count for much in the end."

"He really likes you, though. I can see it in the way he looks at you."

"*Likes* isn't the right word. I don't think he likes anyone, at least not more than he likes himself. I'm a challenge to him. He knows I loved someone else, preferred another man over him, and he can't stand it. So he spent years with me, hoping I would grow to love him as deeply."

Wilder didn't ask who it was she'd loved so much, and Cherry was grateful. She continued, "And he can't take rejection. It wounds his massive, fragile ego. When I left him it was the greatest insult, even though he deserved it. He thinks he should be able to do whatever he wants and still have me hanging on his elbow. He can't get over the fact *I* broke up with *him*. *That's* what you see when you see him looking at me."

The door opened. Two armed men stood outside. One entered and roughly searched them. He seemed to be looking for something. When he came up with nothing he inspected them more closely. Cherry wondered if he was going to make them strip. But when he checked her ears he found what he was looking for. He flicked out her comm and put it in his pocket. Then he did the same with Wilder's. The Earthers had figured out they must have told their shuttle pilot to leave.

The other guard gestured with his rifle.

"Looks like we're going somewhere," Wilder said.

"And I liked it here so much." Cherry joined her as they were forced from the room.

The guards took them deeper into the complex and down another level. They passed Earthers, who eyed them curiously. The place was indeed packed as Itai had said. Things were getting desperate. Two years of living in hiding, watching the skies for the Scythians' return, and now doubling down on their restricted movements, had to have a disastrous effect on the Earthers' already fragile infrastructures.

On the lower level they were taken to a dead-end corridor and put in a room with two bunks, a reinforced steel door, and toilet in the corner.

"Looks like they plan on keeping us here a while," said Wilder.

Cherry noted the dismay in her tone. "Don't worry. It won't be much different from the time we went to the Galactic Assembly. We'll get through this."

The door closed with a clang.

"Do you think the others might leave without us?" Wilder asked.

"Not a chance," Cherry replied, with more confidence than she felt. In fact, they were both expendable. Vessey was desperate to leave, Niall and Dragan could operate the jump drive, and Aubriot... Aubriot would be Aubriot, looking out for number one. "We'll be fine."

THEIR SHARE OF THE EARTHERS' rations at dinner time featured salty porridge, crackers, pickled vegetables, and water.

"We had better on the *Sirocco*," Wilder muttered as she ate.

Cherry stoically chewed a cracker. She'd spent the last few hours going over their options. All seemed bleak. Their chances of escape were minimal. She couldn't take on the guards one-armed, and though Wilder could fight if backed into a corner she was no warrior. Plus, the guards had weapons. Not pulse rifles—they appeared to be similar to the projectile-firing devices the Scythians used—but deadly nonetheless.

Their only hope lay in persuading Buka to let them go, but the old man would never do that without a massive incentive, and she couldn't think of anything to offer him. Would he even believe her if she did? He knew the decisions lay with Vessey. What had he told the captain?

When their meals were finished, she told Wilder they should sleep.

"I don't think I can."

"Then lie down and rest at least. It's going to be a hard few days until this is sorted out. We need to stay focused."

"What's the point?" Despite her words, Wilder lay down. "Do you think they're going to turn out the light?"

They didn't turn out the light.

Long after Wilder had fallen asleep, the cell remained illuminated. Cherry rested on her back, her hand behind her head. She'd given up on trying to figure out what to do. Her mind had traveled back to the early years of the Concordian Colony, to Ethan and Cariad, to Garwin and Twyla, to the arrival of the Guardians, the fall of the *Nova Fortuna*, and to the construction of Sidhe, the underground town the Gens had built to hide from the Scythians.

The remainder of her missing arm ached as she recalled the moment a Scythian spider had sliced it from her body. She didn't remember anything after that until she woke up in the infirmary. She'd learned later that Aubriot and Ethan had saved her and that Aubriot had put her over his shoulder and run with her to safety.

Just like he had inside the Scythian dome.

In his own way, he cared about her. But even if she could forgive his infidelity, which she didn't think she could, she could never be with him again.

What time is it?

The minimal sounds of activity had died away a while ago. Deciding to take her own advice and try to get some sleep, she turned onto her side and closed her eyes.

Footsteps approached along the corridor. It was an odd time of night for visitors. Perhaps it was only a guard come to retrieve their dinner trays. But there seemed to be two sets of footsteps.

When the door opened, Itai stood outside with a guard.

Cherry sat up.

"Please wake your companion and come with me."

"Huh? Does Buka want to speak to us?"

"Quickly, please." Itai glanced at the guard.

Cherry shook Wilder's shoulder. "We have to go."

Wilder groaned. "What?" She blinked and sat up. "Where? What's happening?"

"I don't know." Something seemed odd about the situation. "Get up."

Itai took them with the guard to the stairs that led to the upper level. At their bottom, he told the man something. The guard shook his head as he replied. Itai spoke again, more forcefully. After some back and forth, the guard appeared to relent.

"This way," said Itai, ascending the steps.

The guard remained at the bottom.

"He isn't coming with us?" Cherry asked, her suspicions growing.

"I will explain everything soon. For now, it would be extremely helpful if you don't ask any questions and do exactly as I say."

Was he breaking them out of the place? It was the only explanation for his shady behavior. As the only person who could communicate with the Concordians, Itai must have achieved a measure of trust and authority. If anyone could convince the guards that Buka had asked him to collect the prisoners and that accompanying them was unnecessary, it was him.

But why?

Why was he doing this?

The translator had nothing to gain from helping them and a whole lot to lose. If things didn't go according to plan they could end up cell neighbors.

On the next level the corridors were quiet and empty. Itai took them at a fast walking speed along them to an area that was new to Cherry. "Are you going to tell us where we're going?" she whispered.

He replied quietly, "There's a second exit. It's usually kept locked and therefore unguarded. I managed to get the key."

"Thanks," Wilder breathed. "Thanks so much."

"Wait until we're outside. You can thank me then."

The other exit was at the top of a set of stairs and dusty with disuse. When he tried to open it the key wouldn't turn in the lock. He tried again, twisting sharply. Somewhere distant, a baby began to cry. Itai looked over his shoulder. His attempts to open the door became more frantic.

"It's probably just rust," said Wilder.

"Rust? What's that?"

It was a simple word, but he was speaking a second language. Cherry told him, "You need to hit the lock with something. Do you have anything heavy?"

Itai pulled a hand weapon from his waistband. "Would this do?"

They took a step back.

"You could try," said Wilder, "but be careful."

Itai banged the grip sharply against the lock three times. The noise echoed up the corridor. He shoved the weapon into his pants, and gave the key another sharp twist.

The lock opened.

They ran out.

It was deep night, and frost sparkled on the land under the starlight. The black, blocky shapes of the bunker's surface buildings stood two hundred meters away.

"Can I thank you now?" Wilder asked.

"You're welcome." Itai smiled. "But I have something to ask in return."

Now his actions made sense. Cherry said, "You want to come with us to Concordia."

His smile widened. "Naturally."

19

"We shouldn't be doing this," Nina whispered.

Miki rolled her eyes. It was so typical of her sister to change her mind at the last minute. Not even at the last minute. It was too late to leave their hiding place now. If they did, the pilot was bound to notice. Then he would tell Captain Vessey and they would be in deep trouble.

"We *are* doing it," Miki replied. "So be quiet, or Zapata might hear us."

She did *not* want to get found out. This was their only chance to go to Earth. The captain had ordered an immediate recall of all personnel to the ship, and Zapata was going to collect them. That had to mean the *Sirocco* would be returning to Concordia very soon. It was now or never.

She had to get to the surface. The idea of leaving Dad behind on Earth filled her with so much sadness she couldn't bear it. Losing him had been hard enough. Never being able to visit his grave was a prospect she couldn't even consider. He wouldn't be a few kilometers away, he would be light years from them, alone in the dark.

It didn't make sense. She knew that. She knew he wasn't conscious of anything anymore. But knowing it didn't change the way she felt.

A gentle hum permeated the storage locker they were hiding in.

"That's the a-grav field," she said. "This is it. We can't back out now anyway." The only light penetrating the locker came through the slim gap around the door, so she sensed rather than saw Nina's frown. She added, filling her voice with confidence, "Don't worry. It'll be fine. The Earthers will look after us."

The entire trip down to the surface her heart beat hard in her chest. The source of her fear had changed from the threat of discovery. Now, she feared what might happen to them after they arrived. She hadn't thought that part through carefully. All she knew was they had to remain hidden until after the *Sirocco* left, so there was no chance the Earthers would give them back.

She didn't know how long the Concordians would search for them before they gave up, nor how she and Nina would survive while they waited.

Surely it wouldn't be that hard.

The sensation of flying came to an end as the shuttle's drive cut out and the vessel landed with a small bump. Miki clutched Nina's arm and whispered, "We have to wait until he leaves. Then we slip out."

Nina didn't reply. She must still be having second thoughts. It didn't matter. They were committed.

The clunk and whoosh of the hatch opening followed. There was a click as the pilot's cabin door opened and then heavy footsteps passed by right outside the locker.

Miki softly counted to ten before opening the locker door. The passenger cabin was empty. She climbed out, stood to her full height and stretched. Nina climbed out too.

"Don't forget the bag," Miki reminded her.

Nina reached into the locker for it.

"Hurry up."

Zapata had sealed the hatch but there was an emergency release. Miki twisted the handle and the hatch split from the hull. Cold air swept in. Outside, gray cloud blanketed the sky. The shuttle sat on a concrete pad. In the distance was a group of single story buildings. No one seemed to be about.

So far, so good.

She'd been worried they would be seen by Earthers immediately and reported to Zapata, but this place seemed deserted. It had to be something to do with everyone hiding from the Scythians. That was what Cherry had said. They'd all gone underground.

Luckily for us.

Nina said, "Maybe we should—"

"Come on!" Miki trotted down the steps. When her sister remained at the top, she said, "Give me the bag."

Nina was forced to come down to comply. As soon as Miki was carrying their few belongings and supplies, she walked quickly away from the shuttle. She didn't want to run in case someone noticed and thought they looked suspicious.

There was Zapata!

She hadn't left enough time for him to leave the area. He had his back toward them, heading for the buildings. If he looked back he would spot them.

She turned in the opposite direction.

Two of the Earthers' helis were parked on pads. Beyond them was open countryside. Wide open. The area had once been farmers' fields but weeds covered the ground. Perhaps a kilometer away was a cluster of houses.

Miki checked over her shoulder. Nina was just behind her. Zapata had nearly reached the buildings. He hadn't seen them. When he returned to the shuttle he would find the hatch open, but maybe he would think he'd forgotten to close it.

"We'll go there." She indicated the hamlet.

They waded through waist-high vegetation, moving directly across country. Prickly seed heads caught on their clothes as they brushed past the plants. Soon, they were covered in them. Insects buzzed all around. Something crawled up Miki's sleeve. She flicked it off.

She vaguely remembered a time on Concordia when a cloud of flying pests had descended on her and Dad, and he'd carried her into their house, shielding her from the attack. But she couldn't remember any other life forms on her home planet. Only humans and the biting insects. Earth was so full of life. There had been a time when Concordia had been like this, but now it was a barren place. Earth was better. Once the Earthers had fought off the Scythians, it would be good to live here.

When they reached the first house, she looked back again at the shuttle. The landing area remained empty. Her tension eased. Her plan had succeeded. No one knew they'd left the *Sirocco*. Now all they had to do was find somewhere to stay for a few days while they waited for the Concordians to leave.

At first glance, their new dwelling place didn't appear promising. The little village had clearly been abandoned, perhaps years ago. Doors and windows stood ajar, revealing empty interiors. The weeds from the fields had encroached the streets. An overturned toddler's stroller lay in the middle of the street, rusted and grimy. If she remembered rightly, it had been two years since the aliens paid their first visit to Earth. The people who had lived here might have gone into hiding soon after, judging by the state of things.

"*Don't* tell me we're going to live here," said Nina.

"Only for a little while."

"What will we eat? Is there even any clean water to drink?"

"Stop complaining. Do you want to be near Dad or not? You didn't have to come with me if you didn't want to."

"You didn't tell me we would be living in a dump."

"What did you expect? Did you think we would be living in a palace? Life on Earth is different from how things were on the ship. A lot different. Things are harder here, but they're...richer. Life is more fulfilling." There was only so much she could make up to try to appease her sister. She sought a distraction. "Let's look in there."

The door to one of the houses was closed, as if someone might have taken the time to lock it. Useful things might be inside—things like food, bedding, and warm clothes. She was already feeling cold despite their exercise crossing the fields.

"Is Dad even buried near here?" Nina asked as Miki tried the door. It opened.

"I don't recognize this area," Nina said. "Do you know where we are? Dad might even be buried in another country. Did you consider that?"

Miki was looking at a cramped but comfortable living space. "Hello? Is anyone home?"

The closed door had prevented dust from blowing in from the street. Two small sofas faced a fireplace. It was the first fireplace she'd ever seen, but the ashes and grate told her its purpose. Painted pictures of flowers and landscapes hung on the walls. A rug covered most of the wooden floorboards.

A strange feeling crept over her. She had the impression that in stepping over the threshold she had stepped back in time.

"Hello?" she called again. *Was someone living here?*

The remains of the fire could be days or years old. She simply couldn't tell.

"There's a kitchen through here," said Nina excitedly, all her misgivings apparently forgotten. She'd always been like that. Her mood could change in an instant.

"Check the cupboards," Miki said, following her sister. "The previous owners might have left someth—"

"There's lots of food!" Nina stood in front of an open cupboard filled with packets of dried basic supplies.

Miki couldn't read the writing but she recognized flour, noodles, beans, and peas.

"And here," Nina said triumphantly, opening another door. "And here! There's enough to last us weeks."

A rifle was propped against one wall.

Miki's relief and elation rapidly sank. "No."

"No what?"

"We can't stay here." She glanced into the living room, half-expecting to see it occupied.

"Why not? This is the perfect—"

"Someone already lives here. We have to leave, now."

"But—"

"Now!" She grabbed her sister's arm and tugged her toward the exit.

"Ow, you're hurting me. I thought we were going to live with the Earthers. That's the whole point. What are you frightened of?"

"We're going to live with the Earthers after the *Sirocco* leaves. If they find us now they might send us back to the ship. We need to..."

A noise had come from somewhere else in the house.

"What was that? Did you hear something?"

Her sister shook her head. "What did it sound like?"

"Shhh! There it is again."

The noise had been louder. It had been human. A human voice, but not speaking.

The third time the voice sounded, Nina's eyes widened. "I heard it. It's coming from over there." She pointed at an open door that led into a hall, adding, "It sounds like someone's hurt."

Miki silently nodded. The noise the person was making was the groan or cry of someone in pain.

"We should help them," said Nina.

Miki clenched her hands into fists. She didn't know what to do. They *should* help the person, but that could mean revealing their presence to the other Earthers.

Nina said, "Dad would want us to help them."

Put like that, the answer was simple. "You're right."

While they'd been talking, the person had groaned again. They walked toward the sound. Miki went first. Only two doors led from the hall. Beyond the open one was an empty bathroom. The other door was closed.

She knocked. "Are you okay? Can we come in?"

The person answered but in a language she didn't understand. She looked at Nina, who shrugged.

"We're coming in."

Inside the room lay a man in a double bed. The covers were pulled up to his chin. Closed curtains blocked out the daylight so it was hard to make out much more. The man's hair was straggly and greasy and long stubble clothed his face nearly to his eyes.

"Are you sick?" Miki asked. "Do you need something?"

The man replied in a quiet, grating tone.

She couldn't understand a word or even guess at his meaning. She stepped closer. "My name's Miki, and this is my sister, Nina. We did knock at your front door but no one answered. We can go if you don't want us here, only..." She looked around the room. Her eyes were becoming accustomed to the low light.

A dresser stood open, clothes spilling out. She returned her attention to the man. "Are you ill?"

He didn't seem ill. His eyes were bright and his skin looked healthy, if rather dirty.

As they held each other's gaze, she began to see something in his expression she didn't like. Something hungry and mean.

"If you don't need us, we'll go." She turned to her sister. "We're leaving."

She took a step toward the door.

The man threw back the covers and leapt from the bed. He was fully clothed. He'd never been ill. He'd been pretending.

Miki tried to run.

A large hand caught her forearm and clamped tight.

"Nina, go! Run!"

Her sister froze.

In another instant Nina broke from her trance and moved, but the man was ahead of her, hauling Miki with him as he strode to the door. He flung it open, shoved her into her sister so they tumbled to the floor, stepped out, and slammed the door shut. A key rattled in the lock.

Disentangling herself from Nina, Miki yelled, "The window!"

She raced over to it and tore open the curtains. It was locked too.

"Smash it!" exclaimed Nina.

They looked around for something hard, but the only things that might break the glass were the bed and the dresser, both too large and heavy to lift.

"I'll punch it out," Miki announced.

"Be careful."

She snatched a shirt from the floor and wrapped it around her fist.

But as she drew back her arm, the man appeared on the other side.

He was aiming his rifle at them.

They backed away.

He yelled and gesticulated. He wanted them to sit on the bed.

Would he really shoot unarmed girls? Miki couldn't really believe it, but she had Nina to consider. She must not put her sister in even more danger.

She sat down.

20

The man came for them not long after it turned dark. It was hard to tell night had fallen because the man had hammered planks onto the outside of the window, blocking out most of the light. Miki thought he had come to bring them food or at least some water, or maybe he would allow them to go to the bathroom, but he didn't do any of that. He pointed the rifle at them, tucked under the crook of one arm. He was holding something n his other hand.

When Miki saw what it was she quailed.

Two short lengths of cord dangled from his fist.

"What does he want?" Nina whispered.

"I-I think he wants to tie us up." She hoped she was right, and that he didn't want to do the other, unmentionable thing that sprang to mind—the thing that murderers did to their victims.

He thrust the hand holding the cords at Nina and then pointed at the door.

"He wants you to go into the hall with him," said Miki.

"I don't want to." Nina was clearly on the edge of tears.

"I don't want you to either, but I think you must." *Why, oh why did I bring her here?*

If something bad happened to her sister she would never forgive herself. What was she talking about? Something bad was already happening to her. "Nina, I'm so sorry."

"It isn't your fault. I'll do what he says. Maybe we'll find a way to escape." Nina stood up and went to the door. She gave Miki a single, wet-eyed glance before stepping into the hall.

As soon as the man shut the door Miki flew at it. She thumped it with her fists and screamed, "If you hurt my sister I'll kill you! I swear I'll kill you!" She continued to thump and kick it until it jerked open again so forcefully she was knocked to the floor.

The man kicked her, first in her ribs and then in her head. The second kick dazed her and she lay still, confused and not resisting as he bound her wrists. Then he took a step back and picked up his rifle. He waited for her to come to her senses and stand up.

Nina's hands were also tied behind her back. Jabbing them with the muzzle of the rifle, the man forced them out of the house. No lights were on in the other houses and all was still. The village was as quiet as it had been when they'd arrived. The man had to be living here alone. For some reason, he'd remained after everyone else had left.

He indicated the direction he wanted them to go. He walked behind them.

Starlight glittered in an obsidian sky. Space looked different down here on Earth than from a starship. Here, the stars seemed to move ever so slightly. Looking out from the *Sirocco* they were steady pinpricks of light. Their appearance from Earth should have been more friendly but it wasn't.

They passed the last houses in the village, standing each side of the road, and then they were out in open countryside.

Where could the man be taking them? Was he taking them away from his house to...to...? Miki shook her head. She couldn't contemplate the threatening thought. She focused instead on looking around for possible ways to get away. Vegetation grew tall on the borders of the road. If they could escape into it he might not find them. But he would have time to get one or two shots off before they were hidden. However, he couldn't shoot at both of them at once.

"Nina," she whispered, "we can't let him take us to wherever he's planning to go. We need to get away. When I give the signal, you run into the weeds, okay?"

"No way."

"You have to!"

"I know what you're going to do. You're going to try to distract him so he doesn't shoot me."

"No, I—"

"Yes, you are. And then what happens?" Nina asked quietly but fiercely. "What if he doesn't catch me but you're dead? What do you think I'm going to do with my hands tied and all alone? How am I supposed to go on without you?"

Miki didn't have an answer. For what felt like the millionth time she regretted not bringing ear comms. She'd been so determined they weren't ever going back to the *Sirocco* she'd left hers behind and made Nina leave hers too. She'd been so, so stupid. "Maybe you can find some other Earthers who—ow!"

The man had jabbed his rifle in her back, in the exact same place he'd kicked her. She got the message and stopped speaking. Her burgeoning bruise throbbed and her head ached in sympathy.

They trudged on through the night. The dirt road split off to a narrower, more overgrown track to the left but the man didn't take it. He kept them going straight another few hundred meters, until suddenly he jabbed Miki again. She cried out, not understanding what she'd done wrong.

Nina said, "I think he wants us to go that way."

There was a gap in the vegetation, barely one person wide, where the plants had been trodden down. Miki stepped off the road, Nina followed, and the man continued walking behind them. The little path was hard to see in the dark, and a couple of times the man shouted when she veered off it.

Then she saw where they were heading.

How she hadn't managed to spot it before, she didn't know. Perhaps it was because she'd kept her head down, focusing on following the trail. The structure was still some distance away but it stood out plainly as it glowed gently in the night. A pale silver dome protruded from the surrounding shadowy scrub. It had to be one of the Scythian domes she'd heard people talking about on the ship.

"Oh!" Nina exclaimed softly. She'd seen it too.

He was going to give them to the aliens?!

Why would anyone do that? He had to be mad. The Scythians were the Earthers' enemies. They'd been abducting people all over the globe. Why would he hand over two girls he didn't even know and for no reason?

That was *it*. There was no debating any longer. They had to get away from him. They might die in the attempt but at least it would be quick. Who knew what horrors lay in wait for them inside a Scythian dome?

"Nina, when I count to three, run."

"No!"

"Don't argue. One, two, thr— arghhh!" The rifle dug into her ribs. "Now!"

She whirled and kicked the muzzle. Not hard enough. It flicked up but the man held onto it. She ran at him head down, and drove into his chest. He stumbled backward. Her momentum kept going and, unable to use her arms for balance, she began to fall forward. Her forehead smacked against the man's knee as she went down. It hurt but didn't stun her. The impact seemed to complete the man's stumbling because suddenly he was under her.

Where was Nina?

She had no time to check that her sister had done as she'd asked and run away. The man was squirming under her, trying to get both hands on his rifle. She bit the arm that had hold of the weapon. The man grunted. He was heavier and stronger than her. She had to do something to knock him out, fast.

She thrust the top of her head into his jaw and heard his teeth snap closed.

A yell of pain erupted from him.

Had he bitten his tongue?

She leapt to her feet and kicked his head once, twice. For the third kick she recalled him kicking *her* head and kicked even harder. He groaned and rolled. Still, his eyes didn't close and his grip on his rifle remained firm. Liquid oozed from his lips, black in the low light. She aimed a fourth kick, but before it landed a hand shot out and fastened around her ankle.

He tugged sharply and she fell on her backside. She tried to scramble upright but he was faster. A boot thudded down on her middle. The man was standing over her, the weight on his right foot crushing her. She couldn't move. She couldn't breathe. She brought up her knees and squirmed, trying get out from underneath him but it was no use.

Wavering slightly, the man lifted his rifle.

He'd given up on his plan of taking her to the Scythians.

He was going to shoot her.

Thick drops of blood dripped from his chin and spattered on his boot as he took aim.

Her vision narrowed to the gaping hole of the barrel, through which would come her destruction. She turned her head and shoulders away. Her muscles became rigid as she prepared for death.

Would she see Dad again?

She hoped so, though it was sooner than she'd wished.

There was a cry—a female cry, then a yell of rage. Quick footsteps followed and a thump of impact.

The weight on her chest was gone.

The man hit the ground. His rifle was knocked from his grasp. Nina kicked it further away.

"Run!" she shouted. "Miki, run!"

She turned onto her front and managed to get her knees under her. In another second she was up and running. Vegetation flashed past, snatching at her clothes. She didn't know where she was going or where Nina was. All she knew was she had to put as much distance between herself and the Earther as possible, before he could get his rifle and come after her.

If they could both hide so long he gave up looking for them they could find each other in the morning. Maybe they would even be able to untie their wrists.

A tremendous crack exploded.

She gave an involuntary jerk.

He'd fired at one of them. The noise was far louder than a pulse rifle. Had he hit Nina?

There was another shot.

Please, don't let him hit Nina.

She crouched as she ran and glanced from side to side. She couldn't see the Scythian dome so it had to be behind her.

Where's the man?

Where's Nina?

When Miki had run for a few minutes, she slowed and took a look over her shoulder. It was hard to see much in the darkness, but the Earther didn't seem to be in sight. She slowed down some more. Then, panting, she stopped and dropped low. Peeking over the foliage, all she saw was a sea of dark gray leaves, stalks, and dry seed heads. She ducked down.

Where was her sister? Was she okay?

She rested for a moment, catching her breath, and then took another look. Stillness and silence confronted her.

No.

Over to the left the plants gently rustled and swayed.

Praying she was heading for Nina and not their attacker, Miki crawled toward the movement. The rough ground scraped and scratched her knees and hands. Rarely daring to raise her head, she trusted she wasn't going too far off course as she continued on.

As soon as she found Nina they could hide together and wait out the night. The man would have to give up searching for them eventually.

Her hands grew sore and she stopped to nurse them, tucking them under her armpits as she squatted on her haunches.

Then, somewhere ahead of her, the vegetation crackled and swished.

She held her breath.

It was impossible to get away without making a noise. She could only wait, frozen between fear and hope, unable to see farther than a meter all around. Her arms folded over her chest, she felt the thud of her heart against them.

A head burst into view.

Nina!

"Miki! I found you! I thought I saw—"

"Shhh!" she urged. "He might be listening."

They clung to each other, gently sobbing. They were together again. That was something. Miki didn't know what they should do next, whether they should go back to the place where Zapata had landed the shuttle and try to find some friendly, not-crazy, Earthers to help them, or if they should try to find another way out of their predicament. Whatever they did, at least they would not be alone.

A draft of stinky air hit her. At the same time, something impacted the ground behind her.

Nina's features turned rigid with fear as she focused on something over Miki's shoulder.

"Wh—" Before she could get a word out, steely hands fastened around her waist and she was swept up into the air.

21

"**W**hat does that mean?" Itai demanded.

"It means," Cherry retorted hotly, "we can't contact our pilot."

She'd just explained about the guards removing their ear comms. She wasn't sure how Itai had imagined Concordians communicated with each other. Had he thought they had some kind of inbuilt system? But the information was obviously news to him. He must have anticipated the shuttle arriving soon after they escaped. But without a way of comming Zapata, that wasn't going to happen in the short term, perhaps never.

Itai swung wildly around, recklessly waving his gun. "But it won't be long before your absence is noticed. Buka will figure out how we left and he'll send men after us."

"No, really?" Cherry asked sarcastically.

"Maybe we should go back," Wilder suggested. "If we return immediately, we might make it before anyone notices we're missing."

"That can't happen." Itai said. "I must leave with you. You haven't stated it outright, but it's clear that you think Earth is doomed. I agree, but *I'm* not. *I* still have a chance." He muttered something else to himself in his own language as he peered into the night.

"What other option do we have?" Wilder asked. "It sounds like we're going back in that cell whether we like it or not. There's nowhere to hide in this wilderness and even if there were Buka's guards would soon find us."

Cherry said, "I'm not in love with the idea of going back in there." Her gaze was on the weapon he was carelessly moving around. She made eye contact with Wilder. If they could coordinate they could get it from him. She might have tried alone if she had two arms. But Wilder didn't seem to understand her look. "We should leave. Let's not make it easy for them."

"I agree," Itai replied. "There's a small township not far away. We can hide there and wait for your pilot to return. It's that way." He indicated a direction and waited expectantly. When they didn't move, he added, "You two walk ahead of me."

So the fact he hadn't put his gun away wasn't accidental.

They had no choice except to comply. He guided them through the darkness across long-abandoned fields. She wondered why the Earthers around here had given up farming after the Scythian attack of two years ago. Concordians had continued to grow crops despite the ongoing threat of the aliens' return. On the other hand, the Concordians would have starved if they hadn't. Earthers had survived by farming for a long time after the fall of high-tech civilization. They must have had plenty of stores to rely on. But the food wouldn't last forever. What was their long-term plan? They didn't seem to have one. It was no wonder they were desperate for the humans from outer space in their starship to save them.

She and Wilder walked in front of Itai for about half an hour across the semi-wild landscape until they hit a road. They followed the cracked, weedy surface for another fifteen minutes before they reached the outer buildings of the settlement. The houses had been empty for a long time.

"What happened to the people who lived here?" Wilder asked.

"They're in the bunker," replied Itai, "or they went elsewhere, or they're dead."

"The Scythians took them?"

"They killed themselves." Itai's tone was flat. "There were a lot of suicides in the months after the bombardments. Many people had lost everything, or feared a second attack, or refused to live in hiding."

The sky had lightened in the east. If Buka didn't already know they were gone, he would soon.

"Where are you taking us?" asked Wilder. "It won't be hard to search this place top to bottom. Hiding seems futile."

"I know somewhere. Turn to the left. It's down this street, I believe. It's been a while since I was here and the place has changed some-what, but I think I'm right."

As they turned, Cherry got a look at Itai. He was glancing from side to side as if he expected someone to step out from the shadows.

She asked, "Do you think Buka's men are here already?"

"They would seize us immediately if they were. There's a rumor about someone still living here—someone gone mad from fear of the aliens. I don't know if the rumor is true but I'm not taking any chances."

The madman didn't appear. Itai took them to what had once been a shop. The wide glass window was smashed in and the sign hung at a crazy angle. Inside, shelving ran the length of the place, all picked clean, whether by humans or animals.

"This was a grocery," said Itai. "There's a cellar out the back. We can hide in there."

"That's dumb," said Cherry. "If you know about the cellar so do others. We would stand a better chance of not being found out in the fields."

"It isn't safe out in the fields."

"Why not?"

"The Scythians regularly comb them for humans to take back to their dome."

She had no argument against that.

They waded through debris to reach the rear of the store. Torn and gnawed packaging and dust and plant matter blown in from the street littered it. As Itai had predicted, an open hatch in the floor of the back room revealed stairs leading down to a cellar.

"It's dark in there," said Wilder, peering in.

"Go down," said Itai. "I will find some lamps."

"But..." Wilder's protest dried on her lips as he lifted his gun.

"Please don't argue," he said. "I only need one of you alive."

Cherry said, "If you think you'll be allowed aboard the *Sirocco* after murdering one of us, you're deluded."

"Perhaps, but it's a chance I'm willing to take. I know your captain will be anxious to have her engineer back."

"This is insane," Wilder murmured. But she stepped down the stairs.

When Cherry descended and her head was below floor level, Itai shut the hatch, plunging them into near-complete darkness. Only a faint ray of light escaped the edge of the opening.

"I can't see a thing!" Wilder complained.

Cherry's glimpse of the cellar before Itai shut them in had shown her a small room about four meters square. Shelves adorned the walls, all empty. As before, the floor was littered with the leavings of looters. "Just sit down somewhere. If you blunder about you'll hurt yourself."

She descended the remaining steps carefully, until Wilder's hand brushed her. "There are only a couple more steps."

They sat down together.

"Do you think he'll be back?" Wilder asked.

There were sounds of Itai moving around overhead. The idea that he might just shut them in and leave them here—bargaining for passage on the ship in return for revealing their location—had occurred to Cherry too. "I don't know. But don't worry. We'll be okay, I'm sure."

Wilder's arm snaked around her shoulders and hugged her. "You're not my mom. You don't have to reassure me."

Cherry chuckled. "I never was the greatest mom to you, was I?"

"You mean after my incident with the a-grav machine? Forget about it. I was a bratty kid."

"I'm not going to argue about it. Look, as soon as Itai's distracted, we have to—"

The hatch opened. Despite the short interval it had been closed, the light was blinding.

"I found a lamp," said Itai. "We don't have to sit in darkness." He walked down several steps and placed the lamp on the step next to him. Then he pulled the hatch almost completely closed and fiddled at the edge of it. "I've put a rug over the opening."

Cherry rolled her eyes. His tactic was an exercise in futility.

The lamp burned some kind of oil. As Itai carried it down, it gave off an unpleasant vapor. If Buka's people didn't find them soon they might die of smoke inhalation.

Settling down opposite them, Itai rested his gun in his lap, his hand loose on the grip. The lamplight cast up-shadows on his face, lending him a sinister look. Cherry hadn't managed to fully convey to Wilder her intention to overpower him, but she'd said enough to get her point across. Now all they had to do was wait for an opportune moment, when he was lulled into inattention.

"Something I've been wondering," she said. "You told us a group of refugees had arrived at the GAA's bunker. How did they get there? This place seems in the middle of nowhere, and I haven't seen any transportation except helis."

"They walked and rode horses. One family had a truck they used to transport children and the elderly."

"I didn't see any horses or a truck."

"The truck is in a barn. We ate the horses."

"Gross," Wilder muttered.

"So you have mechanized transportation?" Cherry asked.

"It was one of the first innovations of the GAA, along with roads, of course."

"What do your vehicles run on?"

"Alcohol. How is your planet's transportation powered?"

"Electricity."

"Ah, yes. That's right. I've seen it in old books. Unfortunately, we haven't managed to create the infrastructure for battery-powered vehicles. Before the Scythians came we had some power plants, but they were the first things they attacked."

"They knew what they were doing," Wilder said. "Destroying the frameworks of civilization."

Itai's mouth turned down and his shoulders sagged. "It was a terrible time. I lost my wife and children. I was away from home, in another city, organizing the foundation of an education center for technological subjects. It was the beginning of a new, bright future for humanity. From that school we would have sent out people trained in the old skills, possessing the knowledge of past generations. We would have sent them all over the world to teach others. Eventually, humankind would have regained everything we'd lost. But the Scythians came. They razed every major metropolis, blasted the roads, destroyed factories, manufacturing plants, apartment blocks."

He swallowed and continued, "By the time I made it back to my home, my family had been dead for days, killed by falling rubble."

"I'm sorry," said Wilder, reaching out to touch his free hand.

That should have been the moment. They should have jumped on him then and grabbed the gun. But Cherry didn't move, trapped by her thoughts.

In a sense, what had happened to Earth was Concordia's fault. If she wanted to be particularly egocentric it was *her* fault. The aliens had offered Concordia a choice: to submit to slavery or die. She'd overruled the Leader, Meredith's decision and defied the Scythians. As a consequence, they'd launched the biocide, killing hundreds of thousands of Fila and most other life. It had taken her a long time to come to terms with what she'd done, if in fact she ever had.

After leaving their home planet to die—as they thought—the Scythians had come to Earth. They'd found the coordinates from the Guardian, Faina's database, and they wanted to complete their revenge on humanity.

It was simple. If she hadn't refused the Scythians' proposition, if she'd accepted a life under Scythian rule, they might never have come to Earth. The family of this man sitting opposite her might not have died. Civilization might have advanced here.

Heavy footsteps sounded overhead. Dust sprinkled down lightly, the motes shining in the lamp's glow.

Itai lifted his gun and put a finger to his lips.

The ceiling reverberated as something heavy was dragged across the floor. More footsteps resounded. There was a scraping noise and the shuffle of textile. The hatch flew open.

Itai lifted his weapon to aim at the opening.

Cherry leapt on him. "Grab his gun, Wilder! Grab it."

He threw her off. She landed in a pile of trash. In the time it took her to struggle upright, it was all over. Guards had run down the stairs and Itai was on his face, a boot on his back. Another guard had his gun. Wilder was on her feet, staring slack-jawed at the open hatch.

Aubriot was there, looking in, and next to him was Strongquist.

22

The flight to the Scythian dome was a nightmare Miki would not soon forget. Her stomach grasped painfully tight, she'd been carried aloft so fast it had taken her a minute to figure out what was happening. She recalled Nina's upturned face receding, pale in the starlight. Then a second creature had descended to snatch her sister, and it all made sense.

Pure terror had followed. Would the alien drop her, leaving her to plunge to her death? Or would it take her to its dwelling place, and what would happen then? Perhaps the first possibility was better than what else might happen.

And Nina. Poor Nina.

She couldn't bear the thought of what might happen to her sister.

The alien had flown with her to the dome. All the while a horrible smell had wafted down from its wings. The center of the dome's roof had spiraled open, and they had descended through the opening. Inside, a second portal had opened, barely visible in the scarce light. From then on everything was hazy. She recalled being unable to breathe, or rather, choking on the air. She must have passed out because the next thing she knew she was on solid ground and the pressure around her middle had gone.

A warm body lay next to her. She turned onto her side. It was Nina.

Thank the stars!

Nina was coming around.

"It's all right," Miki whispered. "We're safe."

For now.

She looked around. Others were here. Other people.

She sat up.

Earthers of all ages were staring at them, from little children to a woman so old she only had a few wisps of white hair clinging to her scalp. The group numbered about twenty, and they crowded together in one corner of the room.

It was a strange place. The walls were dark gray and made from a material she didn't recognize. It was smooth, matt, and featureless. Above, high above, was what seemed to be the ceiling of the dome, glowing softly like the sky at dusk. The walls didn't reach anywhere near it, at only about four meters tall. Atop the walls, forming a barrier over the room, was a layer of barely discernible, transparent sheeting.

An Earther spoke. A man addressed her and Nina.

Miki shook her head. How to convey she didn't speak their language?

"We can't understand you," Nina replied, loudly, as if shouting might make her meaning clear.

The man spoke again.

Miki replied, "We aren't from Earth. We're Concordians." She cupped her ear as if trying to listen, and then gave an exaggerated shrug.

The man turned to talk to his companions. After a short discussion, he faced them again. The group stared at them once more in silence.

"What is this place?" Nina asked.

"Some kind of holding pen, I guess."

"How long will they keep us here? Are they going to let us go?"

"I don't know." In fact, Miki doubted very much that the Scythians had any plans to set them free. What did they plan on doing with them? She'd heard snatches of conversation aboard the *Sirocco* about the aliens kidnapping people, but as soon as the speakers noticed she was listening they shut up. If anyone knew what happened to the humans taken into captivity, she hadn't heard anything about it.

Nina said softly, her voice full of fear, "They're never going to let us go, are they? Do you think they're gonna...gonna..."

"Shhh!" Miki hugged her. She knew what her sister had been about to say. The same idea had occurred to her—that the Scythians might feed on humans. But the notion was too terrible to state out loud. "Everyone on the *Sirocco* knows we're missing. They'll be searching for us. They'll find us and rescue us."

"Are you sure?"

"I'm sure. Cherry and Wilder won't leave without us." As soon as the words were out, she knew they were true. What a stupid thing she'd done. Instead of talking to Dad's friends about how she felt, she'd run off and messed up their plans. They would either delay the ship's departure or they would stay on Earth to try to find them, missing their chance to go home.

A shadow crossed the pale light and the Earthers reacted with frightened murmurs. A Scythian was descending, holding something in its feet. It landed on the transparent barrier, which dipped under the additional weight. With one wing claw, it cut a slit and then emptied its burden through the gap. Something fell and hit the ground with wet splashes.

Instantly, the Earthers fell upon it, grabbing handfuls of the material and shoving them in their mouths. The man who had spoken before thrust a cupped, full hand in the girls' direction. He seemed to be holding a kind of cereal mash. Miki wrinkled her nose and shook her head. She was not *that* hungry.

"Is that all there is to eat?" asked Nina.

The question seemed rhetorical. "You should try some if you want." Miki looked up. The Scythian had gone and the cut it had made was no longer visible.

The Earthers cleared the food in under five minutes. They didn't exactly fight over it. They made sure the old and young were fed. But it was clear they were hungry. The aliens weren't supplying enough sustenance, either through ignorance or deliberately. If they didn't give more, eventually everyone would die of malnutrition.

"What do we do now?" Nina asked.

"We should try to get some sleep." It had been night when the crazy Earther had forced them out of his house and over the fields. Then they'd fought him and run from him before being snatched. It had to be late. They needed to conserve their energy for whatever lay ahead.

They moved to a corner of the room. Miki lay behind Nina and wrapped an arm around her, using her other arm as a pillow. The Earthers were settling down too.

"I don't think I *can* sleep," Nina whispered.

"Just try."

All thoughts of slumber were driven from her mind, however, when another foreboding shadow crossed overhead. This time, two Scythians had arrived.

The Earthers reacted with terror, screaming and wailing as they crowded together.

One of the aliens slashed the ceiling open. The Earthers' screams became muffled. They had clapped their hands over their mouths.

It took Miki a couple of seconds to figure out why. "Nina, cover your mouth. Don't breathe."

Her sister's wide, frightened eyes stared out as she did as she was told.

The aliens descended, flapping lazily down. As soon as the first one alighted, it walked awkwardly across to the huddled Earthers and spread its wings threateningly. They were so wide they almost touched the walls.

The other Scythian waddled toward Miki and Nina. Though her hand covered her nose, Miki could smell its stench. She choked and coughed, accidentally breathing in the room's new atmosphere, which made her choke harder.

The alien hopped into the air and reached for Nina.

"No!" Miki thrust a hand against its midriff, pushing it away. The alien's skin had a horrible, greasy feel.

It landed and focused its strange eyes on her. One wing swept smoothly around, the claw catching her cheek and slicing it open. She shrieked and grabbed it. Hot liquid spilled from between her fingers.

"Don't!" Nina yelled. "I'll go with it." She pushed Miki out of the way.

"No!" she shouted. "Not my sister! You're not taking her." She tried to fight off the alien, and in return received two more gashes, one to her arm and another to her hand.

The creature wrested Nina from her grasp and carried her aloft.

"Noooo!" Miki screamed.

23

C herry gazed sourly at Aubriot across the table. He was so full of himself, cocky with the knowledge that he'd 'saved' her again. Yet Buka's guards would have found them anyway, regardless of his and Strongquist's help. The fact clearly didn't stop him from being smug.

Itai's expression was a marked contrast. He stood handcuffed, flanked by armed men, his head down.

Buka trembled with rage as he spoke to him. Cherry was concerned for the old man, fearing he might have a heart attack or stroke. When Itai replied he seemed contrite. Was he apologizing? If he was, Buka didn't accept it. He barked an order at the guards, who grabbed Itai's arms to take him away.

Itai protested and struggled. When Buka ignored him, he turned to the Concordians. "He wants to lock me up but you need me, right? You need me to translate for you."

"Nope," Aubriot replied flatly.

"Your presence won't be necessary," said Strongquist. "I am able to perform translation duties. I have familiarized myself with the local language."

Were they aware he was a machine? Cherry didn't know who she trusted least. She gave Wilder a look, but the younger woman only shrugged. She wasn't familiar with Guardians. She'd only been a kid during the early years of colonization. And Aubriot had turned a hundred and eighty degrees in his attitude. At one time he'd seemed to hate and fear the androids even more than her, if that were possible. Now, because it suited him, Strongquist was his best buddy.

Itai was taken away.

Buka spoke to Cherry and Wilder and Strongquist related his words.

"Please accept my apologies for incarcerating you. I hope you understand we're in a desperate position and as leader of the GAA it's my responsibility to do everything I can to help my fellow human beings in this crisis. I hope you can forgive my actions and move on." He handed them their ear comms.

"I can't speak for Wilder," Cherry replied, "but I don't accept your apology. As far as I'm concerned what you did was unforgivable, and your apology makes no sense anyway. *I'm* one of your fellow human beings and you threw me in a cell. What had I done to deserve that? I came here to find two girls, that's it. And you took advantage of us for your own ends. So don't tell me you're sorry. I don't want to hear it."

There was a soft *tsk* from someone. He gave her a slight shake of his head, as if chiding her. She wanted to punch him.

"It really isn't excusable," Wilder added, though with less vigor. "You can't talk about helping humanity while at the same time incarcerating the innocent. Doesn't make a lot of sense."

"Your responses are noted," said Buka. "I will endeavor to be less hasty in the future. Can we discuss the plan for helping Earth now?"

Cherry was about to answer that there was no plan, that as soon as they found Miki and Nina they would leave the system and Earthers could go screw themselves, but Aubriot got his reply in first.

"The way I see it, there has to be a campaign of mass resistance. Everywhere, all over the planet, you guys have got to stand up for yourselves. Up until now, you've allowed the Scythians to walk all over you, like doormats. You've got to fight back, hard, with everything you've got. Blow up the domes, wage guerrilla warfare, attack, attack, attack. Show the bastards you're not going to be their slaves. If you want your planet back, it's the only way."

Cherry's jaw fell open. What was he talking about? Had he forgotten about the biocide? Did he want Earth turned into another Concordia? "But..."

He turned toward her, hard-faced, and repeated, "It's the only way."

Buka said, "There's no guarantee we will win."

"Right," said Aubriot, "but what you don't get is, it's been like this through most of Earth's history. Go back far enough and you'll discover everyone was at each other's throats for thousands of years. Millions died in wars. Billions, probably, as one leader or another fought for land, or money, or just the love of a beautiful woman. For humans, it's normal. It's what we do. The Scythians are just another catalyst for the same old same old."

She couldn't find the words to respond. Wilder appeared similarly flummoxed.

"History's come full circle," he concluded. "We're back at the beginning."

Wilder spluttered, "I-I don't think that's right. There has to be a different way."

Cherry finally got her brain in gear. She leaned over the table to talk directly to Buka. "What he *isn't* mentioning, and what you have to take into account, is the Scythians' biocide. He told you about it in the early discussions you had with Captain Vessey. Do you remember? The biocide is the reason we're here. It destroyed most life on Concordia. If the Scythians change their minds about enslaving you, if you make their lives too difficult, they'll just kill every living organism here. Not only all humans. *Everything.* And there won't be anything you can do to stop it. Believe me, you do *not* want to see that stuff spreading over the land, through the water, destroying everything it touches. You do not want that."

Aubriot threw her a dark look. She smiled facetiously.

"I do remember you mentioning a devastating pesticide," said Buka.

"It isn't a pesticide as such," Wilder explained. "It's a virus. A virus that targets all living things, multiplying as it spreads. That's how it's so devastating."

"On Concordia," said Cherry, "we managed to vaccinate everyone. You'll never do that here."

"But you have the vaccine?" Buka asked.

"We…" They didn't have the vaccine but they could manufacture it, the same as they'd used Kes's blood to manufacture a vaccine against the Earth virus that had killed him. They had people who knew how to do it. "No, we don't."

"But we could make it," said Aubriot.

"Not in sufficient quantities," Wilder protested. "What's the population of Earth? A billion? Two billion? Do you even know?"

"The number is irrelevant if we can get the information out," said Buka. He knitted his fingers and rested his hands on the table. "Ever since you came here, you've had a habit of acting…how can I put it?… superior? It's clear you think your society is far in advance of ours. But what have you really seen of Earth? When you arrived we'd already suffered one attack, an attack that caught us unawares. You didn't see the level of development we'd achieved before then. You also don't understand the GAA or our workings. This association exists to disseminate information. That's its primary purpose. We delve into the past—old data bases, ancient machinery, archaic books, even— strive to understand and reverse engineer, and then we spread what we know all over the world. We are already aware of how vaccination works. Give us the necessary—"

"You don't get it!" Cherry exclaimed. "Even if you manage to protect every human being, the biocide will kill everything else. How are you going to survive on a barren planet?"

"How did the Concordians survive?"

"We had stores, but—"

"So do we."

She groaned and put her face in her hand.

"You don't understand," said Buka. "People are already rising up. We've been receiving reports from all over the globe of attacks on the domes. Most are unsuccessful, but people are trying. They've had their loved ones taken away from them and they know what's coming next. They know the Scythians are preparing to subjugate all humanity. Many won't tolerate it. With or without your help, there will be a war. Without your help, we don't stand a chance."

"*You* don't understand," said Wilder gently, "Concordia is barely clinging on. That's why we're here—to collect the material we need to revitalize our planet."

"I do understand that very well," Buka replied. "And if you succeed in your endeavor, Concordia could return the favor to Earth. It could be the repository from which we draw in order to re-seed our planet."

"I'm no biologist, but even I know you're underestimating the amount of biodiversity here. It's built up over a billion years. What we've taken from Earth will only recreate a shadow of it on my home planet. I hope it'll be enough to kick start ecological development, then evolution can take over."

"Exactly as it can here."

"He's got a point," said Aubriot. "There's been plenty of mass extinctions on Earth. Each time, life started up again, spreading out, diversifying. If conditions are right, that's what happens, over and over again. Scythians might try to kill everything but a few things will survive, the same as they did on Concordia."

"But...Earth is beautiful," Wilder said helplessly.

Then she was silent.

Cherry had no words either. Aubriot and Buka were set on their course and she didn't have the inclination or willpower anymore to force them off it. But there was something else to discuss. "What about Miki and Nina? We have to find them."

"Now *that*," Aubriot said, "we do agree on. What's happened to the little tykes, Buka? Any ideas?"

"It seems clear they must have gone to the abandoned settlement where we found you, but I'm afraid they aren't there any longer. When my people were trying to find you and Itai, they searched the settlement thoroughly. There was no sign of anyone."

"They would have been hiding," said Cherry. "We need to search it again."

"There's something you don't know." The GAA leader looked uncomfortable, and Strongquist paused as he waited for him to continue. "The settlement was not entirely abandoned. One individual couldn't be persuaded to leave. He is mentally ill, and he was convinced the Scythians were gods who had come to punish humanity for its sins. It seems likely that, according to what the searchers found, the girls from your ship encountered him."

"So?" Cherry asked. "Then you just need to find where he's gone, and Miki and Nina will be with him."

"When I said no one was found at the settlement I was speaking the truth. However, the mentally ill man *was* found, wandering in the fields. From what could be gleaned from his babble, it seems likely that he took the girls to the Scythian dome and—"

"No!" Cherry yelled, leaping to her feet. "No, don't tell me that. It isn't true."

Strongquist continued his translation in an even tone, "...the aliens snatched them."

24

"Are you out of your mind?!" Cherry demanded after Buka had left the meeting room. She was boiling with rage, and she needed a diversion from the news that Miki and Nina had been taken by the Scythians and were probably dead.

There was no doubt who was the object of her question.

Aubriot replied, "Save it for the cowards on the ship."

"*Cowards*? It isn't cowardice to not want to die in a pointless war—a war that has nothing to do with us. Let the Earthers fight their own battles. We have our own problems to worry about. Does Vessey know what you're doing?" She had a suspicion he was acting unilaterally, that the captain hadn't agreed to the message he'd given the GAA. The woman might not even know about it.

"After you snuck off..." Aubriot began.

She restrained herself from hitting him. He'd all but *told* her to sneak away and go to the surface to find Miki and Nina.

"...I reminded the *Sirocco*'s personnel about their heritage, their duty, and what they owed to the people of this fine planet. I also made the very good point that what we learn here fighting the Scythians we will be able to apply on Concordia, when the time inevitably comes."

Her jaw set, she replied, "So you persuaded them to stay."

"In a word, yes."

"You did it on purpose, didn't you?"

He raised his eyebrows innocently. "Did what?"

"If you're going to make me spell it out—you orchestrated everything so I was off the ship while you were giving your little speech, changing people's minds, because you knew I would argue against it. Like you, I've been around since the early years and people listen to me. You wanted a powerful opposition out of the way. You never gave a shit about Kes's kids. You wanted me gone. I'm right, aren't I?"

"That's not nice, Cherry. Of course I care about the girls. I'm not a monster."

"Huh. Maybe. But you care more about yourself and what you want."

Wilder said, "What about the *Sirocco*? If we help the Earthers wage this war, the minute the Scythian backup arrives they'll blast her out of the sky."

"Ah, I thought of a solution to that problem. Wouldn't have got Vessey on my side otherwise. The *Sirocco* only has to make a little jump to be out of danger." He lifted a hand and placed his fingertips on the table. "She starts here..." he moved his hand to one side "...and jumps here. At the right time, she jumps back again..." he moved his hand to its original position "...and picks us up. The Scythians don't have jump tech or they would be here by now."

"*At the right time*?" Cherry asked. "When's that going to be? This war will last years. It'll never be over."

"Millions will die," said Wilder.

"Everyone dies," Aubriot retorted.

"Not everyone. Not according to what I've heard."

Aubriot looked sharply at Cherry. She glared back.

"And what's going to happen to Concordia while we're gone?" Wilder continued. "We desperately need to begin the re-seeding process if it's going to be saved."

"Concordia's an open question," said Aubriot. "We've been gone so long, we don't know what we'll find when we get back. The colony might have died out. That's what Kes seemed to think would happen. In which case, what would be the point of restarting it? We can live here just as well."

"Not if the Scythians do the same here as they did on Concordia! Then we'll have *two* dead planets and nowhere to live."

Cherry said, "You don't want to go back, do you? You've decided you want to stay on Earth. You're home now and you don't want to leave. That's fine. But don't drag all of us into it. You stay here. We'll go."

"He wants us," said Wilder. "He wants me, Niall, and Dragan. We can help wage this hopeless war against the Scythians. And he wants all the scientists. They're the ones with the knowledge to help humanity survive in the face of a biocide attack. He wants the *Sirocco*, too, for everything she can offer. Maybe he plans on taking out as many Scythian ships and domes as he can before she jumps."

Aubriot gave a supercilious grin. "I always said you were smart, didn't I?"

"You're sick," said Cherry.

"And him." Wilder jabbed a finger at Strongquist. "You want him too."

"*It!*" Cherry said.

While they argued, the android had remained quiet. Now the attention was on him, he said, "I will fulfill my programmed purpose and defend humans wherever possible."

Wilder asked, "Are you taking *it* to the Makers' place to look over the equipment?"

Aubriot replied, "You read my mind."

"Stars," said Cherry. "Is there anything you haven't thought of?"

"Something will come up. I'm not perfect." Aubriot knitted his fingers, turned his hands palm outward, and stretched his arms. He stood up. "Sorry, ladies. Lots of work to do. Strongquist, with me."

He left, the android in tow.

"That man's unbelievable," said Cherry. "Blithely committing millions of people to their deaths, like it was just another Tuesday."

"He's in his element. There's no stopping him."

"There is. There has to be. We just need to think of it. In the meantime..." She got to her feet. "We have to do what we came here for. We have to find Miki and Nina."

"But Buka said they must have been taken into the dome. It seems a solid explanation for their disappearance. It's devastating, but—"

"I'm not giving up on them and you shouldn't either. They might still be alive. But before we do anything let's see what we can find out about what's happening on the ship."

They left the bunker and walked to the shuttle, where Zapata was lounging.

He straightened up as they approached. "I-I had to tell Vessey—"

"It's okay," Cherry interrupted. "You couldn't hang around forever, hoping we might comm you one day."

He seemed relieved.

"But," she continued, "if you feel like you owe us one..."

He sighed. "You want me to fly you somewhere? I mean, why not? It's not like Vessey could get any more furious at me."

"No, actually. I was wondering if you were there while Aubriot was turning everyone to his side."

"It was all over by the time I got back. I only got the chance to talk to a few people. Niall and Dragan were telling me they're making progress with the Scythian vessel we captured when Aubriot nabbed me and asked me to bring him and the android down here."

"Did anyone tell you what happened after we left?"

"They didn't say a lot, and I didn't push. I try not to get involved, you know?"

Cherry did know. The pilot was notorious for never having an opinion on anything important. He was one of those people who just did his job, which would have been fine in ordinary circumstances, but in situations like this, opinions mattered. "Do you know if they had the vote of confidence in the captain while we were gone?"

"I'm pretty sure they didn't. Vessey's still in charge as far as I can tell."

Maybe even Aubriot had concluded that was a step too far.

"Do you think the others really agree with Aubriot about helping the Earthers wage a war, or did he just browbeat them into it?"

"Honestly, I don't know."

Wilder asked, "Are you thinking you can get them to change their minds?"

"Maybe, but..." Visions of thousands of dead Fila bodies, floating on the ocean surface, filled her mind. The decision to make a stand against the Scythians had been her greatest regret. The guilt she'd felt had been enormous, unbearable. Yet she could also understand the objection to living in thrall to another species. It was all too much to think about. Better to focus on the things within her control. "It's going to take Aubriot time to set things up. If we want to try to stop him, we still have days—days we can spend looking for Miki and Nina. We should get all the help we can to do that." A realization struck and her eyes widened. "I've had an idea." She asked Zapata, "You're confident Vessey's still captain?"

"As confident as I can be."

"Great. Wait here."

She found the android with Aubriot. The latter was in the midst of setting up an operations room within the GAA bunker. He was energized, barking orders via translation to the Earthers.

"Strongquist, can I talk to you a moment?" Cherry asked.

"Certainly."

"Don't keep him too long," said Aubriot. "I need my translator."

Ignoring him, Cherry said, "I want you to come with me."

"Uhh..." The android's gaze switched to Aubriot, who was overseeing the setup of interface screens. "For what purpose?"

"I need you to help us find two girls who have gone missing. You remember in the meeting Buka said they'd most likely been taken into a Scythian dome? I want you to help us get them out."

"In that case, I will go with you."

"Hey," Aubriot yelled as they reached the door, "Strongquist, where are you going?"

Cherry replied, "He's coming with me. He's going to help—"

"No, no, no." Aubriot strode closer, hands on hips, shaking his head. "Not happening. The android stays with me. Like I said, I'm worried about the kids too, but billions of Earthers take priority."

"Billions of Earthers you're committing to slaughter. Anyway, you can't overrule me. You don't have superior status. You're just another member of the crew."

"Oh, I see. Very clever, Cherry. Very clever. You remembered the Guardians have to obey whoever's highest in command."

"I did. I have a good memory, don't you think?"

"When it comes to hard feelings it's fucking excellent. Strongquist, you're programmed to protect humans, right? So you should stay here and help me plan Earth's defense."

"Defense isn't the same as launching a war," Cherry retorted.

"*That's* what you're actually doing. Strongquist, there are two adolescent girls in immediate and present danger. I order you to help me rescue them."

"I...I..." The android looked from Aubriot to Cherry and back again. "I must go with this woman. When the girls are safe I will return and continue my translation duties."

"You can't leave! How the hell am I going to talk to these people?"

"Try sign language," Cherry said.

25

The Scythians came for Miki later. When the ceiling had self-repaired and the room had filled with breathable atmosphere once more, some of the Earthers tried to tend to her wounds. There was little they could do. Though they wrapped the cuts in rags torn from their clothing she continued to bleed. The gashes were too long and deep, and the cloths were soon sodden with her blood.

She'd been lying down for hours, helpless and hopeless, paralyzed with fear for Nina and regretting everything she'd ever done, when two of the aliens arrived. Whether it was the same ones she couldn't tell. They did the same thing as before—one of them corralled the Earthers into a corner while the other tottered to her side in its ungainly gait.

She did not resist.

Not only was fighting back pointless, she *wanted* to experience whatever happened because that was what had happened to Nina. She'd persuaded her sweet sister to come to Earth. She'd taken her from the safety of the *Sirocco* and risked her life. Now it looked like both of them would die.

Dad would not have wanted this. He would have wanted them to stay safe. He would have wanted her to look after her sister.

Tears streaming down her face stung her cut terribly as the alien took her in its feet. She hung from it loosely, not fighting as it beat upward.

She saw only the dome's ceiling as she was flown across the space, her chest heaving as her lungs fought to draw in oxygen. She could have turned her head for a sight of the aliens' dwelling but she had no will to do it, convinced she was going to a dire fate.

The alien landed. There was the sound of something ripping, and then it unceremoniously pushed her with one of its feet. She fell and hit a soft surface.

She could breathe again.

The ceiling of this room was opaque. Something at the edge of her vision caught her attention. A set of straps dangled from the center of the ceiling. The sight was so odd it made her turn her head.

A Scythian was suspended within the straps, its wings folded tightly and neatly along its back. A transparent globe enclosed its head, a tube leading to the wall hanging from the rear.

The creature was looking at her.

It moved toward her, tiptoeing on its long-toed feet. She understood the purpose of the harness. It allowed the creature to walk lightly, not in the gawky, lumbering manner of the other Scythians she'd seen.

She was lying on a padded mat, raised about a meter off the floor. As the alien approached, she shrank to the edge and lifted her head for a better look at her surroundings.

Another purpose for the harness emerged. Low structures dotted the place. Some were flat, bare screens with displays, others held receptacles and equipment items, a few seemed to be for storage. The floor here wasn't the bare earth of the humans' enclosure, metallic tiles covered the surface. It seemed to be some kind of laboratory, like the ones on the *Sirocco* where the scientists did their analyses.

The Scythian had reached her. She couldn't escape. There were no doors and the walls were too smooth and high for her to scale. Even if she could reach the ceiling, she lacked the aliens' sharp claws to cut through it.

"Leave me alone!"

The alien moved around the mat to her side. She scooted away again, but it must have activated something or issued a command because a web of threads erupted from all sides and pinned her down flat. As she struggled, the webbing tightened.

"What have you done with my sister?! Where's Nina? What have you done to her? If you've hurt her I'll kill you all! Every last one of you." Her threat was empty and ridiculous, considering her position, but it felt good to yell it out.

The Scythian hopped lightly up. It was so close its odor filled her nostrils and she gagged. A foot neared her face. She tried to turn away but the threads held her fast. She had a close-up of the bronze skin before shutting her eyes.

Was this it? Was it the end? Would it be quick, or would the creature cut her open alive?

There was a repetitive pinging sound and the tension of the webbing on her face disappeared. As she opened her eyes the tip of a claw filled her view. She would have reared backward if she'd been able to move a centimeter.

The expected slash didn't arrive. The claw moved out of her vision and was replaced by the creature's toe. The pinging sound must have been the noise of it severing the threads over her face. The Scythian prodded the cut on her cheek and she sucked in a breath as pain knifed from it.

"Don't touch me! It hurts. Leave me alone. I want to see my sister! Where is she?"

The creature bent down until its globe-encased head was only a short distance from her own. Its eyes were round and white. A black line running down their middle widened as they drew closer.

Miki held her breath. Not only was the alien's smell horrible, the *otherness* of the thing was too awful to bear.

A cold, wet sensation hit her cheek. She flinched.

While the Scythian had been scrutinizing her it must have applied something to her face.

The ache from her wound began to ease.

The alien inspected her other cuts. One wing opened out and it reached down delicately to slice the webbing over her injuries before smoothing an ointment over them.

She stopped struggling, transfixed. The Scythian was actually treating her. It seemed impossible, yet she couldn't imagine another explanation for its actions.

When it had finished its claw swooped close to her face again and she gave a little scream, but it only touched her mouth.

She clenched her teeth and hissed, "Leave me alone! I want to see my sister. Let us go!"

The creature angled its head and tapped her mouth again.

"What do you want? Stop doing that."

The Scythian hopped down. She watched it as it tippy-toed over to a flat screen. The long toes scraped the surface in long swipes, causing the display to change. She rested her head. She had no idea what it was doing. When would the ordeal be over? The fact that she hadn't been killed immediately gave her a small hope that Nina might be okay.

There was a hiss to her right. Her head snapped around. A robotic arm had appeared, sporting a long needle. The needle descended to her arm. She couldn't move it away. She couldn't move a thing. As it pierced her she yelped. Several long seconds passed, and then it withdrew. Had it injected her with something?

The Scythian was back. For a third time, its great wing unfolded and the claw drew close to her face. She was not quite so frightened as before when the tip poked her mouth.

"What the hell are you doing? Why do you keep doing that?"

The large eyes watched.

Her rage suddenly dissipated. She was weak and alone, far from her friends. She didn't know where Nina was or if she was alive. She didn't know if either of them would ever get out of this place or even live another day. "Please, please let us go. If you aren't going to kill us, let us leave. We'll go back to our ship and leave the system. I promise. I promise we'll go back to Concordia."

Dad would never have wanted this.

The alien moved away again.

She didn't bother watching it. She was exhausted and heartsick.

She missed Nina already, and she missed Cherry and Wilder. She hated herself for making them worry.

The ceiling opened and a Scythian flew down. It slashed the netting, grasped her around her middle, and carried her up. When it descended she expected to go back to the room that held the Earthers, but it had taken her to a different place. The alien dropped her before she reached floor level. She landed awkwardly and fell to her knees.

"Miki!"

It was Nina! She was here.

She was alive.

26

A ubriot's face was a picture as he strode out of the bunker and across to the landing area. Cherry could imagine what he must have been like as a toddler, screaming himself into a fit whenever he didn't get his way. She could have been the bigger person and resisted the urge to chuckle, but she did not, despite her fears about Kes's daughters. Aubriot's rage-filled expression was welcome light relief.

Her reaction didn't improve his temper.

"Funny, is it?" he spat. "All right, you win."

"It's very gracious of you to come all the way out here to tell me," she replied, "but I already know. So you might as well go back inside and twiddle your thumbs while we try to find Miki and Nina."

Wilder asked, "Can't you use Itai to talk to the Earthers? Buka won't mind, surely."

"Tried that," Aubriot replied shortly. "Buka was all for it, but Itai won't play unless I get a cast-iron guarantee from Vessey he has a berth on the *Sirocco* to Concordia. Man's not stupid."

"And the captain won't allow it?" Wilder asked.

"She says if she does that they'll all want to come."

"She's right," said Cherry. "She can't set a precedent. *She's* not stupid either."

"Short story is, you've got me. That's why I'm here. Not to offer my congratulations."

Cherry blinked. "We've got you?"

"I'm gonna help you in your useless effort. Then, when you finally realize it's a wild goose chase and those kids are sadly departed, I can have the android back and get on with the real business of fighting back against the invasion."

"They're not *sadly departed*," Cherry retorted, her voice trembling. "Don't say that."

"Whatever. What's your plan?"

"Who agreed to you joining us?"

"So you don't have one. No surprise there. But I have. You wanna hear it?"

"*I* want to hear it," Wilder said, interposing herself between them. "Have you thought of a way of getting the girls out of the dome?"

"Like I said, I think it's too late for a rescue attempt, but I know a way to get in and search it if that's what you want to do."

"How?"

"Slice the lid off it. Open it up like a boiled egg. We know the explosive we used before can crack the shell. You remember the Scythian city on Suddene, Cherry?"

How could she forget? Aubriot was the only other Concordian who had ever entered the place, when he'd destroyed the ancient planetary defense system—the system the compromised android Faina had been sent to re-activate.

He continued without waiting for an answer, "The rooms didn't have any ceilings, right? Didn't make any sense at the time, but now we know why. Flying's easier than walking for them. My guess is, the set up inside the domes is the same. And they must be filled with CO_2. If we blast the top off, all their sweet carbon dioxide will escape, Earth's poisonous atmosphere will flood in, and pandemonium will ensue. Exactly the kind of chaos we need to look for the kids."

Cherry had to concede his idea made sense.

Wilder said, "A lot of Scythians will suffocate and die."

"All the better," said Aubriot.

"I'm not saying it's a bad thing, but what about the two equals sixty-four warning? For every Scythian killed in the attack they'll execute thirty-two humans. Does Buka know about that? Has anyone told him?"

Aubriot grimaced. "*They'll* execute them, not us. There are always casualties in a war."

"I don't like it either," said Cherry, "but what are we supposed to do? Let them walk all over us? People are going to die regardless, and we have to get Miki and Nina back. What the Scythians do in response isn't our responsibility. We aren't the aggressors here."

"Now there's the woman I remember," said Aubriot condescendingly. "I was wondering when she would show her face again."

She gave him a withering look. "How do you plan on blowing the top off the dome?"

THEY APPROACHED AT MIDDAY. The sky was clear, the sunlight strong and hot. Buka had given them plenty of the explosive substance they'd used before. It was safe to drop it onto a hard surface. There was no danger it would explode on impact. A thick layer of adhesive coated each lump except for two spots where it could be held.

The GAA leader had allotted a large proportion of the group's military arm, created after the first Scythian attack. With Strongquist's help, Aubriot had outlined the plan. After that, the troops would mostly be acting alone. The android would take part in the mission but real-time translation of orders would be difficult in a time-critical scenario. Buka had also loaned them five of the GAA's helis. The *Sirocco*'s shuttle lacked the maneuverability required for the first part of the mission. Zapata's role would come later—if they managed to break the shell of the dome.

"Cherry," yelled Aubriot, "I'm telling you for the last time, wait outside with Wilder. You can come in and search for the girls when we've secured the place."

She could barely hear him over the whine of the heli's rotors as it rose into the air.

"I don't take orders from you," she yelled back.

"It's not safe dropping into the dome unarmed."

She tapped the muzzle of the rifle she had strapped to her back.

"You know what I mean. You can't hold onto your rifle *and* the line. You'll be a sitting duck."

She didn't know what a duck was but she got the idea. "It'll only take a few seconds. I'll be fine."

"Then at least let me go below you."

She shrugged.

The ground troops and Wilder had set out earlier and were currently waiting, hidden in the vegetation around the dome. Cherry hoped they were well hidden. If the Scythians understood they were about to be attacked it would make the mission all the harder. They might even kill their prisoners, assuming they had prisoners.

The helis crossed the distance in less than a minute. The aircraft circled the space above the dome. The troops dropped the lumps of explosive. In the bright sunlight, the opaque blister glowed soft and shimmering, shining out in the drab grayish green of the surrounding landscape. Cherry was reminded of the opalescent interior of the shell of a Concordian sea creature. How could the horrifying aliens create something so beautiful?

She hoped with all her heart the stunning structure contained an exceptional prize.

A hole spiraled open at the top of the dome. The Scythians were coming out.

The helis swept away. Cherry was thrust into her seat and her stomach lurched.

Aubriot pressed the detonator.

A loud report erupted from the dome. Smoke rose from the sites the explosives had been dropped.

She craned her neck to see the result.

Scythians were pouring from their airlock and beating into the sky on their wide, leathery wings. The GAA's ground troops rose from their cover and began firing at the aliens.

"Did it work?" she asked Aubriot.

He was leaning out of the side of the heli, aiming at Scythians flying their way. "Can't tell yet."

The side of the dome facing them had cracks radiating from the explosion sites. At the distance, and without a full view of the structure, it was impossible to tell if the fault lines joined up.

She squinted in the direction of the bunker. The shuttle had already taken off.

In the years of journeying through deep space after the accident with the jump drive, water had been their number one need for survival. Though the *Sirocco* had the usual water-recycling system, it wasn't leak-proof, and they'd needed additional water to grow crops. Luckily, water hadn't been hard to find in the asteroids and comets of planetary systems. What had been a challenge at first was harvesting it.

The engineers had built a device for this purpose and fitted it into the base of the shuttle. The mechanism fired bolts fitted with backward-facing spikes and attached to thick metal ropes wound around drums. Zapata would fire the bolts into the water-bearing space object and tow it to the ship. It was this device the pilot had used to bring the Scythian vessel to the *Sirocco*, and it was this Aubriot had proposed he used to remove the 'lid' from the aliens' dome.

It was a terrible risk. If they lost the shuttle they had no way of returning to the ship. They couldn't use it routinely in the war Aubriot wanted to wage against the Scythians, but for this purpose, the risk was worth it. If they didn't get Miki and Nina back, Cherry didn't know if she even wanted to return to Concordia.

Aliens continued to stream from the dome. Whatever effect the explosions had caused, they hadn't damaged the Scythians' exit. GAA troops were picking some off from below but many shots were missing their mark. A few holes in the aliens' wings didn't seem to impact their ability to fly. Only hitting their body or their heads had any effect.

A bunch of Scythians were converging on a heli, hammering the occupants with shots. Aubriot turned his attention to the group. Pulse rounds flew from his rifle. But it was too late. The heli's nose tipped downward and it whirled erratically. In another second it had plummeted into the scrub and exploded.

The shuttle had arrived. Lines shot from its base. The bolts disappeared, sinking deep into the surface of the dome. The helis flew closer in an effort to shield the shuttle from attack. Many of the aliens who had emerged were concentrating their fire on the ground troops and the flow of aliens from the dome had slowed.

The vessel heaved upward. The lines tightened.

The dome remained whole.

"C'mon, Zapata," Cherry muttered. "You can do it."

The Scythians had understood what their attackers intended. Every single one that emerged aimed its fire at the underbelly of the shuttle. The vessel must have lost its spaceworthiness but it could be repaired. What couldn't be repaired was the pilot, at least not immediately. If Zapata got hit and the shuttle crashed it was goodbye Concordia.

The GAA troops sharing her heli were yelling.

"What are they saying?" she asked Strongquist.

"They are anxious that the dome won't break open."

Stupid question.

Time crawled as the shuttle strained.

"Come *on*!"

A roar split the air.

Flame flared from the rear of the shuttle.

Of course! As he had ever since he'd been flying it, Zapata had been using the vessel's a-grav drive. but the engineers had also built in the outdated thruster system as a backup. At the last minute he'd remembered and activated it, doubling the pulling force.

A mighty *crack* resounded.

The dome was splitting apart. The top was lifting off. The shuttle pulled away, lifting and dragging the fractured part with it.

Inside their habitation, Scythians would be suffocating, choking, dying.

It was time to go in.

27

Aubriot's head was beneath her as Cherry dropped into the Scythian dome. He clung to the line with one hand and sprayed fire from his rifle with the other. She could only cling on.

The removed lid had revealed a honeycomb of rooms. At the center sat the vessel the aliens had arrived in. Radiating from it were sections of various sizes, some containing equipment, others empty. Aliens flew between them. In the haze of flapping wings it was hard to see what they were doing, but presumably they were rushing to get breathing apparatus now the structure was exposed to Earth's atmosphere.

She had explained to the troops—via Strongquist—that the walls separating the rooms might be soft enough to push through. Otherwise, they would have to blast their way in. A ground team was already assigned to make its way to the outer wall and blow a hole in it to allow the drop team to exit.

Aubriot was only a few meters from the ground. The heli was lowering them into an empty room. That was no good.

"Try to get into the next one," she yelled to Aubriot. The neighboring room contained equipment and perhaps Scythians. It was better than nothing at all.

"What?" His aim and focus remained downward. "What did you say?"

"The next room!"

"All right. I'll try."

They continued on the same downward trajectory, but then the heli swept sideways, bringing his feet level with the upper edge of the wall. He stretched out a leg and hooked his toes over it. When the heli dropped lower, he slid down into the room with the equipment. He took a leap from the line, making it swing. She was twisted around. The next sight she had of him, he was reaching out. He grabbed the line, drawing her close.

She jumped.

Her feet hit dirt.

She looked up. The heli was gone. All its troops dropped, its mission was accomplished.

This room seemed empty of Scythians. She had no idea what the devices inside it did, but maybe Wilder could investigate them if they succeeded in taking the dome.

No. The room wasn't empty. There was movement in a corner. Bronze-skinned wings opened out and a figure rose up. The alien's head was bare. It wouldn't be able to breathe, but in the time it took to die it was still dangerous.

She aimed and fired.

A hole opened up in its middle, oozing blood and smoking.

The wings folded. The Scythian crumpled to the ground, twitching.

A reeking haze hit her—the odor of the burning wound. She swallowed saliva.

Aubriot was probing the wall. "It's soft. I think we can push through."

"Be careful."

The danger with forcing a passage into a room was that it took time. You couldn't leap out and surprise the occupants. With a little observation they would know you were coming.

"I'll go through here," she said, moving to the opposite end of the wall. At least with two of them emerging at once they might reduce their likelihood of being hit.

From all around came the loud bangs of the GAA's troops' fire, interspersed with shouts and the occasional scream. Strongquist was with them, helping to coordinate the attack.

She went low, hoping to avoid attracting attention, and pushed the muzzle of her rifle in first, following it up with her shoulder. When her head was through, a strange sight struck her and she smelled food. It wasn't exactly an enticing smell but neither was it unpleasant.

Aubriot had arrived just ahead of her. He rose to a crouch and scanned the place.

Nothing moved.

She had emerged next to a large steel container. She peeked over the edge and was surprised to see grain.

Aubriot had straightened up and was striding around, poking into corners. "No one's here. Time to move on." He pressed another wall experimentally.

"Wait," she said. A second device seemed to be for cooking. "What's all this for?"

"It doesn't matter. We can figure it out later."

The second item was a small tank, also containing grain, but it was partially cooked and steaming. The cooker continued to operate, heating it contents.

"Do you think the Scythians eat cereals?" she asked.

He joined her. "Who cares what they eat? As long as it isn't us."

"These are Earth crops. I'd swear it. I used to grow these on Concordia. What are the chances that Scythians can eat our food? Their anatomy is entirely different."

"You think this is to feed humans?"

She hardly dared to hope she was right. Her belief that Miki and Nina were still alive had been nebulous—a dream built on guilt that she hadn't done enough to comfort the girls in their grief and fear, and that she would never have the opportunity to try. She nodded.

"That's not a stupid guess, but if they are here we still need to find them. Let's try over there."

He marched to the wall diagonally opposite and thrust it with his fist.

He cursed.

The wall was solid.

"They're inside that room!" Cherry exclaimed. "They have to be. The wall's hard because it's impermeable to gases. The Scythians must keep it supplied with oxygen for humans to breathe."

Aubriot took a step backward. "I'll comm Strongquist. Ask him to bring explosives."

"And kill anyone in the blast range inside?"

"Good point." His brow wrinkled. "Gotta get in somehow."

She checked the room again. "I know. Drag that cooker over here." It was the tallest piece of equipment in the place.

Aubriot hauled the machinery across the room and pushed it up against the wall before climbing onto it. Standing on his tiptoes, he reached upward. Another meter remained between his fingertips and the top of the wall. "Can't reach. I'll have to jump for it."

"Don't do that. This thing could fall over. Give me a hand up." She slung her rifle onto her back.

He squatted and held out his hand, pulling her up beside him.

"And the rest," she said.

"I should go first."

"I don't have two hands. Now shut up and help me."

He knitted his fingers and made a cradle for her foot. With his boost, she easily reached the top.

When she looked over the wall, her heart leapt. "There are people in here!"

Human figures huddled in a corner, their fearful faces turned upward. She couldn't see Miki or Nina, but there were about twenty people. They had to be here but out of sight.

A transparent barrier covered the upper area of the room. She'd been right. The Scythians supplied it with an atmosphere humans could breathe. She pressed on the barrier. It gave but seemed tough.

"Can you see the kids?" Aubriot asked.

"Not yet." She pulled her knife from its sheath and pushed it into the transparent sheet. It split easily.

Booooom!

A shock ran through the wall.

That had to be the troops blasting a hole through to the outside. The captives flinched.

"Don't worry," she called to them. "We'll have you out soon."

She tucked the knife back in its sheath and pulled at a cut edge. Like all Scythian materials she'd encountered, it was odd. Soft and slightly sticky, it clung to her hand.

"Push me up," she told Aubriot. "I'm going in."

"Wait for Strongquist to get here. I've comm'd him."

"*Push me up!*"

Muttering, he did as she asked. She got one knee onto the wall and then the other. As she climbed onto the barrier it sagged. She lowered herself through the gap she'd cut. When halfway through, she gripped the edge as tight as she could and dropped the rest of the way. Holding on with one hand, she looked down. A few of the men had gathered beneath her.

She let go.

The men caught her and set her on her feet.

"Miki! Nina! Where are you?" She searched the unfamiliar faces.

They were pale and gaunt. They looked half-starved. How long had these people been here?

Where were Miki and Nina?

"I'm looking for two girls." No one answered, naturally. They couldn't understand her. She pushed through the crowd.

Where were they?

She spun around to the captives and held up two fingers. "Two girls." She touched her hair. "They look like me."

Unlike Concordians, Earthers came in all colors. Some had very pale skin and blue eyes, some were very dark-skinned and their eyes and hair were black.

"Two girls," she repeated with desperation. "Have you seen two young girls?"

But the captives only answered her with uncomprehending looks.

"Cherry!" Aubriot shouted from outside. "Did you find them?"

"They're not here. They must be somewhere else."

"Get the people away from the opposite wall. Strongquist's gonna blow it."

Her mind a whirl, she pushed the captives away from the area. They might not understand English but they seemed to understand what she was trying to do and why. All of them quickly moved to the other side of their cell.

She covered her ear with one hand and the other with her shoulder.

Just in time.

The wall exploded, showering them with lumps, shards, and dust.

Strongquist leaned in. "We must leave, quickly." He beckoned to the humans.

"Have you found Miki and Nina?"

"No, but the Scythians are successfully repelling the attack." He stepped aside to allow the people to pass and then stuck his head in again. "There's a safe passage to the outer wall but I don't know how much longer we can hold it."

"We have to find the girls. We can't leave yet."

"We must, Cherry. The dome has been searched. This is the only place humans have been found."

The captives had gone. The room was empty. But she was sure Miki and Nina had been here. They must have been. The Scythians hadn't killed the people they'd snatched. They were keeping them alive. Miki and Nina weren't dead, but where were they?

Aubriot ran in. "It's time to go."

"I know, but..." Her desperate gaze roved the bare room.

Where are they?

"No more heroics," Aubriot said. "We've done our job. There's nothing more to do. We have to get out of here."

Reluctantly, she had to agree.

28

After the Scythian had brought Miki from the examination room to Nina, she had shown her how to wear a respirator. Under the watchful eyes of the guard, her sister had put on her own, demonstrating how to place it over the face and tighten the straps. The devices were awkward things, poorly made. The aliens were still learning about human anatomy. Miki hoped it worked. She'd had enough of choking while being transported within the Scythian-occupied areas of the dome. But Nina had assured her it did and that the tasks they had to perform weren't too bad.

"At least they aren't going to kill us," she'd said.

Not yet.

When Miki took an experimental breath she heard the click of a valve opening. Air tainted with an odor she couldn't place filled her lungs. When she exhaled, the valve clicked again.

Nina gave her a questioning thumbs up.

Miki had been exhausted. She hadn't slept since arriving in the dome, not since they'd left the Sirocco, in fact. They'd had the long walk to the settlement and then across the fields. They'd been terrified so many times, she'd been cut, and now they had who knew how many hours of work ahead of them And then to eat they would have to fight the other humans for the horrible mash. She marveled at Nina's resilience.

She adjusted the tank on her back to a more comfortable position and returned the thumbs up.

Her sister beckoned her to follow.

They passed through an air lock into a round tunnel, leading down. There were lights but, like everywhere else in the Scythians' areas, they were turned down so low it was difficult to see where she was going.

She guessed they'd walked for ten minutes or so, steadily downward, when the tunnel opened out into a large chamber. It was so big it had to be outside the dome. The Scythians were spreading out underground.

Long, narrow vats occupied the space. Each vat held a liquid. The light reflected in it, creating ripple effects on the ceiling. Grids divided the liquid into sections, and running along one of the longer sides of each vat was a tray filled with a dark substance.

Nina took her hand and guided her through the vats to the far end of the chamber. Two other workers were there but they ignored them, perhaps due to the Scythian sitting in a corner, watching.

Nina picked a pair of tweezers from a pile and handed them to her before taking a pair for herself. Then she showed her what to do. She leaned over the vat to reach the tray and dug around in the dark material. After searching for a few seconds, she retrieved a little worm-like creature. She dropped it into one of the sections in the vat.

Miki peered at it. The creature squirmed, as if shocked by the sudden transformation in its environment, but then its movements became less urgent. It relaxed and swam downward. Miki peered more closely, squinting, but she couldn't see it anymore. She checked another of the sections. In this one a larger version of the worm undulated languidly.

Nina poked her and gestured with her tweezers, glancing pointedly at the Scythian.

"I get it," Miki said, though she doubted Nina would be able to make out her words.

She'd spent time with the scientists on the *Sirocco*, learning about living organisms. She'd guessed they felt sorry for her after Dad's death, and maybe they thought she might become a biologist like him. She'd learned how animals went through growth stages. She guessed what she and Nina were supposed to do was to help these alien organisms move from one growth stage to the next, from a soil-based environment to an aquatic one. These creatures probably ended up as Scythian food.

So she and Nina were factory farmers now?

Like her sister had said, it was better than dying.

That session with the tanks, Miki had observed several growth stages of the farmed animals. They appeared in the trays—perhaps hatching from tiny eggs. When they were a couple of centimeters long they were large enough to go in the liquid. She hesitated to call it water though that was what it looked like. She couldn't smell it through her mask so it might have had an odor. The Scythians breathed carbon dioxide, so maybe other things about their planet(s) were different too. On the other hand, Concordia had water and that was their origin planet, so...

Pondering questions like these helped to pass the time, though they also reminded her of Dad, and the familiar painful knot would form in her stomach.

The creatures grew larger in the liquid medium. In the hours she spent working she didn't see anyone feeding them, and she wondered if they absorbed nutrients through their skin. At around four centimeters, they moulted. The shed skin would float to the surface and had to be removed. Then the worker had to find the creature, often submerging their arm up to the armpit to feel for it in a corner of its section. The new version had pincers and being nipped by them seemed unavoidable. Miki's fingers were soon sore and bleeding while performing that task.

She had to transfer these secondary stage creatures to another, communal tank. There, the food was others of their own kind. They cannibalized each other. Despite her own difficulties, she felt sorry for the latest additions she dropped into the tank. They would be immediately set upon by older, larger rivals. It seemed odd to allow the produce to destroy itself, but she guessed the Scythians saw it as a necessary part of the life cycle.

The 'winners' in the group tank would moult several times, growing as big as her hand and fearsome. The Scythians provided a scoop with a lid for getting them out, which was just as well. The workers would have been quickly rendered incapable of working otherwise. After a final moult, the creatures spent their last growth stage breathing the atmosphere. They were housed in individual cages under the tanks, fed meal, and grew about thirty centimeters long. By this time they were vicious. They would throw themselves at everyone who passed by, pushing their heads between the bars and snapping their teeth.

From what she'd seen, she imagined the animals growing on the Scythian planet. She guessed they started life on a river bank or shore. When a seasonal flood came or there was a particularly high tide, the wriggling first-stage creatures would be swept into the water —or other liquid. While growing larger, they would encounter others of their kind and fight and eat each other. Then, when they'd reached maturity, they would haul themselves out onto dry land, find a partner, and mate.

Only here what happened was the Scythians ate them.

How did they eat them? Did they consume them raw, biting off their heads and spitting them out before feasting on their bodies, breaking apart the carapaces to reach the flesh? Or did they neatly dispatch them, chop them up and put them in a stew? Or maybe they barbecued them on sunny days, sprinkled with a little salt, and ate them with friends they'd invited over, sharing beers.

She giggled.

Nina gave her a questioning look.

She was so tired. She wished she could rub her aching eyes. How long did they have to work? Until they dropped?

A piercing whistle sounded.

The other workers put down their tools and walked to the exit.

It was finally over.

They should be able to sleep now, at last. She wasn't hungry and she didn't know if the aliens would give more of the cereal mash anyway. But her stomach pangs would return in the end. She and Nina would either have to eat the slop or starve. Or, rather, they could eat the slop and starve more slowly.

How long would they last? Cherry and Wilder would never find them, and eventually the *Sirocco* would depart.

When she'd told Nina they should live on Earth to be near Dad, this wasn't what she meant.

INSIDE THE DOME it was impossible to tell if it was day or night. Miki had a feeling they'd worked through the day and it was now night-time. Not long after they were returned to the cell with the Earthers, another allotment of cereal mash arrived. This time, she ate it. In the short journey back, it was as if her stomach had woken up. She found she was suddenly famished. Nina ate too. Their cellmates had been fair in portioning out the food. They were given two handfuls. It was not enough. As Miki settled down to sleep, her stomach rumbled.

She curled up with her sister in a corner of the room. The Earthers no longer stared at them and the atmosphere was friendlier. They were all in this dreadful situation together, united in their imprisonment and suffering.

"What happened to your face?" Nina asked quietly.

She'd forgotten about the cut she'd received from a Scythian's claw. She touched the spot. The ointment had dried and as it flaked away the skin beneath it felt tender but whole. The bleeding had stopped and her injury seemed to be healing.

"Do I have a scar?" she asked.

Nina nodded. She added, "It's not bad. It's a little bit cool, in fact."

She smiled, straining the damaged skin. "Let's sleep."

The Earthers were also settling down. What did *they* do in this place? She didn't remember seeing any of them in the animal nursery, though she wasn't sure. It was hard to make out people's faces behind the respirators. Maybe there were more underground chambers where the Scythians grew different types of food.

As her imagination took over, it conjured scenes of aliens

waddling in their strange gait through golden fields of wheat, cracking whips on toiling humans. An inescapable heaviness descended on her eyelids and she slipped into a deep slumber.

Seconds later, it seemed, something grabbed her.

She snapped to alertness and flailed, slapping and kicking the thing gripping her. As she recognized the feeling of Scythian skin, she froze.

Why couldn't the aliens leave them alone? Where were they taking them now? She felt as though she'd only slept an hour or so. Surely they didn't have to work again already?

Where was Nina?

Another alien was here. It had her sister in its grasp and was flying upward.

As Miki was also carried aloft the Earthers huddled and watched.

She held her breath.

The Scythian holding her flew out of the cell and continued up to the top of the dome. A portal spiraled open and the alien flapped through it. The creature was wearing a transparent globe over its head.

They were going outside.

The hatch closed. They were inside a chamber. Above, through a round hole, stars twinkled in a deep blue sky. The night air was fresh, cold, and moist. Miki inhaled deeply.

The alien didn't fly out with her as she'd anticipated. It flew across the chamber to a small vessel, dropped her into it and then climbed in too. The seat reclined so far she was almost lying flat. It was much too large for her and protrusions from it dug into her back and legs.

Straps snaked out and closed over her, holding her tightly against the ridges.

Next to her, the Scythian had folded its wings into a receptacle behind its seat. Similar straps held its body in place. Its legs were angled forward. With its long, prehensile toes it gripped the flight controls.

The vessel started up and lifted into the darkness.

re you from another planet?

Miki stared at the interface screen, almost unable to take in the words, though they were written in plain English.

How did the Scythians know that? How did they know her language?

Had they captured the *Sirocco* and taken everyone captive? She'd thought the ship must have left the system by now.

She lifted her gaze to the alien. It stared back at her unblinkingly, the black slits of its eyes narrowed to slivers. The light in the room was too bright for it, she guessed. To her it was a normal level, though stronger than the usual light levels in Scythian domes. They must have turned it up to help her read the text. The room was like the one in the other dome, where she'd been examined, only this time she wasn't restrained by webbing.

How was she supposed to answer? If she nodded, would it understand the gesture? Should she speak?

Should she answer truthfully?

If she answered correctly, would that mean she was collaborating with the aliens? What would the knowledge she was from Concordia mean to them? She didn't know if it was meant to be a secret.

The Scythian reached out with a claw and tapped the screen, as if to re-direct her attention to it.

"Y-es?" she replied doubtfully.

It tapped the screen again. When she didn't understand it moved its claw toward her hand.

She snatched it away, drawing it to her stomach.

The alien touched the back of it so lightly she barely felt the contact, and then tapped the screen again.

"Oh!" It wanted her to touch the interface.

When she did, a keyboard appeared. She hesitated and then typed Yes.

The Scythian didn't look at the screen. Did it have another way of understanding what she'd written?

The question disappeared and another took its place.

What is the name of your planet?

Suddenly, she understood what must have happened. At the other dome, the one near the bunker where Zapata had landed the shuttle, the alien that had healed her wounds had also touched her mouth a few times. She'd been shouting, demanding to know what had happened to Nina. It must have realized her words were different from the other humans'. It had gone to a console. Had it recorded her?

And yet, things still didn't make complete sense. On Earth, people living in different places spoke different languages. Why did the Scythians think she was from another planet and not just another country?

The alien tapped the screen.

She clutched her hand to her stomach again and shook her head. She would not answer any more questions. Why should she? How would it benefit her to tell them anything?

"Let me go. Let me and Nina go. You have no right to keep us here."

It tapped the screen.

It was horrible. They all were.

On the flight from the previous dome the small vessel had filled with the pilot's odor. She'd nearly vomited several times. They'd flown for hours, through the night and into the morning. When the sun rose the cover over the cabin had darkened and the sun became a glowing ball in a dark blue haze.

What was their planet like?

Was it covered in a layer of thick cloud? Or perhaps it was so far distant from its star that daylight was like dusk on Concordia? And what were the landscapes like? She imagined many seas and shorelines where the creatures in the vats wriggled and crawled. Did plants grow there? And if they did, were they green? Could their plants photosynthesize in the low light? Dad had told her about plants and animals that derived their energy from chemicals exuded from below ground. Was that how things worked on the Scythian world?

Her questioner tapped the interface again, more forcefully.

"I'm not telling you anything else. I demand to be released, along with my sister." She tilted her chin upward and looked down her nose at the creature. It was a haughty stare she'd practiced and used when she wanted to get her way. It had worked on Dad sometimes. Other times he'd only chuckled.

The Scythian's claw approached her cheek. She stiffened. The tip traced the line of her scar.

What did it mean? If she didn't answer would it cut her?

Her eyes became wet and she sniffed. Drawing her chin into her chest, she gave a little shake of her head. The Scythian didn't withdraw its claw. The tip remained resting against her cheek. The pressure increased.

She moved her head but the claw followed. She felt a sharp sting and the tip sank into her skin. "Ow!" She batted at it. "Leave me alone!"

The alien moved away.

Tiptoeing on its long toes, it swung away in its harness to a console, leaving the interface next to her.

Blood trickled down her cheek and she wiped it. She lay down on the pad and stared morosely at the ceiling. Through the transparent barrier she could see the underside of this new dome. It was much bigger than the other one and very, very far from it. She hadn't been able to see the landscape she'd passed over on her flight, but she'd flown for so long she supposed she might be in a different country.

At least Nina was here too. She'd been brought in another vessel. It had been such a relief to see her waiting when she arrived. But they had to be thousands of kilometers from Dad's grave now. The whole point of them coming to Earth was lost. They would probably never escape from the Scythians. Along with the other humans being held captive, they would spend their days growing the aliens' food while slowly starving to death themselves.

But she would not answer any more questions. She regretted saying she came from another planet. Why should she tell them anything?

A Scythian approached overhead. At first, she didn't take any notice. Several had flown over while she'd been in the examining room. Then she noticed it was carrying something and it was descending.

Nina!

It held her sister in its feet. She hung limply like a doll.

Their gazes met.

Miki leapt to her feet. "What are you doing with my sister? Don't bring her here. Take her back."

The alien at the console was watching.

The Scythian above landed with a thump, depressing the barrier. It put Nina down but it didn't cut a slit to push her through into the room.

"What are you doing?" Miki demanded. "She can't breathe out there."

Nina was spreadeagled, her mouth open and eyes staring. She clutched at the barrier, trying to tear it.

"Let her in!" Miki screamed. She tried to jump to reach her sister but the distance was too great.

Nina was coughing and clutching at her throat. She scrabbled at the surface, her movements growing weaker.

"All right," Miki said. "All right! I'll tell you the answer. I'm from

Concordia. That's the name of my planet." She picked up the interface and began to type.

The Scythian above took Nina in its feet and lazily flapped away.

"I'll tell you everything," Miki said, sobbing.

30

The last of the Earthers who took part in the raid—the walking wounded—were arriving at the bunker. Cherry stood to one side as they staggered in. Some would never make it back. They'd died in the fight or afterward during the mad dash to safety. The helis had been reserved for the badly injured. Everyone else had been forced to return on foot, making the best use of the vegetation as cover while the Scythians took pot shots from above.

The aliens might have several disadvantages here on Earth, unable to breathe the atmosphere or go face to face with humans on the ground, but in the air their capabilities were vastly superior. It was lucky so many had died of suffocation when their dome had been ripped open. Otherwise, no one would have stood a chance of getting away.

"Thinking of helping?" Aubriot asked, finding her at the bunker entrance. "Leave it to the medics."

"I'm watching the sky."

He peered into the clouds. "Any sign of anything?"

"No, but they must have noticed where we went. It won't be long before they come for us."

"If they do attack, it won't be from space. Vessey's parked the

Sirocco right overhead. Won't be a Scythian starship dares come within a thousand klicks of her."

"Yet."

He shrugged. "Best enjoy the respite while we can."

"I don't get why we had to leave so soon. I thought we'd defeated them."

"A second wave of Scythians arrived, all togged up with respirators."

"A second wave? Where did it come from?"

"Don't know. Strongquist reckons they might have dug out more space underground."

"But maybe Miki and Nina are there! We have to go back."

"Is that a joke? They're already repairing the dome, we lost two helis and half the troops are dead or wounded."

"But they could be—"

"Forget it. The kids aren't there. Either they never were or they're dead. End of. It's time to move on."

"Huh, for you maybe. I'm not giving up on them."

"Let's leave it for now, okay? We need to debrief, go over what we learned."

"Later."

"Suit yourself."

He disappeared inside the bunker and Wilder approached from the heli landing area. Stragglers from the raid continued to limp in.

Wilder said, watching the troops, "I'm glad you got out of there in one piece. Was it bad?"

"Not as bad as it could have been."

"No sign of the girls?" she asked, her tone softer.

Cherry shook her head. "Can you repair the shuttle?"

"It shouldn't be a problem. Buka has the materials and Zapata's already on it. Should take a couple of hours. Are you planning on going up to the *Sirocco*?"

Cherry gave a huff of exasperation. "I don't know what I have planned. I don't know what we do from here. There might be areas beneath the dome we didn't get to search, and I don't know how we

will now. If only we had the equipment we have on Concordia. We
could blow that place open."

"Well that wouldn't exactly be safe for Miki and Nina, would it?"

"I know, I know..." Cherry rubbed her forehead.

Wilder touched her arm. "You look exhausted. Go inside. Get
some rest. I'll fix the shuttle, and then we'll talk with Buka and
Aubriot and see where we go from here."

Strongquist walked up the stairs. "Mr Buka would like to speak
with you, Cherry."

"What about?" She wasn't in the mood to be pushed for more
promises on how the Concordians were going to help protect Earth.

"He has some news about the missing adolescents."

Two Earthers sat with the leader of the GAA in the meeting room.
From the state of their garments and the gauntness of their faces, she
guessed they'd been rescued from the dome.

Of course. In her despair over failing to rescue Miki and Nina,
she'd forgotten the possibility that other captives might have seen
them.

Aubriot was here too, pretending he gave a shit.

"Please, sit down," Buka said via Strongquist. "I would like to
thank you for helping to free our people."

"I heard you know something about the girls from our ship?"

"I have some information, yes. As soon as I discovered you hadn't
found them, I enquired among the former captives. These men say
they remember two girls who didn't seem to be from around here.
They spoke a foreign language and wore strange clothes. One was
about fifteen and the other perhaps twelve or so."

"That sounds like them!" Cherry gripped the arm of her chair.
Would the news be good or bad? "Do they know what happened to
them? Are they okay?"

Strongquist translated the question. Buka spoke to the men. They
replied, their gazes on her. Strongquist translated,, "The girls were
alive the last time they were seen, but they were taken away. These

men don't know where, and they're sure no one else in their group knows."

"Is it possible they were taken underground?"

The frustrating chain of dialogue repeated.

"There is an underground chamber, but it's unlikely the girls were there. They had just returned from there when they were taken."

"But if they weren't in the other chamber and they weren't in the cell with the others, where else could they have been?"

A short conversation took place.

"That seems to be a puzzle. These men say the only way for anyone to escape—prior to their rescue—was by dying, yet the girls appeared healthy the last time they were seen."

The stark reality of what life must have been like in the dome hit Cherry forcefully. She swallowed. "They're sure they were okay?"

Buka said something in a tone that didn't require translating. "They were well the last time they were seen."

"When was that?"

"Not long ago. The captives had no way of measuring time, but it appears the girls were taken away recently, perhaps only yesterday."

"How long were they in the dome?"

"Again, only a short time."

She asked, bitterly, "So if you hadn't locked me and Wilder up we might have found them?"

Strongquist translated the question but Buka didn't answer. The Earther men's attention traveled from Cherry to the GAA leader, and they shifted uneasily.

Aubriot said, "There's no point in getting on your high horse now. What's done is done."

"Your concern for Miki and Nina is touching. Really touching."

"Don't start that bullshit, Cherry. I'm just saying there's no point crying over spilt milk."

"Or anyone's life except your own."

Buka raised a hand. "I will make further inquiries. I may be able to discover more information. Please wait here." He got to his feet and shuffled from the room, leaning heavily on his cane.

"This war had better be over soon," Aubriot remarked, "or he won't be around to see the end of it."

Cherry ignored him. The war would not be over for a very long time, if ever.

She asked Strongquist to ask the men for more details about Miki and Nina, what they looked like, how they acted, and so on. It was clear from their answers there could be no mistake. Kes's daughters had been in the dome, and they'd only just missed them.

Buka returned. He lowered himself carefully to his seat and propped his cane against it before saying, "You may not be aware the GAA has a network of observers tracking the Scythians' movements. We know where each dome is and keep a record of the vessels that fly between them. These journeys are rare and usually only one vessel makes the trip. Two Scythian vessels departed the dome you attacked yesterday night in quick succession. I asked our network if they'd picked them up, and the answer came back immediately. They traveled south."

Two?

If the ships in question were two-seaters like the one brought back to the *Sirocco*, that would mean they could have been carrying a girl each and a pilot.

"Do you know where they went?"

"We are still working that out. The observers are all over the globe. If the girls were aboard the vessels, we should be able to discover where they were taken."

31

This chamber for growing the Scythians' food was much larger than the other one. The vats stretched out so far it was hard to see where they ended, and tens of human workers tended to the creatures living in and under them. The walls echoed with the scrapings and scratchings of the mature animals in their cages.

The respirators were just the same. Miki tightened the straps on hers a little more and lifted a set of tweezers. Nina was already at work a few rows away, but she dared not go over to her. Here, three Scythians watched them, stationed on platforms spaced out across the chamber. Besides, she couldn't talk to her sister. Communication was nearly impossible with the masks over their faces.

Also, what could she tell her?

That she'd told the aliens everything about Concordia, and the *Sirocco*, and why the Concordians had come to Earth?

That she was a traitor?

It was bad enough that she'd dragged her sister into this mess. Now she'd doomed everyone else too.

She dug in the soft, brown substance, looking for a worm to transfer to the liquid. Tears blurred her view and she blinked hard, unable to wipe them away.

Maybe she should take off her mask and suffocate herself. Maybe she should stick her head in one of the vats.

One of the wriggling creatures appeared. She snipped it in two spitefully. It was the smallest revenge for what the Scythians had made her do but it felt good. But the creature seemed unfazed. Each half continued to wriggle. She heaved a sigh, fogging her visor. When the mask cleared, the severed animal remained alive.

Something sharp poked her arm. A Scythian was at her side. The slits of its horrible eyes were wide in the dim light as it inspected her. She'd lingered too long. Hastily, she picked up a half of a worm and dropped it in a section of the vat, quickly following with the other half in another section.

The Scythian moved away. She exhaled.

She moved along to another area. There were no worms here but some of the older creatures were large enough to face battle with their rivals in the communal tank. With distaste, she transferred them to their almost-certain deaths.

Then something new happened.

On one side of the chamber a large hatch opened. A Scythian stood each side of the opening, and two humans were dragging a cage full of snapping animals toward it. Something emerged—a questing foot. One of the watching Scythians thrust it back, and then the humans arrived with the cage. They pushed it against the hole and pulled up the adjoining section. The creatures raced out and were gone. The hatch closed, and the event was over. The humans hauled the cage back to its original position.

So what she'd thought was the final growth stage wasn't? The leg that had emerged was much bigger than those of the creatures in the cages.

There was no point in speculating. She couldn't ask anyone for information and what did it matter anyway?

By the time she reached the end of her shift she was sore, tired, and hungry. The cereal mash was the same as in the other place and her stomach rebelled as she ate it, but she forced it down. She couldn't look at Nina as they ate, let alone speak to her. Shame filled every fiber of her being.

When they'd finished, they sat away from the others. Their cell companions had quickly established they couldn't communicate and left them alone.

Nina put an arm around her and rested her head on her shoulder. "What happened to you before you came to work? Was that Scythian examining you again?"

She meant the interrogation.

Miki hugged her sister back. "Did you get hurt when they brought you over? Did you pass out?"

"It was horrible, but I was okay. Why did they do that?"

"They were trying to make me..." She couldn't say it. How to confess what she'd done? "They know we're from Concordia. I don't know what difference it might make, but you should know that. They know we're from the *Sirocco* and we're different from the Earthers."

Nina sat up and faced her, her eyes wide. "Do you think the Scythians will use us as hostages? They might threaten to kill us if the captain doesn't do what they say."

Miki hadn't even thought of that particular disastrous scenario. "I think the ship's probably left by now anyway."

Nina gave a sigh and returned her head to Miki's shoulder. "That's something, I suppose." But she sounded disappointed, as if she hadn't imagined they would be abandoned so easily.

The knowledge that her sister was withholding entirely justified blame was a painful knot in the depths of Miki's chest. "I-I'm sorry," she whispered. "I'm sorry for everything."

"It's all right, sis," Nina said, softly stroking her hair. "It's all right."

Their cellmates were settling down to sleep. Above, the dim light inside the dome remained unchanging. She'd already lost track of whether it might be day or night outside. The briefest of glimpses of their surroundings before she'd been brought inside had revealed a vast jungle landscape, such as she'd only ever seen on ancient vids of Earth. Nothing similar existed on Concordia, certainly not now but also before the devastation caused by the biocide.

It had been her last sight of freedom.

"What are we going to do to get out?" Nina asked.

Get out? "I don't think we can."

"But maybe there's a way. We only need to think of it."

"If it was possible to get out, do you think all these people would still be here?" There were double the number of humans in this room as in the other dome, and she'd noticed another room containing people adjacent to theirs.

"Just because they didn't manage it," Nina replied, "that doesn't mean we can't."

"They're older than us, bigger and stronger. We're smaller and weaker. If they can't do it, how can we?"

"Maybe you don't need to be big and strong. Maybe it helps to be small. I don't know. I just don't think we should give up."

"If there's a way..." Miki's chin trembled and her shoulders shook.

Nina grabbed her arms and peered into her face. "What's wrong?"

"Oh, Nina. I told them everything. *Everything*! All about the *Sirocco*, and the long journey we took to come here, and...and..." Sobs overcame her.

"How? How could they ask you all that?"

"They know English. The questions were on a screen."

"But how could they know English?"

"I don't know. It isn't important. But now, even if the ship's left, the Scythians know the biocide didn't work and that people survived on Concordia. Now they'll go back there to finish them off. What have I done, Nina? What have I done?"

Her sister wrapped her arms around her. "You couldn't help it. It isn't your fault. If you hadn't answered them they would have let me die."

It was true, but somehow the fact didn't make things any better. She felt as though there must have been a third option, only she hadn't thought of it.

"We have to escape now," said Nina. "If the ship's still here, we might be able to warn them."

"But we can't escape!" she exclaimed wretchedly.

"Miki." Nina's tone was serious. She sounded ten years older than she was.

Miki stopped crying and looked at her.

"What would Dad say?" Nina asked.

"I don't know. What do you mean?"

"Do you remember when the jump drive failed?"

She did, though only vaguely. "Do you?"

"No, of course not. I was too young. But I do remember Dad talking about it. He said it was the worst moment, when everyone realized they'd been thrown years off course, and that even if they did try to make it to Earth they would starve long before they arrived."

Miki recalled her father speaking about that time occasionally too, but she still didn't understand Nina's meaning.

"Don't you remember that time when he told us they could have given up then? He said some people did. They just gave up on life. But most of them didn't. They kept on trying. They looked on planets for plants they could grow for food, they converted the Ark into a farm, and they *kept on trying*. And they made it. After all those years as we were growing up, they made it here. He told us, when he was..." Nina wiped her eyes "...when he was dying, that we must remember that and never give up. We have to keep on trying. Always. Don't you remember?"

She did not. Their father's death was almost a blank in her mind, and it wasn't something she wanted to dwell on.

"I know it looks hopeless," Nina said, "but we have to do what Dad said. Right?"

Miki nodded numbly. "Right."

32

"No," Cherry said firmly. "We go directly there. Now."

"I never heard anything so stupid," Aubriot replied. "And what do you propose we do when we get there? Walk up to the dome and knock on it, asking to be let in? Or if the Scythians aren't accepting visitors, ask if we could please have the kids back?" He made a dismissive *pfft*.

"If we don't go there right away who knows what might happen?" she argued. "We could be too late. If Buka had let me and Wilder search for the girls as soon as we arrived we might have found them. A little bit of time can make all the difference. We have to act immediately."

"And if we go off half-cocked we could ruin everything. I know you care about the kids. We all do. That's why we have to plan this carefully. I'm sure they're safe for now. The Scythians must think they're important, otherwise why transfer them somewhere else?"

According to Buka's sources, Miki and Nina had been taken to a Scythian dome far in the south. It was the largest alien structure of all and the site of one of the first abductions. It was also the place where the massacre of the villagers had occurred. Cherry agreed that it did seem the aliens valued the girls, though she didn't know why.

"Another thing," Aubriot added. "They'll know all about the

earlier attack by now. They'll be prepared. We can't try the same trick again. Besides, from the sound of it, it wouldn't work anyway. Zapata struggled to lift the lid off an ordinary-sized dome. This one's bigger. The biggest. We need different tactics."

Strongquist said, "If you would like my opinion—"

"We wouldn't," Cherry retorted.

"I would advise returning to the island."

"We can work out different tactics right here," Cherry said, ignoring the android. "Everything else is speculation. Am I right, Wilder?"

Their friend hadn't said a word during the argument. She folded her arms over her thin chest and said, "Actually, Aubriot has a p—"

"Fine!" Cherry snapped. "Fine. Let's waste some more time. Why not? I'll be outside." She stomped out of the room and slammed the door.

That was one thing to be said for the Earthers' old-fashioned, low tech portals. They were certainly useful for something to take out your temper on.

She marched up the stairs and out into the sunshine.

A migration was underway.

Buka had decided the bunker had to be evacuated as it was no longer safe. Revenge for the attack on the dome was expected by the hour. A small military contingent would remain to keep the communications hub going as long as possible, but everyone else was moving out. The remaining helis would take the worst-injured. Nearly every vehicle was being utilized to transport the rest.

She watched the activity. Itai walked past, his hands secured behind his back. He glanced at her and then looked down.

What a fool.

She checked the skies. If it were not for Vessey's protection the bunker would be a smoking ruin by now. That was for sure. How much longer could the Earthers rely on the presence of the *Sirocco*?

Zapata approached her, wiping his hands on a rag. "Is Wilder around? I finished the repairs."

"She's inside," Cherry replied woodenly.

"Something wrong?"

"Nope."

He looked bemused at this clear denial of the truth. "Where are we off to next? Back to the ship?"

"We have a few detours to make first."

"So where are we going?"

"To the Makers' site."

A WAVE of sadness hit Cherry as the shuttle touched down. On one side was the ocean, on the other the forested mountain she remembered from her last visit. When she'd come here with Kes he'd been healthy and happy, keen to find the seeds to re-green Concordia. He'd been his usual positive, energetic, courageous self. She missed him so much.

"Wakey, wakey," Aubriot chided, snapping her from her memories. "Are you coming or not? We haven't got all day. Weren't you the one saying we have to hurry?"

Throwing a dark look at his retreating back as he made his way off the shuttle, she followed him wordlessly.

"It's quite a walk," Wilder said once they were outside, "whichever route we take."

"There's more than one?" asked Aubriot.

"There are two."

"There are actually three," Strongquist corrected. "But the third route isn't important for our purposes."

"We either go through the seed vault or over the mountain. The distance is the same." When Strongquist opened his lips as if to speak, Wilder added, "Give or take."

"Over the mountain," Aubriot and Cherry said simultaneously. After sharing a mutual glance, he continued, "I'm no fan of that vault. Too many skeletons to trip over."

She didn't want to go in because the place would remind her too strongly of Kes.

Everyone was armed. The possibility that the Scythians might have found the place had been discussed on the trip over. Wilder thought it was unlikely. The Makers' beacon had deactivated, and if the aliens had managed to find an entrance anyway, they would find getting inside difficult if not impossible. But it wouldn't hurt to bring rifles just in case.

Strongquist led them under the trees and along the narrow, rocky bed of a dried-up stream. The path soon began to climb, and Cherry quickly found herself out of breath. She began to lag the others, struggling upward. Her rifle seemed unusually heavy. After some time, Wilder noticed her and halted to wait for her to catch up.

"It's hard work, isn't it?" she asked when Cherry reached her.

"It's been a while since I got any real exercise," she puffed. "Spent too long sitting on my ass aboard that ship."

"I can carry your rifle if you like."

Cherry hesitated but then handed her weapon over. "Thanks. That would be a big help." They continued to climb. "The raid on the dome took its toll on me too, I guess."

In truth, she'd been feeling tired for a while. Bone tired. And not just physically, mentally too. The struggle to survive never seemed to end. She'd known it all her life, ever since disembarking the *Nova*. First it had been the sluglimpets, the Woken, and the Guardians, then it had been the Scythians. And running through all of it was the effort to build a civilization. She had conjured life from the soil. She had fed the colony with crops teased from almost nothing. Food for the hungry.

And she hadn't even chosen her destiny. It had been chosen for her, many generations ago, somewhere on this planet, by her fore-bears. They had elected to spend the rest of their lives aboard a colony ship and assign their far-off descendants, willing or not, the task of creating a new home for humankind.

She felt as though she'd lived several lifetimes already. How did Aubriot manage it?

She'd had enough. Her will to battle on was finite. She would use her remaining energy on rescuing the girls. She owed Kes that much. But then she reckoned she would be done.

The entrance to the Makers' site was a small door tucked behind a protrusion of bare rock, almost impossible to see unless you knew where it was. Strongquist took them through it and down many steps before they reached the cavern where the *Mistral* had been crafted.

The sight of the massive underground space took Cherry's breath away. She paused at the entrance, taking it all in. It was as if she'd stepped back in time to the early days of the Concordia Colony.

"You all right?" Aubriot asked, noticing she'd stopped.

"Doesn't it make you feel weird, knowing this is where they built everything? The Guardians, their ship, everything?"

"It's impressive, I'll give it that. But we don't have time for being awestruck. We've got a job to do. We need to find something to help us get in that dome and get the kids out."

"I still think it's a fool's errand. What could there be here that would help us? Even if we do find armaments or a bomb—which, let's face it, is very unlikely because the Makers have zero reason to leave something like that here—what good is it going to do? We can't blow the dome up with Miki and Nina inside. And other humans will be with them."

"If there's any high tech on this planet, it's here. Until we search the place thoroughly we don't know there's nothing we can use, if not to rescue the kids, then in the war."

She had been walking with him across the main chamber, but at his comment she halted, her fist clenched. "That's what this is about, isn't it? You aren't interested in saving Miki and Nina, you're looking for stuff to use in your war."

"Keep your hair on. Anything we find to help us get the kids out will be useful in other ways too. Stands to reason. We're just killing two birds with one stone."

Wilder had gone ahead with Strongquist to a small room adjoining the chamber. Through the open door, Cherry spotted another figure and she froze. But then she relaxed as she realized it was only a holo. She recalled Wilder saying the Makers had left a message for later generations who might stumble across the site, but she hadn't listened to it.

Curious to see one of the builders of the *Mistral* she walked over to the room. Aubriot went in another direction.

The android was working at a control panel and Wilder was idly watching the holo.

She explained, "Strongquist is uploading the language Buka and his people speak and creating a language database we can use for translation."

"I suppose it'll save us having to use him all the time."

"Exactly."

"He says he can do it for all Earth languages eventually if we want him to."

"I hope we won't be here that long."

"Itching to get home?"

"Yes, but not without Miki and Nina."

Strongquist turned to face them. "It's done. Now all I need to do is build some simple translators. I'm sure I can find the materials around here somewhere. If you wouldn't mind waiting?" He moved toward the door.

"Actually," Cherry retorted, "I *do* mind. This excursion is a waste of time, but I'm overruled, so..."

Wilder winced.

Strongquist said, "Would you like me to unmute the holo and translate his speech to English?"

"I'm interested to hear what he has to say," said Wilder. "I had a look around in here before but I didn't understand what some of the equipment is for. The holo's message might give us a clue."

Judging from the man's expression, Cherry was doubtful he would tell them anything useful. He looked livid.

"Hm," Strongquist murmured. "This is interesting."

"Can't you do the translation?" Wilder asked.

"No, that isn't a problem. There's a later message, recorded after this one."

"Oh, in that case, can we have the later one? That's probably more relevant."

The holo disappeared and another appeared in its place. The man was the same but his clothes were different. His expression was different too. He seemed much happier.

When he spoke, his first words were unintelligible before an artificial voice cut in.

"... did you find us, I wonder? I hope you didn't break in via one of the hidden entrances, and that you figured out our little puzzles at the bottom of the seed vault. If you did, that means civilization has returned to a reasonable level of development. If you broke in, well, you probably won't understand a word of what I'm saying and it doesn't matter anyway."

He waved a hand as if dismissing his audience. "Go away, and don't come back until you've figured out how to understand me." He chuckled. "If you *do* understand me, that makes me very happy. It means our time has come. Science and technology are no longer feared and hated. People like me and my friends aren't despised and persecuted. The world has become a better place. It's safe for us to wake up and rejoin society."

The holo continued to speak, but Cherry didn't hear it. She and Wilder were staring at each other, open-mouthed.

Wake up?!

She flew to the door, leaned out of it and screamed, "Aubriot, get in here!"

Wilder said mildly, "You have your comm, you know."

"Oh, yeah." While she comm'd Aubriot to come to the room, Wilder asked Strongquist to halt the recording and take it back to the beginning.

When Aubriot arrived, they watched the message the whole way through and then watched it a second time.

The Makers hadn't left the site, or at least not all of them. Some had elected to return to the world and live out their lives the best they could, but forty engineers and scientists had entrusted their bodies to the same cryosleep used aboard the *Nova Fortuna*. They had set a date for the system to revive them or it could be triggered externally. The man in the holo, whose name was Steen, explained that if the visitors could understand him and human society was no longer hostile to his kind, they were invited to start the process.

At the end of the second viewing, the three watchers were silent.

"Holy *shit*," Wilder breathed.

"No kidding," said Cherry.

She'd thought Aubriot was the last of the obnoxious Woken.

33

One thing that puzzled Miki was where the other Earthers went. Several of their fellow captives also worked with the odd worm-turned-carapaced creatures, but the others went elsewhere. When they returned they looked tired, so they'd clearly been working, but what at? Like in the other dome, it was impossible to ask them because they didn't speak the same language.

"What are you thinking?" Nina asked as they settled down to sleep after another day's labor at the vats.

"Just wondering what other things the humans do around here. What do you think it is?"

Nina covered her mouth with the back of her hand as she stifled a yawn. "I don't know. Who cares? Have you had any ideas about how we can escape?"

The question dragged Miki back from the realms of speculation to harsh reality. "I haven't. Have you?" Nina had been the one talking about never giving up. Why couldn't *she* think of something?

As soon as the thought popped into her mind, Miki chided herself. She was the older one. It was her job to look after her sister, especially now Dad was gone. "I mean, if you have any suggestions, I'd love to hear them."

Their conversation was interrupted. A woman from the group of

humans they lived with had walked over to them. She was gesticulat-
ing, as if she wanted to talk. Miki paid her more attention. The
woman rubbed her stomach and said something.

"I think she's asking if we're hungry," Nina said.

Miki thought so too. "No, we're fine. Thank you." She smiled and
gave a thumbs up.

The woman looked questioningly at her hand. She didn't understand thumbs up?

Miki pointed at her and rubbed her own stomach. "Are you
hungry?"

This appeared to be understood. The woman grinned before
reaching forward and grabbing Miki and Nina into a hug.

It was nice to be welcomed into the group.

A shadow passed overhead. A Scythian had flown over. The
woman had noticed too. She pointed to where the creature had been
a moment ago and then performed a series of actions. Miki and Nina
watched closely.

At the third repetition, Miki got it. The woman had been miming
picking out worms with tweezers and putting them in the vat. "Yes!
That's what we do." She nodded vigorously. "We grow the Scythians'
food. What about you? What do you do?" She opened her hands in an
inquiring gesture.

But their new companion didn't seem inclined to answer. She
pointed above again and then, chuckling, drew her finger across her
throat.

"Wh-what?" Miki asked.

The woman laughed wickedly, mimed cutting her throat again,
and pointed upward. Then she nodded, her eyebrows raised.

Nina said hesitantly, "She...wants us to kill the Scythians?"

"I think so. But that's dumb. How could we ever kill one of them?
They're much bigger than us and they have those horrible claws on
their wings."

"I think she might be crazy," Nina said, "like that man who took us
to the dome."

"You could be right. There certainly seem to be a lot of crazy
Earthers."

The woman was making her way back to the other side of the cell. She said something to her group and they laughed, throwing appreciative glances at Miki and Nina.

"Did we agree to something?" Nina asked.

"I have no idea."

THE FOLLOWING day they were back at the vats, performing their tasks. Miki hadn't slept well, not only due to worrying about their troubles, but also over concern she and Nina were sharing a cell with someone who was mentally unstable. As if things weren't bad enough as they were. They didn't need threats from within their prison too.

Neither she nor Nina had been allotted the chore of dragging a cage of snapping animals to the hatch in the wall yet, but she knew it was an inevitability. It was the most hated job—she could tell from the demeanor of workers who had to do it—and there was no reason she or her sister would be excused. It turned out today was the day.

The Scythian that came up behind her made her jump.

It poked her in the back and waved its claw at a cage full of particularly large creatures. Her shoulders slumped and she looked around for someone to help her. She couldn't possibly drag the cage by herself.

Everyone promptly looked away.

Except one person.

A young man caught her gaze and gave a short nod.

She breathed a silent *Thank you.*

As she reached for the cage, the animals grew more agitated, as if they guessed what was about to happen. Did they face the same fight to the death they'd faced in their earlier growth cycle? A closer view of what was through the hatch might tell her—not that she really wanted to know.

Shell-encased, articulated limbs flashed out from between the bars, trying to grab her. The creatures' jaws clicked and ground. She kept her legs and feet as far from the cage as she could as she and the young man hauled it over the sandy floor. When they reached the wall they shoved it tightly up against the hatch. If one of the creatures escaped it could do serious damage. Miki had already seen cuts and slashes on the legs of workmates who got too close to them.

The hatch jerked open. One hand on the back of the cage, while keeping a safe distance from it, Miki crouched a little to see what lay on the other side. The young man tapped her shoulder and gave a small shake of his head. But she wanted to see. It couldn't be that bad, could it?

The caged creatures were crawling through the portal, exploring the newly opened space. A loud bustling and rustling leaked out. One creature remained at the back of the cage, sitting on its scaly behind, hesitating to take advantage of the new freedom.

A Scythian waddled over and gave the cage a kick, and the reluctant straggler moved.

Still, Miki couldn't see properly what awaited the animals. The light levels on the other side of the hatch seemed even lower than usual.

Something darted into the cage, grabbed the remaining creature, and disappeared. It happened so fast it was over almost before Miki could register the action.

The hatch slid shut. The spectacle was over. What had she learned?

As she returned the empty cage to its former spot, she mentally replayed the sight that had flashed before her eyes.

What had she seen?

An arm or leg of some kind had reached out to take the animal into the other room. But *had* it been an arm or a leg? She didn't recall seeing anything resembling grasping fingers or toes. What kind of appendage had it used?

Now, in her mind's eye, she could see it.

It had been a claw. A small one, but a claw nonetheless. It must have hooked the creature rather than grasped it. What had made her take so long to figure it out was the fact that the claw had been surrounded by webbed material, like...

As she'd been musing the question in her mind, she'd picked up some tweezers and was absent-mindedly transferring a worm to the liquid.

When the realization hit, the tweezers and the worm fell from her frozen fingers. Both sank out of sight but she barely noticed.

She'd seen a Scythian's wing and claw. It had been a smaller version of the aliens' wing and claw that had snatched the young creature from its cage. The room beyond the hatch held young Scythians in the final growth stage, feeding on and fighting each other for the younger stages. The animals she'd thought were their food were the Scythians themselves.

34

S trongquist had known all along. He'd been truthful when he'd said Wilder and Niall had triggered his activation when they'd entered the site, but ever since then he'd been following instructions to not divulge the presence of the sleeping Makers until he'd assessed the state of things on Earth. If a certain level of human civilization had been reached again, he could—with or without the visitors' knowledge or approval—trigger the process that would bring the engineers and scientists back to life.

If his assessment was that Earth remained uncivilized and unfriendly to their kind, he was to return to Svalbard, close up the site, and deactivate, ready for when another opportunity might arise. If no visitors ever found their way in, the Makers would awaken at the time they'd set. Strongquist would have been waiting.

The Makers could not have anticipated the current situation. They hadn't even known that other intelligent species existed in the galaxy when they entered their sleep, let alone imagined they would have invaded Earth. Of that, Wilder was sure. She wasn't as knowledgeable about the history of the creators of the Guardians as Aubriot or Cherry, but she could guess that much.

What would they make of everything when they woke up? It would take days to find out. The cryosleep revival procedure took a long time and couldn't be hurried. Even if followed correctly to the last detail, problems could still result. She recalled Woken affected by blindness and paraplegia. Some had not survived.

It was lucky they had Strongquist to oversee the process. On the *Nova* trained personnel had performed the revivals. She had no clue what to do, and neither did Aubriot or Cherry. Not that Cherry would have cared. She'd been in an even more foul mood than usual.

"The first stage has initiated," said Strongquist. "All the capsules are operating within normal parameters."

The cryosleep chamber was beneath the floor of the vast cavern. The android had opened an invisible door and led them down to it. Twenty capsules stood each side of a steel-lined room that looked as pristine as the day it had been made. The capsules were windowless boxes reminiscent of coffins, and each had functioned perfectly according to the data reports. The fusion reactor had been put to good use.

"How long until we can talk to them?" asked Aubriot.

"A week at least," the android replied. "Some may take longer to return to full consciousness than others."

"A week? That's a long time."

"It will take longer for the Makers to return to normal functionality."

Aubriot stretched his arms out to each side. "Yeah, I remember that feeling. Stiff and cold, like you'd fallen into an icy sea. But, still, great news. Fantastic. I came here thinking we might find something we could turn into a devastating weapon for the war. The last thing I expected was the weapon would be human."

"Huh?" Cherry lifted a lip scornfully. "What makes you think they'll agree to fight? They're expecting to wake up to a fairly normal world."

"What choice will they have? It'll be either fight or die. Of course they'll help their fellow humans."

Strongquist said, "This was a question I asked myself when I was debating whether to reveal the existence of the Makers. It's my belief that, knowing them as I do, they would want to participate in the effort to save Earth from the aliens' exploitation.

Not least because a world in servitude is not one they would
want to encounter when they awoke at their chosen revival
date."

"See?" Aubriot sneered. "They will want to fight. And what a
difference they'll make. These people built a *starship*, from scratch."

"So did Wilder," Cherry said.

He opened his mouth but nothing came out. Finally, he said,
"Yeah, well, that was different." He lifted a finger. "And the Makers
created the Guardians too."

"You say that like it's a good thing. Don't you remember all the
trouble they caused? And didn't they sedate you because they thought
you were a danger to the establishment of the colony?"

He tutted and shook his head as if she was crazy, but he also didn't
come up with an answer.

"Someone needs to tell Vessey what's happening," Cherry
announced. "I volunteer to climb those damned stairs and direct
comm the ship. Unless someone else wants to do it?"

"Be my guest," Aubriot said.

"I'll come with you," said Wilder. "It's a lot harder going up than
coming down, but I'd like to speak to Niall and Dragan. I want to find
out what they've discovered about the Scythian ship."

They returned to the main chamber and then began the long
climb to the outside.

"Unbelievable," Wilder commented. "Who would have thought
the Makers were still alive."

"More's the pity."

"You don't think it's a good thing?"

"Do you remember the Woken?"

"Sure. A few of them, anyway. Cariad...Anahi...and Kes, of
course."

"He was about the only decent one. Cariad was okay once you got
to know her. The rest were a bunch of stuck-up egomaniacs. Like
Aubriot."

"Surely not that bad?" Wilder asked.

"No, not as bad as him, but not much better. They all thought *they*
should be running the colony, not us Gens."

They continued to climb for several minutes until Cherry halted. "Can we take a breather?"

"I don't remember that time very well," Wilder said, stopping on the step below. "I was just a kid. But I'm sure the Makers won't be the same as the Woken. The situation here's entirely different."

"The situation might be different. Doesn't mean the people will be." When her panting eased, she said, "Come on, let's go."

They climbed all the way to the top and stepped out into bright sunshine and a strong, cool breeze.

"That's nice." Cherry rested her hand on her knee as she caught her breath. The view over the forest canopy as it spread down the mountainside was beautiful. In a cleft sat the neat triangle of the distant ocean and above it a clear blue sky.

Wilder was looking in the same direction. "I spotted the Scythians that attacked us from here. I didn't realize what they were. I thought they were two huge birds."

Cherry chuckled. "Two huge, very ugly birds."

"How was I to know? I hadn't seen a single bird before coming to Earth. I didn't know their normal range of appearance. I still don't. And I only got a glimpse of them. I wish I *had* recognized them. It would have saved us a world of trouble, and," she added sadly, "that village wouldn't have been massacred."

"You mustn't blame yourself. The Scythians are going to do a lot more damage before their time on Earth is over. Shit. I sound like Aubriot. Ugh." She put a finger to her ear. "Time to update Vessey." After a pause she said, "That's weird."

"What's up?"

"She's not answering."

"She's probably asleep. Try the ship."

Watching Cherry's face after she sent the comm, Wilder asked, "Still nothing?"

She shook her head slowly. "You try Niall."

"I'll try Dragan. Niall's been off with me lately." She comm'd her workmate. When Dragan didn't respond she comm'd Niall.

Nothing.

Their gazes met.

"You don't think...?" Cherry asked.

"No, it can't be that. I know—Zapata." She sent a comm request to the pilot, who was supposed to be waiting for them at the landing site on the other side of the mountain.

Her request melted into the ether, unanswered.

"No answer." She added, hopefully, "But he would never just abandon us."

"Not deliberately," Cherry agreed, "but who knows what Vessey's told him? She could have tricked him somehow."

"Wait, have you tried to comm anyone since Buka gave back our devices? I haven't."

"I haven't either. You think they might be broken?"

"Buka's people could have done it by accident."

"We could tell Aubriot to come up and try comming someone," said Cherry, "but I'd rather not. Look, we're going to be here days waiting for the Makers to wake up. Why don't we walk back to the landing site? We can use the shuttle's comm." She was silent on the other, awful possibility.

They trekked the same route along the stream bed. Daylight began to fade as they walked. If they didn't hurry, they would be journeying back in darkness, but that was the least of Wilder's worries.

The view of the landing site was obscured the entire way. Her fears were not confirmed until they stepped out of the forest and onto the flat land leading down to the water. Here, they could see clearly the spot where the shuttle had landed.

It was empty. Their ride was gone. Zapata had flown her away. He must have returned to the *Sirocco* under some pretense of Vessey's.

The shuttle was absent, and no one on the ship was answering comms. The two facts could mean only one thing: Vessey had ordered a jump.

The Concordians had abandoned them.

35

L ife in the Scythian dome had become a monotonous, boring routine consisting of long hours of work and short rest periods, mostly spent sleeping. Meager meals punctuated the days twice only—once before work and once afterward—when the humans would portion out the scant amount of tasteless mash as fairly as they could. No one was so self-sacrificing as to refuse their allotment yet no one demanded more, not even the strongest men.

It was a sad testament to the altruism people could show, Miki thought, in these extreme circumstances. The sadness came from the fact that no one on the outside would ever know of the kindness humans had shown each other within the domes.

She'd tried to count the sleeping periods as they passed, but she'd become muddled. She wasn't sure, but she estimated they'd been brought to this dome ten or eleven days ago. Judging from the gauntness of her cellmates' bodies, they'd been here longer. They tried to communicate with her and Nina sometimes but their efforts were generally no more successful than the first time, when the woman had pointed at the Scythian sweeping overhead and mimed cutting her throat.

What had *that* been about?

One of her points was clear: she and Nina were working with

young Scythians, either growing their food or growing the aliens themselves. That part she hadn't quite figured out. Not that it mattered. She might want them dead too, as the woman had, but what could any of them do about it?

Then, on the twelfth or thirteenth night, when she was deeply asleep curled up next to her sister, someone shook her shoulder. A figure crouched over her, softly silhouetted by the dull lighting above.

She sat up.

No Scythians were flying overhead and the dome seemed particularly quiet. If any of her fellow prisoners were awake they didn't look it, none except this one. It was one of the adult men.

Now he had her attention, he dipped a hand into his shirt and drew two things out. In another second the objects were in her hands and he was on his way back to his side of the cell.

She lay down, tucking the things under her. Clearly, neither he nor she was supposed to have them. What had he given her and why? Surreptitiously, she ran her fingers over the objects. They were made from metal, a little shorter than her forearm, curved, long and narrow, finishing in a point. She took a peek. It was hard to make them out in the near darkness, but in the end she saw they were implements for digging, similar to tools used in the *Sirocco*'s Ark.

They must have come from another section where the workers had to dig small holes. How odd that the man had given them to her. What was his intention? As there were two tools, she guessed one was meant for Nina. She would give it to her later when she woke up. They would have to find a place to secrete them. No items could be taken from the work sites. The Scythians made sure they put all the tweezers back at the end of their shifts. They conducted random searches, though rarely of Miki or Nina, perhaps because they were young and weak.

MIKI HAD TUCKED the digging implement under her top and down the back of her pants. It made bending difficult but it was the best she could do. She knew it was important to keep it hidden, she just didn't know why. Nina had done the same. As they put on their respirators, she hoped she wasn't about to get her little sister into trouble yet again. What would the Scythians do to them if they were found out?

They walked down the tunnel to the room full of vats. Inside, everything seemed normal. The three Scythians sat on their podiums, the creatures in the cages rustled and gnashed their scaly teeth, within their earthy substrate the worms would be wriggling. It seemed to be just another working day.

She took Nina's elbow as they walked to the far end of the vats. She wanted to keep Nina close beside her. They began work, transferring half-grown specimens to their almost certain deaths, victims of older members of their species. As they worked, Miki watched the room from the corners of her eyes. She kept her head low and her movements steady, though her heart raced. The other humans must have something planned, but what? And when?

Hours passed. The skin on her hands and arms grew wrinkled from constant dipping in the liquid. Her fingers grew sore from the nips of the livestock.

A small *thunk* came from the other side of the vat. Miki looked up and met Nina's eyes, wide with panic. Nina's gaze flicked to the nearest Scythian and back to Miki, pleading written in her look.

What was wrong?

Nina had stopped moving.

Keeping her pace slow and nonchalant, Miki walked around the tank to join her sister. Before she reached her, she saw the problem. Poking out from the leg of her pants was the end of the metal tool. It had slipped to the bottom. Nina would have a hard time retrieving it and returning it to her waist without attracting notice.

Miki reached for a pair of tweezers, pretending to fumble them, and dropped them on the ground. She stooped, tugged the tool from the leg of Nina's pants, and stood up behind her, quickly lifting her shirt and shoving it into her waistband. Then she dug in the soil with the tweezers.

Nina's hidden contraband was a problem. She'd lost weight since coming to the dome and her pants hung loose on her hips. The tool could easily drop out again. She must have been moving carefully all this time to try to prevent it.

But, the next second, that was the least of her concerns.

The workers nearest the three watching Scythians jumped on them. Instantly, the podiums became a whirl of human and alien limbs, thrashing, slashing, battering, stabbing. The workers had brought in the digging tools and were using them to attack the watchers.

Miki watched in horrified fascination. Would they manage to kill them? But what did it matter? They were—

A woman grabbed her to get her attention. She motioned to the vat and shouted something.

"I-I don't understand."

Shaking her head in frustration, the woman climbed onto the vat, balancing on the section separators, and held out a hand.

"You want me to come up there?"

Still confused, she allowed the woman to help her up. The woman pointed at the ceiling.

It was low, only just above her head. Miki hadn't taken much notice of it before. Between supporting metal beams, the soil was bare and crumbly and the roots of plants hung from it. Now she saw it more closely, she realized how unstable it looked. They were lucky there hadn't been...

"You want me to dig!" she exclaimed. She turned to her sister. "They want us to—"

"I know! I know." Nina was already climbing up and pulling out her tool.

The woman ran off, heading for one of the groups tackling the Scythians.

Together, they hacked at the soil. Miki worked with all her strength, driving the point into the surface over and over again. Clumps of earth rained down, battering against her visor.

The Earthers must have guessed this area was not far underground, and like at the other dome, it lay outside the above-ground structure. If they could just break through, they might escape.

But was she tall enough to reach the surface? What would she do when she'd dug as high as she could?

The sounds of fighting continued. For the first time, she heard what she guessed was a Scythian sound. Amongst the pants and gasps of the humans there was a noise between a whistle and a grunt. Were they killing it? She hoped so. She hoped they killed them all.

She and Nina quickly excavated what seemed like a tonne of soil. It cascaded into the tank, turning the liquid into mud. Then it began to pile up around their feet.

Her arms and back ached with the effort. The visor of her respirator steamed up with her heavy panting. But she didn't slacken her pace, not for a millisecond. The Scythians would crack down hard after a failed escape attempt. They would probably execute everyone. If she and Nina didn't dig through to the outside they would die.

But she couldn't reach high enough! She was on her tiptoes, extending her arms as far as they went, and the point of her tool was only scratching the soil. Nina had given up digging upward and was digging outward in an apparently desperate effort to do *something*, even something that didn't help. Yet there was no sign of daylight.

Hands grabbed her thighs. She looked down in shock. Men, their arms and hands cut, their hair slick with blood, were holding her legs.

They lifted her up.

In a frenzy, she drove her tool into the soil with power she didn't know she had.

She had to break through. She had to. If she didn't Nina would die.

She—

The point of the tool met no resistance.

A ray of sunshine shone in her eyes. She blinked, unbelieving.

She believed.

She threw the tool down and tore at the earth with her bare hands. Plants filled her fingers. Green, fresh plants, and the light blinded her.

The hands on her legs lifted her higher.

She was looking at a sea of vegetation. It was alive with insects, and above was the dear, sweet, blue sky.

Grasping the nearest stalks, she hauled herself out. The soil was unstable so close to the hole. She lay flat on her stomach and peered in. Nina was on her way up, lifted by the men. She grabbed her sister's shirt and dragged her the rest of the way.

A smooth, pale white wall rose in a curve over to the right: the Scythians' dome. It was as the Earthers had guessed. The room with the vats lay outside the dome's perimeter.

To the left was jungle.

She ripped off her respirator. "Come on, Nina. We have to run."

An Earther man appeared in the hole, dripping blood.

She hoped he made it out. She hoped they all made it out, but she couldn't wait around to see.

She took her sister's hand, and they raced for the trees.

36

The man lay on his side, covered in a blanket, shivering. Cherry pulled the blanket higher over his shoulders and tucked it in. His skin was so pale it was almost translucent, and his hair was auburn tinged silver. Cherry was reminded of Kes. Was this how he'd appeared when he was revived? She'd never witnessed someone undergoing the final stage of the process, alive yet not quite aware, not completely conscious. She'd only ever seen the Woken when they were up and walking around. He hovered, drifting in and out of dreams, murmuring indistinctly. She didn't speak his language so couldn't understand his meaning. It didn't matter. He was talking about a time centuries past and, aside from his cryo companions, about people long dead.

"How's this one doing?" Wilder asked, sitting down beside her.

"Not too bad. Of them all, I'd say he's recovering the best. Do you recognize him?"

"Huh?" Wilder peered closer. "Holy shit. It's the holo."

"Took me a while. He looks different, right? Older."

"Yeah. Do you think they waited a while before entering cryo?"

"Maybe there was a problem that took a few years to fix but they didn't bother re-recording the message. We'll soon find out. He should be coherent in a day or so, according to Strongquist."

"And then what will we tell him?"

"Everything. We'll have plenty of time to do it."

Wilder nodded her agreement sadly.

They were stuck on the island. Now that Zapata had flown away in the shuttle and the *Sirocco* had apparently jumped from the system, they had no way of getting off. Not unless the android built them a boat and they rowed away. Which, going by his—*its*—performance so far might not be beyond it.

If it hadn't been for Strongquist, they would already be feeling the effects of starvation. Thinking they would only be here a few hours they hadn't brought any supplies. Zapata had taken away the emergency rations on the shuttle, and the seed vault no longer held anything edible.

But they were surrounded by an ocean, and the water was full of life. Through various ingenious methods, the android had supplied them with seaweed, shellfish, and fish to eat. In truth, with Strongquist's indefatigable efforts, they could probably live out their natural lives here, though for Aubriot that would be a very long time.

The man muttered something.

"Did you catch that?" Wilder asked.

"How could I?"

"Uh, I forgot." She pulled a lanyard with a small device attached out of her pocket and handed it over. "Strongquist gave me two a minute ago. I'm wearing mine already. I came here to give you yours."

"He made translators?" Cherry asked, slipping it over her head.

"Yes, *he* did. It transmits to your ear comm. So you're finally thinking of him like a person?"

She didn't answer.

"Look, I get it. You had a bad time with the Guardians in the early days of the colony. But Strongquist's done nothing except help us in every way possible. I think you should be nicer."

"Why? It doesn't have feelings," Cherry said stubbornly.

"I'm not so sure about that. He kind of grows on you. When I first met him I asked if I could call him Strongquist II, but now he's just Strongquist."

"Who are you?"

The man from the holo had spoken. The translator repeated his words in English, clear as day, in Cherry's ear.

He'd turned onto his back while they'd been chatting, and now he was staring at them, looking a little frightened.

"It's okay," Wilder replied. "We're friends."

His eyes widened and he tried to get up.

"Take it easy," Cherry said, placing a gentle hand on his chest.

He pushed it away and looked around wildly.

Wilder said, "He can't understand us."

"Get Strongquist."

She managed to restrain the man while waiting for the android to arrive. He was weak anyway, as well as obviously disoriented. As he took in his surrounding his struggles eased.

"Steen," Strongquist said, striding between the rows of revived Makers.

At his arrival, Steen visibly relaxed. His head sank into his pillow. "It's good to see you again. What year is this? And who the hell are these people?"

THE FOLLOWING days were what Cherry could only describe as 'interesting'. The Makers continued to slowly come to full consciousness. The cryosleep chambers they'd built turned out to be a superior design to the ones used on the *Nova Fortuna*. All forty men and women survived the process physically and mentally unharmed.

As they began to walk around, eat, and talk, she was struck by the deep camaraderie between them. Then, as time went on, she upgraded her description of their relationship to love. They bickered, teased, and nagged, but their deep familiarity and affection was apparent. How couldn't it be so? These people had suffered the same persecution, they'd toiled to find each other, and they'd undertaken a massive endeavor together, an endeavor spanning years and requiring every gram of their cooperation, intellect, and ingenuity.

She understood at last what had bound the Woken on Concordia, the scientists who had created the *Nova Fortuna* Project. At the time she'd only seen that they kept themselves separate and seemed aloof. Perhaps that was so, but what she hadn't taken into account was their long history of laboring as a group toward a common goal.

What also made the days interesting was bringing the Makers up to speed on all that had happened since they entered their chambers. When they heard that the *Mistral* and Guardians had made it to Concordia they'd been giddy with relief and joy. When they learned that Cherry and Wilder were among the first Gens to set foot on the planet, they gasped in wonderment and touched them as if to make sure they were real. When they were told that Aubriot was *the* Aubriot, the Project's founder and main backer, they laughed, some saying, "No way!" and "It can't be true!"

When all that was explained, it was time to tell them about the Scythians. Cherry started with the attacks on Concordia and the trip to the Galactic Assembly. Then she explained about the biocide. The Makers listened in silence. She grew tired of talking and asked Wilder to take over. Wilder told them about the *Sirocco* and the purpose of her visit. Then she told them about the state of things on Earth.

She concluded with the reason she'd returned to Svalbard and Strongquist's revelation about their existence. "It was quite the surprise," she said finally. "I never imagined I would ever meet you guys."

"Likewise," said Steen.

Aubriot hadn't said a thing for hours. He'd stood, hands on hips, watching and listening, as the remaining details were explained. "So now you're all compos mentis and up to speed, do you have any ideas about fighting off the invasion?"

"Stars," said Cherry, "give them a minute. They only just woke up."

"We've been here weeks. The time to fight back is long past due. If we don't do something soon Earth's never going to be free."

"I haven't told them the last bit," Wilder said.

"What's that?" Steen asked.

"The shuttle that brought us here left, and we think the *Sirocco* jumped from the system. It's just Cherry, Aubriot, and I here, and we have no way of leaving this island."

"No transportation?" Steen asked, eyebrows lifting. "That shouldn't be a problem."

"You're gonna build a boat?" Aubriot asked. "That'll take weeks. We need something now. I was thinking we could reactivate your signal beacon and rig it to comm the GAA."

"No need." Steen rose to his feet. His pallor had improved and he looked more like the holo he'd recorded. "Come this way, ladies and gentlemen."

He led them to the exit of the area under the floor of the cavern and out of it. Then he crossed the vast chamber. When he reached the opposite side, he said, "Strongquist, deactivate the security." After waiting a moment, he pressed a panel on the wall. A section popped out.

Wilder said, "You guys and your hidden compartments. What's in here?"

"What's in here," he announced, sliding the section to one side, "is our way off the island."

Within the newly revealed room stood six vehicles. They were not the most streamlined or attractive Cherry had seen. They were simple and blocky, though large. Each could hold around ten or fifteen people. They reminded her of something.

They had no wheels.

"Hey," she blurted, "are these—"

"I believe you called them skimmers."

37

The reality that she wouldn't be returning to Concordia didn't begin to hit Wilder until she was traveling over the plains of Earth on one of the Makers' skimmers. Up until then, all the time she'd spent at their site on the island, waiting for them to recover from cryo sleep, the fact that the *Sirocco* was gone and wouldn't be coming back hadn't seemed real. But looking out over the flat, grassy landscape stretching to the horizon on all sides really brought the fact home to her. Maybe it was because Kes was buried out there somewhere. Like her, he would never go back.

Or maybe it was because she couldn't quite believe that Niall and Dragan would desert her. She'd been with them through thick and thin, racing to build the *Sirocco* to the Leader's insane deadline. Dragan, in the depths of his madness and affiliation with the Final Day cult, hadn't been able to bring himself to hurt her—because they were friends. Niall had blown hot and cold in his affection for her, but she'd counted him as a friend too. How could they do this?

She grasped the handrail of the skimmer and told herself the wind was stinging her eyes.

"I hear you build starships too," said a voice.

Steen had appeared beside her. She still found it hard to reconcile the physical presence of the man with the holo. "Who told you that?"

"Your little friend."

"Cherry? You'd better not call her 'little' within her hearing."

"I thought it was better than 'one-armed'."

Wilder chuckled.

"It's good to see you laugh."

Huh? Was he getting fresh with her? She guessed several centuries in cryosleep might do that. "I haven't had much to laugh about lately. Sorry if my glum face brings you down."

"Not at all. It would take a lot more than a frown to bring me down. When I got in that cryo chamber I didn't know if I would ever wake up, or what I would find if I did. I used to be an angry, bitter man. I loved life. I was *not* happy about the group decision to expend our remaining resources and years of our finite lives on the hope of saving a colony on a far-off planet, on complete strangers who might not even have made it there." He smiled. "But my opinion didn't count. I was overruled, and so if I wanted to stay at the site I had to do what everyone else wanted. We didn't even think of building cryosleep capsules until after the *Mistral* had departed. I had a chance at a new lease of life, the opportunity to live in a new world right here on Earth. A world of the future. It's a pretty amazing one, don't you think?" He gazed out across the plain.

"From what I hear it's a better place for you," Wilder said, "and it *is* beautiful, but it isn't home. My home is that far-off planet you helped to save."

"I'm sorry your ship left without you. Maybe one day we'll build a new starship, together, and journey out into the stars." His hand moved to slide over hers.

She quickly moved hers away.

He shrugged, smiled again, and returned to his seat.

She cringed. Steen was a little creepy. But maybe his flirtatious comment wasn't only wishful thinking. If the Makers had built the *Mistral* here, maybe she could build a starship. But, she realized sadly, that had been a long time ago, when Earth was rich with the remains of the peak of technological development. All that was gone now. Getting back to Concordia might take a lifetime.

Several hours later, they arrived at the new headquarters of the

GAA. They had set up in the heart of a bombed-out, deserted town. The people Buka had tasked with disguising the site had done a great job. Wilder didn't see it until they were right in front of it. The garage door of a destroyed department store rolled up, and the skimmers glided in.

All the Makers insisted on being at the meeting with the head of the GAA. They had no single representative, not even a small group of people. Everything was decided democratically after long—sometimes very long—discussions. Sometimes the discussions dissolved into arguments, and then they would agree to go away and cool off before returning to talk.

The room was crowded. There weren't enough chairs, so half the participants stood at the back and sides or sat on the floor in the middle.

Buka arrived and hobbled to his seat. His rheumy-eyed gaze traveled from one intelligent, alert face to another, as if he couldn't believe his luck. He *was* lucky. Everyone on Earth was. The planet had just received an injection of humanity's brightest and best, the cream of the crop.

The Makers chattered noisily, apparently unaware of Buka's arrival.

Aubriot stood up and raised his hands. "All right, shut up everyone. Shut up," he repeated, louder. As the noise quietened, he swept a hand toward Buka. "May I introduce Mr Dakarai Buka, Head of the Global Advancement Association. Over to you, Mr Buka." He flopped into his seat and rested his elbow on the table and his chin in his hand, as if he expected to be in for a long, boring meeting.

His prediction came true, for the first part anyway. The Makers had to hear the details of the Scythian invasion, details Wilder already knew. She zoned out. A while later, when the topic moved on to a plan of action to repel the Scythians, things became more interesting. Aubriot rose to his feet again. "If we talk about this bit by bit with everyone having their say, we're gonna be here all day. I propose we split into teams. Maybe you can organize yourselves according to your expertise. I'll coordinate."

The Makers stared at him in silence.

"Come on, chop chop." He motioned with his hands, chivvying them.

Steen said, "That isn't how we, er..."

Someone opened the door, hitting a Maker in the back. After apologizing, he walked to Buka and whispered in his ear.

The old man nodded and spoke to him. When the messenger had left, he said, "Two people of great importance have arrived. What they can tell us may have a large bearing on what we decide today. I have asked that they be brought here immediately. I would like to ask for your patience for a few moments."

Wilder wondered who it could be. She didn't know of any Earthers of influence except Buka. She wasn't aware there even were any.

Quick footsteps sounded outside and the door opened again.

In stepped Miki and Nina.

A shriek went up from Cherry. She flew across the room and grabbed the girls, weeping with joy and relief. Wilder was simply dumbfounded. She couldn't believe they were here, alive and well.

"I apologize for not telling you sooner," Buka said. "I couldn't be absolutely certain they were safe until the heli bringing them up from the south touched down."

It took Cherry about fifteen minutes to calm down. The two Makers who had been sitting next to her gave up their seats for the girls, and though she stopped crying she couldn't take her eyes off them.

Miki told their story.

What a story it was. Wilder listened intently as she described the interior of the domes, the trapped people, and the work they had to do tending to the alien creatures. She explained how she suspected the creatures were actually baby Scythians and the aliens were growing their young in chambers beneath the ground outside the domes.

The Makers seized on this fact, and Miki lapsed into silence as they ran with it. She caught Wilder's gaze and looked away. Something was bothering her. Was there something she hadn't said?

But Miki was young and probably overly concerned with unimportant things. Perhaps she felt bad about absconding from the ship. She would have to reassure her later that she was completely forgiven.

The chatter in the room was rising. A Maker was proposing blowing up the 'alien nursery' Miki and Nina had escaped from. "Did most of the people get out?" she asked Miki.

"Uh huh," she replied softly. "Most of them."

"Then it's perfect," the woman went on. "We want the least collateral damage possible. That'll send a firm message. And if they don't leave, we'll blow up another, and another."

Cherry shot to her feet. "You can't do that. The minute the Scythians think they might not win this war you want to start, they'll launch their biocide and destroy the whole planet. We told you about that back on Svalbard, remember?"

Buka cleared his throat. "We have begun a vaccination program, based on the vaccine your captain gave us before your ship left."

"Oh, she did, did she?" Cherry asked icily. "That was so kind of her. But it's beside the point. You can't vaccinate all living things. I've seen the biocide effects on Concordia. You do not want that here on Earth."

The Maker said, "We might be able to find a way to neutralize the virus before it spreads."

"You won't. It works too fast. Depending on the conditions, it can travel faster than a man can run." Cherry made eye contact with Wilder and held it.

"She's right," Wilder said. "You should listen to her."

"I am listening," said the Maker tetchily, "but there's more than one opinion here."

"I'm not stating my opinion," Cherry retorted through her teeth, "I'm stating a fact."

More Makers spoke out, others responded, Aubriot had plenty to say too. The noise began to overwhelm Wilder. The consensus seemed to be moving toward blowing up the Scythians' nursery, but she didn't want to stick around for the final agreement. She crossed the room to where Cherry, Miki, and Nina sat, picking her way through the Makers sitting on the floor. "How about we get out of here?"

They heartily agreed.

38

"We're lucky to have you guys here, with all your experience of fighting the Scythians. We would be clueless otherwise." The woman who had argued with Cherry at the meeting seemed to be speaking sincerely, but Wilder had the impression her words were only a sop to Cherry's feelings.

Cherry seemed to think the same. "Lucky for you, maybe," she replied in a neutral tone, though her eyes displayed her dislike, "not for us. We have our own home to protect."

"I'm sorry you feel that way," said the Maker stiffly. "We're all human after all."

Cherry was being a little churlish, considering the efforts the Makers had gone to in order to help the Concordians, but she didn't blame her. She was down about being abandoned too, though Miki and Nina's safe return mitigated her sadness.

Aubriot strode in. "You guys ready?"

"Very ready," Cherry replied, as if she couldn't wait to get out of the place, or more particularly, away from the Maker and her fake compliments.

They were setting off for the south and the Scythian dome where the girls had been held captive. From other things Miki had said, it seemed the place was central to the aliens' activity on Earth. Buka had confirmed it was the largest dome on Earth, and large numbers of people had been abducted from the surrounding area. Fortunately, many had escaped at the same time as Miki and Nina.

The fact that the dome was important had fueled everyone's determination to make it the first strike in the coming war—everyone except Cherry. She feared what the Scythians might do as a counter-strike. The voice of one person counted for little, however, despite her 'experience of fighting the Scythians'.

As they got up to leave, the Maker said, "You know, in a funny way the Scythians' arrival might be good for humanity as a whole."

Cherry froze and stared at her. "How the hell do you figure that?"

"I know it must sound strange but, well, my specialism is human psychology, so I am speaking from a place of knowledge. I was the person responsible for programming the androids you called Guardians for their interactions with the colonists."

"Oh," said Aubriot, an edge in his tone, "that was you, was it?"

"You see," the Maker went on, "the common person needs someone to hate, an enemy or 'other'. That's how they form a favor-able picture of themselves, by comparison with a group they dislike, and for some it's how they understand society, by dividing it into acceptable and unacceptable people. Their relationships are based on this worldview. When the Natural Movement started up, the world was divided according to a new paradigm—or perhaps a very old one, depending on how you look at it—those who accepted a scientific understanding of life and those who didn't. Scientists, engineers, technicians, doctors, physicists, mathematicians, all these and similar people became the 'other'."

She looked at Aubriot. "You were around to see the first effects."

He grimaced. "Yep. It wasn't pretty."

"It was the beginning of the end. My friends and I were the remnants of the remnants, clinging on to rationality and the scientific process. Civilization was in full collapse, and it appears to have only just begun to recover. But now the Scythians are here—"

"They will be a common enemy," Wilder interrupted.

"Exactly. Humans will stop fighting among themselves, killing each other in endless wars. They will band together, unite against the alien invaders. Ideally, they should also have a figure to follow, a leader, dead or alive, to worship. A redeemer who takes on their sins."

"People will die," Cherry said.

"Sadly, yes. It's an age-old question: is it better to die than to live as a slave? I can't speak for everyone, but for me the answer is yes. I will do all I can to defeat the Scythians, even at the cost of my life."

They were brave words, but she was not going south to the jungle. Along with the rest of the Makers, she would remain far from the fighting. The GAA wanted to preserve humanity's new and greatest assets.

Would her opinion be different if she were to see agony, terror, and death close up? Wilder didn't know.

"We have many more ideas on what we can do to fight back," the Maker said. "With time and effort, we will rid Earth of their presence."

"Time's getting on," said Aubriot.

~

MIKI AND NINA came with them on the journey south. They would stay well away from the action zone, but they could help advise on the placement of the explosives. Cherry also didn't want to let them out of her sight and Wilder felt the same. Strongquist would be with them as well as a group of locals.

They landed in a clearing in a hot, steamy jungle. The local people were waiting to meet them. A man and woman greeted Miki and Nina warmly. Miki explained they were former captives of the Scythians who had taken part in the escape. The couple had two boys with them, but they left them behind for the trek down to the dome. The pale hemisphere glowed in the valley, an easy-to-spot navigation beacon.

They walked down the trail between tall trees, each person carrying an item of equipment needed to blow up the Scythians' nursery. Sweat soon covered every inch of Wilder's body and her palms grew slippery. Insects buzzed in her ears.

Then Aubriot and Cherry began to bicker. Perhaps he'd tried to be friendly again and she'd rejected him—again. He alternated between being sarcastic and nice to her. Neither tactic worked. Wilder didn't know why he kept on trying. Cherry was never going to forgive him for what he'd done all those years ago. At least, maybe not unless he begged, and he was not the type to beg.

Suddenly, he exploded. "I'm sorry! All right? Is that what you want to hear?! I'm fucking sorry. Now, for fuck's sake, forget about it and move on."

Wilder winced with second-hand embarrassment. Everyone in the group was pretending to not hear the argument, though, naturally, everyone could. The local people wouldn't understand what was being said but it didn't really matter.

"I don't give a shit," Cherry yelled back. "Why are you even telling me that? I haven't cared about you in a very long time. Why can't you understand that and leave me alone?"

"That's a lie and you know it. If you didn't give a shit about me why treat me like a pariah?"

"Because you deserve it! Because you're an asshole who only ever thinks about himself. You know what? I *did* sleep with Kes."

Oh, stars!

Wilder glanced up the trail. Had Miki and Nina heard? She hoped not. If Cherry wanted Aubriot to stop bugging her this wasn't the right time for it.

"You know what else?" Cherry continued, raging. "He was better than you. He was a better person than you in every way. The wrong man died!"

Holy shit.

Wilder halted. She had to say something to make them stop fighting.

But Cherry stomped past, her mouth tightly shut. She seemed to be done.

Aubriot passed her too, head down. Cherry's words had been harsh but perhaps he needed to hear them. Maybe she'd succeeded where everyone else had failed, bringing his ego down a notch.

39

Cherry dug a hole in the dark soil. She was helping to place the explosives, following the Makers' instructions. They had to be buried below the surface and facing in a certain direction.

Dusk was falling. If any humans the Scythians had captured remained alive they would be returning to their cells, according to Miki's estimates. It was also the time the aliens would be emerging from the dome. Local intel said they had stepped up their efforts to seize people since the escape.

Luckily, there was plenty of cover at the edge of the clearing, and the explosive devices didn't need to be right up against the Scythian nursery to destroy it and everything inside.

When she'd dug a hole sufficiently deep to submerge the device she slipped it in and covered it up so only a short antenna protruded. Crawling backward, she returned to the trees. The dome glimmered in the half light, fifty or so meters away. The place where the captives had made their escape was no longer visible. The Scythians must have filled it in.

How were the rest of the team doing?

Stooping low, she made her way through the jungle to the rendezvous point. Most of the locals had returned already. Miki and

Nina were retreating with Wilder at the top of the rise, moving out of sight. She was conflicted about having them close by, even though they were far from the explosion zone. But Miki's help had been invaluable in estimating the location of the nursery. The local couple had gotten it wrong at first until she had corrected them with pointing and gestures.

A dark shape swept overhead.

Damn.

The Scythians were coming out for their night patrols.

Leaves in the undergrowth rustled and another local man appeared. He gave a nod. His device had been placed. She counted ten men and women. That was nearly everyone. Only Aubriot was missing. He'd volunteered to undertake the placement farthest from cover, but he should be back by now. Of all of them, he needed to make it. He was carrying the trigger that would set off the explosion.

She peered into the deepening gloom. Where the hell was he? If they didn't blow the place soon the Scythians were bound to spot the humans lurking beneath the forest canopy.

Guilt nagged at her over what she'd said to him. She'd been over-heated, tired, despairing of never seeing Concordia again, worried about being responsible for Miki and Nina now Kes was gone. What she'd told Aubriot was true, all of it. But he didn't need to hear it right now, and especially not in front of everyone like that. As he'd stated a few times, he was not an actual monster, annoying though he was.

He was coming.

The tall man was nearly doubled over as he crept stealthily through the long grass.

A shadow blocked the light of the rising moon.

Another Scythian!

That was two in less than a minute. They had to be stepping up reconnaissance of the area surrounding their dome.

Aubriot had disappeared, sinking into the vegetation. He must have spotted the threat too. He had about thirty meters to go to reach cover and be a safe distance from the explosion. Just thirty meters. She peered at the top of the dome. A winged shape rose from it, gray in the failing light. Another alien, so soon.

Aubriot, hurry up.

The creature swept a wide circle, cutting out the light of the first stars, and flew away.

Now's your chance.

Where was he?

There he was.

Aubriot had risen and was heading for them. His gaze met Cherry's across the open space. Despite all his self-aggrandizement, he was actually quite brave, braver than he'd been in the early years of the colony. And she couldn't deny he'd protected her from danger more than once. She decided to cut him some slack from now on.

A Scythian swooped.

She hadn't seen it coming and neither had Aubriot. The creature descended from his rear, wings opened wide, legs outstretched.

"Aubriot!" she screamed.

It was as much warning as he got before the Scythian's feet fastened on him. But it was enough to foil the creature's attempt to drag him into the air.

He swung around and punched the alien in the throat. The creature was stunned and its grip slipped. Aubriot tried to wrestle free, but then the taloned toes tightened once more. The great wings beat, lifting into the air. Aubriot kicked and punched, hitting its stomach, chest, legs, anything he could reach. He grasped its neck and squeezed, bending it. The Scythian faltered, wobbled, and toppled to the ground.

Cherry had her rifle out and aiming, but she couldn't get off a shot without risking hitting Aubriot.

As he grappled with the creature, cuts opened up on his back, welling blood. The alien was attacking him with the claws on its wings.

And still she couldn't get a clear shot.

He'd got it underneath him, a knee on its neck, while the dreadful claws did their work. He was trying to get the globe off its head, but the claws were tearing into him.

The sky filled with flitting shapes. More Scythians were coming.

Aubriot!

She ran out. She had to kill the thing.

He saw her. "Get back!"

It was like Garwin's death all over again, sliced to shreds by the Scythian spiders.

"Get back," he gasped. "I'm gonna blow it."

He reached into his pocket.

The Scythian's claw cut across his face.

With a final, despairing look, she ran back into the trees.

The others had gone, and so should she, but she couldn't. She couldn't leave.

Aubriot and his attacker had morphed into one struggling shadow, a writhing heap of darkness in the grass. Scythians were alighting all around and waddling closer to witness the spectacle.

A *whoompf* resounded, a shockwave traveling through the ground and air. Cherry's legs jerked from the impact and the wave passed up her body. Soil and vegetation erupted in a gigantic fountain and rained down, filling her hair and mouth, spattering against her hastily closed eyes.

When she opened them again, devastation spread out before her. The Scythians on the ground in the blast zone were prone, motionless or twitching. What had been a simple forest clearing was a mess of earth, roots, and shredded foliage.

And something else.

Here and there within the devastated space lay smaller Scythians and weird animals with carapaces. None moved.

They'd destroyed the nursery. They'd begun humanity's counterattack.

She heard a groan. A very human groan.

Aubriot was still alive.

The sound had come from somewhere nearby.

She saw him.

The blast had blown him toward the forest, and now he lay only a few meters distant. Closer to the dome, Scythians were landing, but they were distracted, inspecting the corpses of their dead offspring.

She crawled out to Aubriot on her stomach.

He was barely recognizable. His face was a mask of blood and his limbs were bent at strange angles.

"You did it," she whispered. "We've begun to fight back."

His chest labored and his eyes were turning glassy. She wasn't sure he'd heard her.

"I love you," he said.

"I know." Her tears dropped onto his face. "I hated you, but I love you too."

This seemed to register.

He swallowed. "See ya, Bandit."

40

A   s Wilder reached the spot where the heli was waiting, a
        familiar but very unexpected voice sounded in her ear.
        "Wilder, are you guys ready for pickup? I have your
location. ETA seven minutes."

"Zapata?! What the hell? You're back? What happened?"

"It's a long story. Is there a clear landing site nearby? Get to it
ASAP. I hope you got the girls."

"Uhh..." The only available open space that wasn't the clearing
below was occupied by the GAA's heli. For the *Sirocco*'s shuttle to land
the heli would have to leave. Even so, she wasn't sure it would fit. "We
did, but we're in the middle of a jungle."

"Listen. I don't have wiggle room. Either I pick you up in seven—
six—minutes, or I don't, ever. I repeat, is there room for me to land?"

"Yeah," she replied hastily. "There will be. We'll be waiting."

Miki and Nina were staring at her.

"The *Sirocco*'s back," she announced. "We're going home."

"That's good news," said Strongquist. "Do you want me to tell the
heli pilot to move his vessel out of the way?"

"Yes, but..." she looked down toward the dome in the valley. A
black hole had opened up in it. "The Scythians are coming out. Tell
him he needs to get far away." She told the girls to get deeper into the

trees and went with them. The local people helping with the attack were already melting into the forest.

She saw the expressions on Miki and Nina's faces. "You do want to go back to Concordia, right?"

Miki looked doubtful.

"Yes," Nina replied, "we do." She nudged her sister.

"I guess so," Miki murmured, "but I'm gonna miss Dad."

"You'll miss him just as bad here as there," Nina said. "It's time to go home. He wouldn't want us to stay here just for him."

Miki didn't answer.

Wilder said, "You have six minutes to decide. You leave now or you'll never have another chance. You understand?"

Miki nodded, biting her lip.

More Scythians were flying out of the dome. Surely it was past time to detonate the explosives. What was Aubriot waiting for? She peered into the valley but all she could see was the tops of the trees and the semi-luminous dome. Another creature swept into the air. She recalled the time the Scythian had carried her aloft and shivered.

So she would see Niall and Dragan again, and everyone else on the *Sirocco*. So they hadn't left. She couldn't imagine what had happened, but there would be plenty of time to hear about it later between jumps back to Concordia. They should be there in only a few weeks, finally bringing the seeding material the planet needed so desperately.

Where were Cherry and Aubriot? If they weren't here in five minutes, Zapata couldn't wait.

She was about to comm Cherry when a dull roar resounded and the ground trembled.

They'd blown up the Scythians' nursery.

Humanity had finally hit back at the aliens, but she wouldn't be around to see the fallout. She had work to do elsewhere. Cherry and Aubriot would be on their way back now. The heli had taken off and Strongquist had returned to her side. "Are you coming with us?" she asked.

"Coming with you to Concordia? I hadn't considered it as an option."

"You could be useful there. We have a lot to do."

"There is much to do on Earth too."

"Do you *have* free will?" It was a question that had only just occurred to her. "Can you come and go as you please?"

"Within the restraints of my programming, I can choose my own path."

"So you aren't programmed to serve the Makers?"

"I am not. In the remaining time, I will consider your offer."

Wilder trotted to the head of the trail. It was empty. She comm'd, "Cherry, where are you?"

"I-I'm on my way."

She sounded out of breath.

"And Aubriot? Is he with you?"

"He's...he's..."

Shit. She'd been mistaken. Cherry wasn't panting, she was crying.

"I'm sorry, but you have to hurry. Zapata's on his way."

"What?! How?"

"I don't know yet. We only have a few minutes."

Cherry's head appeared, bobbing as she trotted up the trail.

"We're over here," Wilder called out.

Distantly, she heard the whine of the shuttle's a-grav drive.

Cherry ran up. Her face was grimy except for tear tracks running from her eyes. "The *Sirocco* came back?"

"I can't believe it either. Zapata says he can't wait around, so we must leave now."

Cherry's chest heaved and she nodded. "Aubriot didn't make it."

"I got that. It's a shame he's gone." She didn't feel a hypocrite saying it. She meant it, even though she hadn't liked the man.

"Maybe he'll turn into that person the Maker was talking about." Cherry wiped her eyes on her sleeve.

"What person?"

"Someone for the Earthers to rally around, a figurehead. His story might grow over time, you know, how the stories of famous people do. He would have liked that."

"Yeah, he would."

The shuttle's whine increased.

Zapata comm'd, "I see the landing site. Coming in. Be ready."

The imposing vessel appeared in the night sky. Scythians flew straight for it and whirled around it.

"He'll never touch down," said Wilder. "It's too dangerous."

Cherry marched toward the clearing. "Get the girls." She had hefted her rifle to her shoulder.

"Nina, Miki, you're coming?" Wilder asked.

"Yes," Miki replied, "we're coming."

Pulse rounds lit the night, but Cherry hadn't begun firing. It was Strongquist. He was picking off the aliens, aiming through the canopy, laying cover for the descending shuttle. "I have decided to decline your offer," he shouted. "I wish you luck in all your endeavors."

They ran for the landing site.

Cherry began shooting too.

The shuttle was down, the hatch opening.

Wilder reached it and helped the girls board. "Cherry, it's time to go!"

"I'm not coming."

"What? You have to come back to Concordia!"

"You go. I'm going to stay here to help the Earthers. Good luck."

"But—"

"Take off in ten seconds," Zapata comm'd.

"Wilder!" Nina called. "Come inside. Close the hatch."

With a sense of unreality, she climbed into the shuttle. The hatch closed. Before she reached a seat, the shuttle rose into the air. She sat numbly on the deck for several moments until she summoned the willpower to sit in a seat and strap in.

She comm'd Cherry, her voice trembling. "What are you doing? I don't understand."

"The Maker said the Earthers needed someone to advise them about the Scythians."

"But we need you on Concordia too."

"You'll be fine without me, and you'll be great for Miki and Nina. I was never the motherly type."

"None of those things is true." Wilder's tears were flowing freely.

"I'm done," Cherry said. "I'm tired, and I'm done. Maybe the GAA will give me a room somewhere far from the fighting, and I can annoy the Makers by telling them they're wrong."

"I don't get it."

"I'm not sure I do either. Tell the girls I'll visit Kes's grave for them. You take care. You'll be the last of the first Concordians. You have a reputation to uphold. It was good knowing you, Wilder."

The comm went dead.

41

The shuttle zoomed into the bay and landed. Heavy clunks echoed through the cabin as the clamps snapped into place.

"Stay right where you are," Zapata ordered. "It's the safest place right now."

"Are you going to tell me what's going on?" Wilder asked.

"When we came back to get you the Scythians' military ships had arrived. They weren't so shy about attacking us as the transports."

The entire ship shuddered.

"That's the Parvus's weapon firing," Zapata explained. "We've taken a couple of hits, but we're giving as good as we're getting. It won't be long until the ship runs out of juice, though, hence the deadline for picking you up. If we waited too long we wouldn't have the energy to jump."

"We're going to jump?"

"Imminently."

"With us in the shuttle?"

"You're welcome to try and run for a capsule if you think you can make it."

"I'll take my chances here."

Miki and Nina had only heard her half of the conversation, so she told them the bits they'd missed.

"What about Cherry?" Miki asked.

"She isn't coming." It was blunt, but she didn't know a gentler way of explaining it.

"Will we ever see her again?" Nina asked.

"Maybe one day. She said she'll go to see your Dad from time to time."

"That's good," said Miki. "It's good he won't be alone."

And then the *Sirocco* jumped.

VESSEY HAD TRICKED THEM. She'd told Zapata she needed him to fly her to the GAA's headquarters to hand over vaccine samples. That much had been true. But after he'd returned her to the ship she'd confined him to his cabin, spinning a tale about him defying her and disobeying orders.

Only a few of the ship's personnel were fully in the know about what she was doing. She'd told the ones she trusted about her plan to abandon the five Concordians on Earth and take the ship home. She'd told them that time had run out, and they had to sacrifice a few for the sake of the majority.

She announced to the rest that the ship would make one jump, leaving the system as a safety precaution. They would return later, by which time Aubriot, Cherry, and Wilder would have found Miki and Nina. But the waiting period stretched out, and in the meantime Vessey's cronies tried to persuade the others that it wouldn't be safe to go back, that the might of the Scythian military must have arrived, and if the *Sirocco* returned to Earth everyone would be going to their certain deaths.

The persuasion worked on some. Opinion began to turn in favor of continuing the journey home. They had everything they needed to re-start ecosystems on Concordia. Abandoning a few people was hard, but, after all, two of them were half-Earthers anyway, and one of them was mostly disliked.

But the persuasion hadn't worked on everyone. Niall and Dragan figured out Vessey's scheme and broke Zapata out. With the help of the personnel who hadn't been turned, they mutinied.

The former Captain Vessey was now the person confined to her cabin. Her erstwhile supporters had faded away, and a sense of normality had returned, somewhat.

The days sped past. After each jump the *Sirocco* appeared in the vicinity of a star. Then it was just a matter of waiting for the ship to build sufficient power to move on again. And so they continued, leaping across the galaxy, taking a single second to traverse a distance that, on the outward journey, had taken years. Traveling to Earth had cost many lives: the suicides of those who had given up hope, the plant-hunters who had died in the search for crops to keep everyone alive, Kes, and, finally, Aubriot, perhaps immortal yet not indestructible. But they had completed their mission. The Ark was full from decks to overheads with the material to rejuvenate their ravaged planet. If any survivors remained, the *Sirocco*'s return would seem like a myth made real, history come alive, replete with riches.

They were preparing for the final jump, which would take them into Concordia's system, when Miki approached Wilder. The girl had been subdued and quiet the entire journey so far. It wasn't surprising. She had to be grieving for her father and missing Cherry. But this time Wilder read something new in her eyes.

"Miki, what's wrong?"

She collapsed into her arms. "I'm so sorry. I've messed everything up. We're all going to die!"

Wilder almost laughed. It was such a ridiculous thing to say. But the girl was only fifteen and had a taste for the dramatic. Wilder swallowed her chuckle. "I'm sure we aren't all going to die. Tell me what's bothering you. I'm sure we can put it right."

Her head pressed against Wilder's chest, Miki replied in muffled tones, "I told the Scythians everything. They knew I was from Concordia, and they interrogated me."

Wilder was still. Then she gently pulled Miki away and looked into her downcast eyes. Miki wouldn't meet her gaze. "I don't understand. How could the Scythians possibly know you were from Concordia?"

"I don't know for sure, but I think they analyzed my speech, and, somehow, they knew. They asked me lots of questions, and I had to answer or they would have killed Nina. I told them all I knew. I couldn't let them kill her."

Miki seemed completely sincere. Wilder was confident she was telling the truth, but it didn't add up...

Except it did.

The Scythians had discovered Earth's coordinates from the Guardian, Faina's database. They would have learned about the language spoken on Concordia in the same way.

Miki's experience must have happened exactly as she'd related it.

The Scythians knew the colony hadn't died out. They knew where the *Sirocco* was from, and that Concordians were returning to re-seed the planet. They knew they would be arriving soon.

After one more jump they would be home, but what would they find there?

The story of the Concordia Colony concludes in:

REPRISAL

Sign up to my reader group for a free ebook *Night of Flames*, the prequel to Space Colony One, and for more free books, discounts on new releases, Review Crew invitations and other interesting stuff: https://jjgreenauthor.com/free-books/

With deepest thanks to patrons:

Paul Hanrahan, John Treadwell, Joseph Lau, Peter Samuel Harness, Geeraline Marrs, Bobby Borland, John Stephenson, Chris, William Retsin, Dan Archibald, Grant Ballard-Tremeer Dale Thompson, Jean Gill, Christopher E. Marshall, Cheryl Kuchler, Shan Shwe, Steve Glasper, Donald Swan, Wayne Lampel, Janette S. Mattey, Brian Kelly, Jim, Sarah Woods, Richard L. Adams, Frank Menendez, Patti DeLang, Elizabeth Hickey, Linda Liem, Russ Kirkpatrick, Kate Wilson, Duff Kindt, Catherine Corcoran, Shaun, John Gancz, Dave, Archie Strong, Struggle Session, Susan Cook, Annie Hsiao-Wen Wang, Julian White, Dane Elliot, Iffet a Burton, Gary Johnson, Tracey Paine, Randy Berlin, Ed Cleeves, Amaranth Dawe, Neil, Alex Green, Ann Bryant, Neil Holford